I0691493

You Don't Know Jack

By

Don Ross

W & B Publishers
USA

W & B Publishers

For information:

W & B Publishers
9001 Ridge Hill Dr
Kernersville NC 27284

www.a-argusbooks.com

ISBN: 978-0-6922742-3-1
ISBN: 0-6922742-3-5

Book Cover designed by Dubya

Printed in the United States of America

Jackson Odum
2525 North Hyde Street Apt #2
Duck, North Carolina 27949

White Pages Publishing Company
1015 Guilford Avenue, Suite 5
Greensboro, North Carolina 27401

Dear Publisher/Editors:

I hereby present for your edification and your readification the manuscript for my premier masterwork, "The Journaller: My Novel: Written and to be Read Out Loud," an exact but sometimes fictionalized look at my down-home North Carolina family and friends with only minimal mention of myself. It was a truly heart-wrenching project bringing this heartfelt tome to the printed page, which I'm sure your editors will immediately discover and take to heart. I have self-edited this manuscript at least once but it may not be quite perfect. Your eagle-eyed editors and wordsmiths may catch one or too spelling or punctuation errors: but thank God and the Geeks for inventing Grammar and Spell Check. Am I right? They are miracles of modern word processing except when Auto Correct replaces the word you meant with one that doesn't make sense but is funny enough that you can't help but launder.

I highly recommend and anticipate publication during the Thanksgiving holiday period as the story takes place during the Thanksgiving holiday period. This dramatic account of my journey to my childhood town of my birth will likely prove movie-worthy. There are very few Thanksgiving-themed films out there, if you think about it. While you're trying to come up with a Thanksgiving movie, also contemplate what a new holiday oriented blockbuster might mean to our collective bottom lines.

Upon publication, I'm well prepared to embark on an extensive national tour to guest lecture at writing seminars where I would be honored to answer questions from authors-to-be and to be asked to read exceptional passages aloud. Indeed, I wrote this book to be read OUT LOUD as suggested by the title, because it's how I wrote it, speaking every word as I typed it. Annoying to those around me, yes, but all writers have their idiosyncrasies-- and idiotic critics who don't understand the CREATIVE PROCESS at work. Just then, as I typed CREATIVE PROCESS in caps, I was once again struck with inspiration and a capital idea: let's publish my book in large print which would add depth and substance to my writing by making the book thicker.

Sincerely yours (y'alls) in print,

Jackson Odum

"The Journaller: My Novel: Written and to be Read Out Loud"

A work of faction by
Jackson Odum

(SURE TO BECOME A MAJOR MOTION PICTURE)

Dedicated to my father, Ralph Odum,
who saw life as a lavatory.

"I used to write fiction all the time as a newspaper reporter."

--Anonymous (for now)

MANUSCRIPT PREFACE
MANUSCRIPT FOREWORD
MANUSCRIPT PROLOGUE

(Dear manuscript editors: As you no doubt noticed above, I couldn't decide if what to follow is a Preface, Foreword or Prologue. It is these kinds of issues and/or publishing standards that I'm reasonably sure y'all are up-to-date on. Before we get started, may I suggest that I communicate with all y'all throughout my manuscript with occasional italicized, (parenthesized) and emboldenized inserts like this. I promise not to be too botherative in making editing and/or publishing suggestions. One thing though, I like it when the first letter of the first word of a chapter is printed in a LARGE funky font like the example shown below. I think it's a nice subtle way to let readers know they're in for something BIG. We can discuss that once we work out first and second printing schedules. So, let's get going. Here with: my premier literary effort: "The Journaller: My Novel: Written and to be Read Out Loud" by Jackson Odum):

*N*ever in the storied history of Jefferson County, North Carolina has there been a more difficult birth of a baby boy recorded at Jefferson County Memorial Hospital during the second week in the month of July!

Except for the big N, that is how my first attempt at writing the all-important first sentence of my first autobiography about myself began.

- 5 -

When I wrote that I immediately thought to myself, *y'know what? That's not bad, Jacko. Not bad at all.* For some reason when I think, I think in *italicized* New Times Roman. *Odd.* Anyway, I read it and then reread it and thought about it further and refurther and said to myself out loud, since there was nobody else in the room to say it out loud to, that it was, indeed, "a solid, dramatic, catchy lead sentence. An attention grabber!" I patted myself on my back and encouraged myself to keep it up. "Good start. Way to go, Jacko!" I also realized at that moment that I call myself Jacko, and not Jack or Jackson, when I talk to myself out loud. It's amazing what big and small things you learn about yourself when you decide to sit down and write your own autobiography.

Hello out there in book buying and reading land. My name is Jack Odum, newspaperman (currently between jobs) and aspiring author of note.

To make a short story long-- this is, after all, a whole book I'm writing here and not some high school essay-- I had decided to write my autobiography when I suddenly found myself with a great deal of extra time on my hands. I had stopped working, for one thing; and for another, made some personal decisions and got involved in certain matters I would rather not discuss at this point, that brought my life to a temporary but extended screeching standstill. So, I figured that having all this time on my hands created the right time to try my right hand at writing this book.

Someone told me sometime somewhere that the lead off sentence in a book will bring it to life or kill it dead. "You gotta capture the reader's attention right off the bat, Jack, or that book of yours will go directly to the bargain bin at the bookstore or onto a pile of discarded junk for Goodwill if it gets published at all and it probably won't," said who(m)ever it was that said that to me. "And write what you know" who/whom also knowingly advised me. I thought, *y'know, you certainly know alot about yourself,*

Jacko. So, write about yourself. And try to figure out exactly when, why or where to use who or whom. Maybe the editors of the book, who(m)ever they are, will know.

I read that first sentence again and I thought that while it was great, it really wasn't as great as it had to be for a book as important as this. *No*, I thought to myself since nobody else was around to think to, *it's great but not great great. A little weak. A little too weak. Honestly, it's more grating than great, Jacko. In fact, it's bad. Badder than bad. Terrible. Crapo to the maxo.* So, I deleted it and took another crack at it.

Everybody felt that Jefferson County Memorial's reputation would be forever changed because never in the storied history...

"No." (Delete).

Anticipation had overtaken normal thought processes at Jefferson County Memorial...

"Even worse, Jacko." (Delete).

It went on like this for days.
For weeks!
For months!
4 months, as a matter of fact.
COME ON JACK. You're a wordsmith! So, start SMITHING some words worth reading, WORDSWORTH, I yelled silently in my head at my reflection in the computer screen that had gone blank yet again. I'd found that yelling out loud made my nose bleed.

The next three pages are the result of my writing on-and-off-and-on-for-FOUR-months-or-so-or-more-or-less.

(Blank)

(Blank)

(Blank)

Well, there you have it.

"That's all she wrote," as they say. In this case, "she" is a he, that is to say, me -- Jackson Odum, your author.

I was unable to come up with a great and wonderful first sentence let alone write an entire book. I had certainly written alot of words but I cursed my cursor almost as soon as it typed them.

//D////A///M///N////////YOU/////////C////U////R////S////O////R!!

Blank pages of deleted former words and sentences were all I had to show for it.

(Dear editors: I considered using some of my old rejected writings instead of blank pages but I decided that might be a bit over the top and confusing. Also, I felt I was over using the words "me," "myself" and "I" which is easy to do when you're writing about yourself. I believe I was coming off as self-absorbed. So, I think the blank pages not only work better than my many failed attempts and add an element of surprise previously never seen before in any previous book. JO)

Still, those pages dramatically illustrate-- if nothingness can be illustrative-- of how gut-grueling, braindraining, sleep-depriving, hand-cramping, eye, ears, nose and throat straining writing an autobiography can be.

It occurred to me that perhaps I should tackle a biography about an important historical figure but my grey matter seemed incapable of thinking-up a better subject matter than myself. I kept trying and deleting. I honestly believed it would be as easy as pie (or a piece of cake, a slice of sweetbread) to tell you all about me, myself and I. I would start at the beginning and detail my difficult birth and childhood, struggles to find myself in an ever-changing world, teenage trials and tribulations, near death experiences, successes and failures, marriage, divorce, jail... whatever. Then it came to me in a slammed-hand-against-the-ole-noggin-moment: *my life story centering on me was simply not autobiographically strong.*

Nuts, I said out loud.

So, that's why this book, that was going to be about me, is not about me at all, per se. It's about per sons I know or knew or might have known. It's not an in depth biographical character study as one might expect from a writer of my depth and per sona. Indeed, I've taken quite a large tad of literary license since discovering that "telling it like it is" isn't (is isn't?) always the best way to write a true story. If truth were told, writing fiction is probably closer to my true per suasion. Therefore, some of what I'm writing here and now and hereafter is, frankly, made-up. I'd guess in the neighborhood of twenty percent.

It was then that I thought *I don't know why you hadn't thought of it before, Jacko.* I mean I can write fiction with my eyes wide closed, as you'll see if you continue reading this with open eyes. The made-up stuff will jump off the page for its originality.

"How do I know this," I'm quoting you, the reader, as I know you're probably asking me right about now? Well, I know because I used to write fiction all the time when I worked as a daily newspaper reporter. Who believes everything they read in the newspaper, right?

Ah, but newspaper writing! Journ-a-lism! Yes. That is where my heart and soul, and other internal organs and spirits, will always remain. It's the profession I was born to profess an interest in. However, book writing is where my head is at the time of this writing because of a temporary setback in my chosen field of expertise.

In Chapter One of this book, which is coming up next, I write about my newspaper career where I wrote articles that often-blended fact and fiction. I was writing what amounted to true fiction. "But that's an oxymoron, Jack," I hear you saying out there. You are correct. Some literary types have come up with a term that makes true fiction sound unoxymoronic: "biographical fiction." Moviemakers get away with it by running the disclaimer "Based on a True Story." Many literati, like me, prefer the term "faction," the combining of fact and fiction.

(Editors: I'm in consultation with my local librarians to establish a Faction section. They're going with the term "Biographical Fiction" but the head librarian said they might consider it. I'm waiting for a call back any month now. I Googled "Faction and Biographical Fiction" and it turns out that it's an up and coming form of literature. Who knew? I'm edgy! We're edgy, editors! JO)

This book is a major work of faction. Here's the thing. Writing faction and writing fiction is fundamentally the same, and that's a fact. Let me put it like this, in **bold** Times New Roman font:

Writing fiction is the simple act of creating interesting characters, placing them in interesting situations and describing the circumstances in interesting words, sentences and paragraphs to build chapters until there are a whole bunch of pages. Writing faction is the same except that some of the characters, situations and circumstances may or may not be real or exactly accurate.

You can "quote" me on that.

Still, because of my journalism background and integrity, I'm trying my best to make this book more true than false. Let's say 75-25. Well, maybe, 60-40. Much the same as the newspaper stories I used to write.

Now then, here's how this factional tome you're reading came about:

It was dusk on a Tuesday. 6:23pm. Right out of the blue cyberspace, via Verizon, my mental block was broken when my brother, JJ, back home in Gosling, North Carolina, sent me a text inviting me to a Thanksgiving family reunion. In a bright-light-bulb-burst-above-the-ole-noggin-moment-of-realization, it dawned (dusked?) on me that my family back home in good ole Gosling was _fit fodder for_ a _factional_ (fi fo fo fa?) novel. _I don't know why I hadn't thought of this before,_ I thought again in _italics: a simple mostly true story highlighting the personalities and manners of an unassuming and authentically small town American family and their small town American friends gathered to celebrate that most American of holidays in the beauteous backdrop of a southern autumn day in America's South. I'd throw in a little reference about myself, here and there, but only where absolutely necessary and appropriate for narrative purposes. I, Jack Odum, your author, am not the subject of this book. I'd take you, the reader and other readers, on my weeklong return to my roots in order to, somewhat faithfully, novelize the people and experiences of my youth that shaped my character and professional writing career; introduce readers to my family, the good and the bad, warts and all._

Or something along those lines, say...

I have an aunt, Hazel, who(m) I'll eventually get around to telling you about who(m) suffers from warts, boils and bunions-- and deservedly so.

This book is the result of that burst of cranial activity my brother's text set in motion: "The Journaller: My Novel: Written and to be Read Out Loud" by, me, Jackson Odum. Enjoy, and read these pages for the ages out loud to anyone who asks, or is blind.

(Editors: Can you make arrangements to have this book printed in Braille? And is there such a thing as

large print Braille, y'know, for the *very* blind? Thanks. JO)

And now, as promoted a page or so ago: Chapter One:

MANUSCRIPT CHAPTER ONE

For Writing Out Loud!

Many a scribe has bemoaned and begroaned the challenge of the blank page and I've certainly done my share of both.

(Editors: Now that's a memorable, "quotable," notable and imaginable firstable book sentence. Where does such inspiration come from? It's a mystery. JO)

The writer whose very words you're reading at this very moment on this very page came to very believe that writing an entire book was beyond his (my) ability and that his (my) short, cut-down, over-edited newspaper blurbs were all he'd (I'd) ever see in print. (For simplicity-sake he'll (I'll) stick with first person narrative from here on out.

I've worked briefly at two newspapers so far in my fifty + or - years. I don't think I need to tell you that newspaper reporting is tough duty, unless you don't agree with me. At newspapers you're required to write, as Sergeant Joe Friday on "Dragnet" says on the Reruns Channel at two o'clock in the morning, "just the facts, ma'am, just the facts." That's why I find fact-driven, hard-hitting newspaper journalism so damn hard, ma'am. As much as I love newspaper writing my brain seems unable to refrain from adding its own facts and figures and "quotes" -- *to improve the story, Jacko. Like the "Six Million Dollar Man" on the Reruns Channel, you want to make the story "bet-*

ter...stronger. "While this book is certainly not about me, I think it will read better if I set the stage here with my backstory:

My first newspaper reporting job was an extremely demanding but boring one at a *PennySaver* in Corolla, North Carolina. Small time, yes, but a *PennySaver* is a newspaper and writing is writing and reporting is reporting. I wrote a list of weekly community activities and store advertisements for eight very long, very boring hours a day for two-- no, three-- very long boring years. Then one day I decided to make the work more enjoyable by putting some originality into the ads. To my dismay, regular advertisers rejected the way I promoted their events and businesses. I saved (*PennySaved?*) this one to reproduce here so you can see what I mean:

Pleasant Valley SOuthern Baptist Church will hold its
annual Pastry Auction this Sunday
All SOBs Welcome
Praise the Lord and Bid your Tithe
2-4 pm in Vacant Lot beside the Cemetery
The Devil's Food Cake will be:
TO DIE FOR

And, what the devil got into Big John Scarpello's craw? He rejected my piece for his Pizzeria:

Big John's Pizza Parlor, exit 33 Highway 12 Corolla
Yo Paisano?
You wanna getta BIGA like-a Big Johna?
Ciao down on hisa Pizza every day.
Itsa oily, itsa fatty, itsa heart attacky
3-meats 3-cheeses 333 fat grams
Justa $12.00

Anyway, it was shortly after that that I was invited to leave the *PennySaver*. A few months after that that, I landed a reporter gig at *The Coastal Carolina Times* newspaper in the North Carolina Outer Banks' village of Duck, which is the next town down from Corolla. Apparently, and thankfully, the HR honchos at *The Times* failed to fact check my work experience at the *PennySaver*.

The Coastal Carolina Times is called *The Coastal Carolina Crimes* by the locals because the police blotters from the various towns in the county make up most of the front-page news: car wrecks, beach house break ins and tourists-gone-weird reports. Muck in Duck stories, I call them. The rest of the rag is fluffy filler features, civic boosterism and obituaries.

I was assigned only pap and crap stories because I was the newest hire and least experienced. I never got to cover a big or breaking story.

"You're not ready Jack," they'd say. "Hone your writing on features and obits first," they'd say. "You should consider sticking with features and obits," they eventually said. When I (byline: *Times* Correspondent Jackson Odum) was handed these newsworthlessness stories, I'd prep myself by thinking of the country wit and wisdom from my father, Ralph Odum, and apply it to my writing. He told me once, and I quote here in **bold font**, separate paragraph and in "quotes":

"If'n you pour some likker in the water bowl of a no good lazy bird dog or coon hound he still won't hunt worth a damn but the hooch might just give him courage to howl if he gets a-whiff of some critter."

Now, every newspaper person has been handed a dull, bone dry, dog of an assignment that some editor insisted was going to be "a talker." Well, I'm here to tell you that you can write and rewrite that bitch but, doggone it, sometimes she just won't bark.

I had been given so many "talkers" so many times as a *Times* reporter in this small town, where nothing much newsy ever happens, that I finally had to rebel. For years, I dutifully dug up what little facts there were and handed in my assigned number of words, which were then cut down and edited to the point that I didn't recognize my own story anymore. All I was getting were features about some local do-gooder biting the dust or an old salt catching a big fish or a Chamber of Commerce breakfast speaker telling businessmen how to grow their businesses with fewer employees and lower wages. My five-hundred-word report on that Chamber story was edited down to four sentences, none of which were mine.

> (Duck) The Duck Chamber of Commerce held its monthly breakfast meeting Wednesday. The guest speaker was Randall Scott, president and flounder of the Duck-in-Dick-out Fish Camp on Coast Highway. He was presented with the Chamber's "Businessman of the Year Award." Mr. Scott's speech, entitled "Doing Business as Unusual" was enthusiastically received by members for its insight into spurring business growth through imaginative cost saving methods.

But, the journalism gods rewarded me when the paper had to make a correction on its story the next day.

> *The Coastal Carolina Times* meant to identify Randall Scott's

> position as president and founder
> of the Duck-in-Dick-out Fish
> Cramp in yesterday's coverage of
> the Chamber of Commerce break-
> fast. We regret the error.

Better yet, the next day they had to correct the correction:

> *The Coastal Carolina Times* inad-
> vertently misspelled the name of a
> local restaurant, the Duck-in-Duck-
> out Fish Camp. We regret the error.

That was all very satisfying from my point of view but my copy of the story had been rejected for being "inaccurate, opinionated, verbose and scrambled," by an editor who'll remain unnamed for the moment.

I can handle destructive criticism. Sure, I was disappointed but I didn't let it get me down. If you think I would let something like that bother me, well, you don't know Jack! Well, okay, so it did depress me! In a deep dark funk that dark and stormy night; I decided I had had it with routinely, factually and dutifully writing Page 5 snoozers. I began adding a little color here and there, fudging a fact or two and improving a "quote*" to make the job more fun and the stories more interesting, y'know* at least to my mind -- thus the *italics*.

The truth is that reporting just the facts, the way my boss, Ernest "Ernie the Hernia" Presenca and Sergeant Joe Friday insisted, can drive a highly creative writer like me a bit batty.

To repeat myself-- something I seldom do-- but to repeat myself, my newspaper pieces were always essentially correct, if slightly embellished. For instance, I was sent to do a story one day about a cat being stuck in a tree. Some old lady called the paper all spazzed out that the cat would starve to death up there. By the time I got to the scene of the action, the fire department had successfully rescued the kitty. I talked to the cat crazy lady and more or less quoted her about how so very happy she was now. I reported that she said, "I'm so very happy now. Oh, my goodness, I'm so relieved and thrilled. I've just started breathing again. Phew. I'm grinnin' like a Cheshire." What she actually said was, "Goodness gracious. Why, it sure took them long enough to git here. I'm goin' in the house now. Please leave." An elderly man across the street complained about the cost to taxpayers of having the fire department rescue a cat in a tree. "What a gawd damned waste of time and money!" he said. "That pussy cat woulda come down from there when it wanted to. Now get off my lawn 'fore I call the po-lice." But I quoted him as saying, "No cat is gonna stay stuck in no tree. They can climb on down as sure as they can climb on up. If they slip and fall they just land on their feet. It's the way they are. One thing you'll never see is a skeleton of a cat in a tree."

(Editors: By the way, please read that last line I just made up there but read it out loud this time. "ONE thing you'll never SEE is a skeleton of a CAT in a TREE." I would like to think it has a Dr. Seuss flavor. In fact, I think I'd like to point out that characteristic to the readers reading this book so I'll just go ahead and include it in the manuscript right now. What do you think? JO)

By the way, please read that last line I just made up again but read it out loud this time. "ONE thing you'll never SEE is a skeleton of a CAT in a TREE." I'd like to think it has a Dr. Seuss flavor.

My dad would've been so proud. I made a nothing, no good story about a cat "howl."

I hear my fellow reporters howling. But, c'mon, O righteous news writers out there in Big Time News Media Land, I reported the story mostly factually correctly (ly ly ly); that is, that a cat was rescued from a tree and the populous rejoiced. Who(m) was harmed by my taking a little license with a little story and juicing it up a little?

My two on-the-scene sources called the paper to complain that they'd been misquoted but I took the call and told them I was the main editor and would reprimand the reporter in question. "JACK," I yelled loudly with the complainers still on the line, "DON'T MISQUOTE PEOPLE OR YOU'RE FIRED." That seemed to satisfy them.

People in the newsroom were used to my being loud like that, as I'll explain in later pages.

That cat tale was, in fact, my very first factually altered news article and Ernie the Hernia loved it. He said those "quotes" were "quote," "almost too good to be true" unquote and praised me for noting them in my notes and "quoting" them in my story.

Amazingly, I kept getting away with it. So, I started having regular fun with the news copy to see how far I could go while still giving the gist of the story. And then, near the end of my employment, I was even making up words to see if they'd make it into print.

There is actually a word for the making up of words, which I discovered one night when I Googled the question, "Is there a word for the making up words?"

ne·ol·o·gism *[knee-ol-oh-jizm] noun.*
    1. A new word or phrase.
    2. A new use of an existing word or phrase.
    3. A new interpretation of sacred writing.
    4. In psychiatry, a new word or words understood only by the speaker occurring most often in the speech of schizophrenics.

Definition number three does not apply here. Honest to God, I swear it! Definition number four, however, has me a little concerned.

Nevertheless, my favorite neologism is "oceanous." The way I see it, if something is mountainous in the mountains then something is oceanous at the ocean. You always hear how fluid the English language is, so I fluidate.

It turned out that my using oceanous, in an obituary of a man I knew causally in Nags Head, was a firing offense:

> Jason Anthony Crump, 58, died Saturday at his humble home in Nags Head, North Carolina. Mr. Crump, a whole nother kind of partier passed (out) away while hiking in the mountains near his much nicer house in Asheville. In addition to his love for partying and trekking in mountainous terrain, Mr. Crump enjoyed partying and stomping around in the oceanous environs of Nags Head.

Jason would have died laughing at that had he not already been died. That obit, and an accusation by a nosy secretary who'll remain anonymous in this sentence that I routinely pilfered the storage room for office supplies, cost me my job. I figure the printing paper and ink I took were part of the money they paid me to work there. What is money but paper and ink? Okay, so I stand guilty as accused by Jennie Cramer of 412 Ocean Drive Apt-5 in Duck, NC 27949. Cell: (910) 555-0983, email: jencra1487@cctimes.com.

Then there's the aforementioned editor I didn't want to mention before, Assistant-to-the-Hernia, Sam Cooke. Sam calls everything huge and/or awesome: {"My '68 Mustang is so awesome" *(which it is)* ... "My new dog is the awesomist" *(it isn't)* ... "I have an idea for a headline that'll be hugely awesome" (*it wasn't used)*}. AweSam even believes he has an awesome singing voice because of his name. He accused me of being flippant, sarcastic, self-centered, aloof and not taking journalism seriously. I told Sam I was just following my father's advice by likkering-up lazy bird dogs. Sam looked hugely confused by my awesome reasoning.

Now back to my word "oceanous" apparently being so onerous and back to what I was writing about writing:

I think wordplay qualifies as creative writing but Ernie the Hernia said he didn't want to see puns in his newspaper-- as if he personally owned the rag. (His father does). That's "craptive writing" he said hernialy. It's too bad he didn't like puns because he was actually quite good at coming up with them. I complimented him once on his punnery in a brownnosing attempt to get a raise. He stood there with hands on hips and legs spread wide cowboy-style and glared at me in his usual pained expression --thus the Hernia nickname-- and said "puns are turd words." See what I'm saying? Some people don't realize their own talents. Other than being an occasionally good punster, Hernia Presenca had no newspaper writing credentials. At least I had some *PennySaver* copy to show off my newsprint-stained fingers.

Incidentally, I hesitated using a big word like "onerous" in the paragraph above because someone in the newsroom, I think, told me one time that news articles should be written at about the seventh-grade level. But this is a whole book that I'm writing here and not a brief newspaper piece, and I just thought that oceanous and onerous sounded nice together since they rhymed and were alliterative. Like all writers, I always keep a Roget's Thesaurus handy to help me find different words so I don't keep using the same words over and over repetitively. In fact, I keep two thesauruses (thesauri?) handy (handi?). You can also see by my use of such words as "onerous," "alliterative" and "repetitively" that I am most definitely not hippopotomonstrosesquipedaliophobic. I always wanted to use that word, which means the fear of long words, in a story at *The Crimes* but was let go before I had the chance. I'm using it in this book because it's too good a word to waste. I found it while Googling (and doodling) one day at the office and also discovered that some people have a phobia of phobias, a fear of fear. They're called phobophobiacs. That's another word that's just too good not to use and abuse, so there it is. I'm wondering now if there are Googlephobiacs, people afraid to Google? I'll Google that and try to get back to you.

But I digress, which I seldom do. So, back to where I was:

"I don't get you," Ernie the Hernia said when he fired me last year. "You've damaged the credibility of this newspaper."

C'mon, Bernie, all I did was improve some stories by changing a couple of "quotes" and adding a little drama where there wasn't any, I said silently to myself trying to defend myself to myself. Out loud I said, "Huh?"

He said the Jason Crump obit was the last straw. I wanted to tell The Hernia that "last straw" was a poor cliché choice (choicé?) from an editor who surely climbed to such journalistic heights on his writing abilities.

"Have you gone batty?" he asked. As I implied several sentences earlier I had, indeed, gone that.

"Well, yes," I said batting my eyes. At least I didn't make chirping bat sounds although I thought about it in my head where only I heard them. I just smiled and told The Hernia that I had become bored by all that standard journalism who(m), what, when, where, why and how ho hum.

"Well, we're a straight news place here, Jack. We report the news as it is not as we want it to be. I'm sorry but I just don't get you, Jack. I'm afraid we'll have to let you go." And then he added the bits about harming the paper's credibility and not to ask for a recommendation and that I should clear out my desk immediately and on and on and blah and blah and mumbo and jumbo. As I left his office, I bat chirped out loud. The Hernia heard me. *He heard you, Jacko.*

Yes sir, I suppose my college journalism professors would be appalled at how I did my job at *The Crimes*-- had I actually studied journalism -- or gone to college. No sir, I learned how to journalize the old-fashioned way. I accepted a minimum wage job nobody else wanted at a penny-pinching-two-bit daily and was told to "just do it, now, fast." Armed with my 3.5 GPA high school education, notepads, pencils, computer, tape recorder, dictionary, thesaurus and a natural gift for writing and telling stories, I was a legitimate newspaperman.

(Editors: Actually 2.1 GPA but, honestly, would anyone question that once my name is better known in literary circles? Besides, I've already mentioned that some of what I'm writing is fiction. Let's go with forty five percent fiction. JO)

On the way out of the building, I grabbed my laptop and boxed up a bunch of office supplies. I knew they'd never ask me to return the company-owned laptop because it was the oldest, slowest computer in the newsroom. If they had, I'd tell them I had already donated it to Goodwill. I sold it on Craig's List for three hundred dollars, a tape recorder for twenty dollars and a stapler for eight. I did not spend the money foolishly. It went to a very good cause, which I'll get around to telling you about eventually.

At this point, you might be wondering about why and how I write the way I write, right? Alright, well, you're not alone there. Sam, The Hernia and others at the newspaper actually complained about my writing style. I suppose they had a point. You see, I tend to say out loud what I'm writing-- which is what I'm doing as I write this. I'm alone right now so there's no one here to complain. I like to hear the printed words spoken out loud, since it's impossible to actually hear words said silently, if you hear what I'm writing. Because I write out loud, you'll notice that this book is easily read out loud, an advantage I hope to use at writing conventions and publicity tours, where I'll be asked to read certain memorable passages when this becomes a bestseller. That's why I've subtitled it "to be Read Out Loud."

(Publisher: Please feel free to schedule as many reading and speaking engagements as possible. Have writer will travel! I'm ready to hit the road on your and my behalves? (bewholes?). JO)

One day I discovered I was being called Jack the Hack behind my back (another Dr. Seussian sentence) in the newsroom. I've also heard people call me Jerk, Jock Strap, Jack O'Dumbo and Jagoff Odum. Those don't bother me since I've heard them since grade school. I'll admit that AweSam Cooke, at the paper, came up with a clever new one. He called me "Jack the Hack Ovum with a "v." That awesomely got my goat. Or should I say "zygote." I laughed but had to immediately Google "ovum" to see what Sam was referring to and that's where I found the word zygote:

Zygote (noun) the cell resulting from the union of an OVUM and a spermatozoon.

"That Jack Ovum slam was awesome, Spermatozoon Sammy," I zygoted him back the next day.

There's so little real news in Duck that I'm surprised my firing wasn't a bold two-inch Dr. Seussian headline:

JACK THE HACK SACKED!

I suppose my speaking the words as I typed them may also have been a contributing factor to my firing. If so, it would just be wrong to get fired for writing out loud, FOR CRYING OUT LOUD! But if you think that's going to quiet my writing than you don't know Jack Odum.

To my credit, I repeatedly offered to accept a private office if they'd provide me one so as not to bother others who write in the silent-mouthing method. Whatever the reasons, my employment as a professional journaller at *The Crimes* ended a year ago a month ago. That's one of two reasons I suddenly had a great deal of time on my hands to write this biographical novel, or if you prefer as I do, work of faction.

You'll discover the second reason much later on, but first my second chapter and more faction action.

Thank you.

(Editors: We may be making history here by this simple act of an author thanking his readers for reading his book without their having to wait long hours in long lines at his simple book signing. JO)

Manuscript Chapter Two

-Er vs -Ist

As an attentive reader, I'm sure you noticed that at the end of Chapter One, I referred to myself as a professional "journaller." "Why journaller and not journalist," I'm asking myself for you? Well, the thought occurred to me that *a writer is never called a writist nor is a reporter called a reportist. A biographer is not a biographist and a chronicler is not a chroniclist. It only reasons, therefore, that it should be journaller instead of journalist. Furthermore, if a wordsmith is a writer of faction, Jacko, then he and we are factioners.* "We?" Now that's an interesting development. All of a sudden, my mind and I are a we.

I remembered hearing from a journaller I once journalled with that all working journallers know they had a book inside of them trying to get out. That got me to thinking in my head-- where all of my thoughts tend to happen-- *to set free the book lurking in your loins, or more likely, in the right (write?) side of the brain, Jacko.* Those of us with the God given gift of being able to express ourselves through the written word should dedicate at least a few weeks, and maybe even a few months of our lives, to getting our thoughts down on paper to share with non-writers. However, as dramatically shown in the Preface/Foreword/Prologue by blank pages, occasionally the brain drains and the words won't come.

Then, six months ago, I received that text I told you about in the Preface/Foreword/Prologue from my younger brother, JJ, about attending Thanksgiving Day dinner with family and friends at his farm back home in Gosling, North Carolina.

> Yo, jacko. am doin annual tgiving dinner reonion again this time. yall think yall can finely make it this time? awsom time last time we did it. many fam & naybers comin. my place again in gosling tgiving day. & thanx for the money help. will pay u back asap. pleese cum. hows duck? jj

I texted back that, while I'm very busy writing my autobiography right now, I would think about going and would get back to him ASAP and that everything in Duck was, as everybody always says in Duck, "just duckie." Being jobless again, I should have texted that things were "just yucky." I also advised him to watch his spelling.

Now, about family reunions: I must spell out here (O.U.T.) that I dislike such get-togethers and traditionally avoid traditional holiday and family group-eats. They often mean sitting hours on end on folding chairs or lawn furniture staring at each other; trying to think of something to say to very old people with no memory of you or much of anything; or to very young people you don't know who(m) they belong to; or to folks you can't relate to despite being related to them.

Then I thought it over and the thought occurred to me, and me alone, *that the reunion might just provide food for thought-- as well as some good food, Jacko-- for writing your Great American Faction Novel.* It would be a simple story highlighting the personalities and manners of an unassuming and authentically small town American family and their small town American friends gathered to celebrate... *wait, Jacko, you already described that in the Preface/Foreword/Prologue*, my thought processer reminded my word processor. So, just ignore that "simple story" bit and continue reading on, please...

Also, I hadn't seen my brother JJ's family since they vacationed in Duck two years earlier. And maybe my globe trotting sister, Bonnie, might even show up. I hadn't seen her in two years either. I hadn't actually been in my hometown of Gosling for over eight years. I wasn't avoiding my relatives there. It's just that I have been relatively busy writing.

Yes, the time seemed right to duck out of Duck for a week's vacation. Take a break from the day-in-day-out routine of being unemployed... from sending out resumes... from spending days alone in a two-room apartment... from... from trying to... to self-biograph.

Well, as it turned out, that week long pilgrimage to my hometown resulted in this, my first and edgy biographical fiction novel "The Journaller: My Novel: Written and to be Read Out Loud" by Jackson Odum. That's Odum with a "d".

(Dear Publisher: Can't promote the title too much or too often I've always said from now on. And may I take this private space to thank you and everyone at White Pages Publishing involved in getting this manuscript into **(large?)** *print and state that it is an honor to work with, and be associated with, the fine literary talents I'm sure y'all are. JO)*

MANUSCRIPT CHAPTER THREE

Oil and Water DO Mix

(Editors: I'm jumping ahead here but when I was at the reunion, which I'll write about in a minute, someone I used to be related to brought up something somewhat unusual in our family: the Odum Oil. It's nothing very important and I hope mentioning it here, before I even get the reader to the reunion, doesn't interrupt the flow of my narrative but I thought I would write about it now to fatten up the beginning of my manuscript which hasn't added up to very many pages so far. JO)

"There must be something in the water."

I don't know how many times I've heard that said about us (we?) Odums. That's because we/us are definitely a rather quirky, colorful clan as you'll see if you continue reading this, and I hope you do because I need the money the sale of this book will bring. I suppose I also need the attention. So, while I have yours, let me tell you a thing or lots about some of my Gosling kin and a little more about my Gosling self.

First of all, folks in Gosling call themselves Goslingers and not Goslings because goslings are baby geese. My ex-wife, Susan, called Duck "Birdland East" and Gosling "Birdland West" and felt that both towns were "for the birds." We had our differences, which I'll eventually get around to telling you about.

Now then, many Odum Goslingers seem to have a different and/or unusual approach to life, for better and/or for worse. In my case, I am a gifted writer, which you'll see if you continue reading this and I hope you bought this book and didn't just borrow it from somebody who did, because I need the money as I mentioned a few sentences ago. It's fair to say and/or write here that, literarily speaking, I am the creative one in the Odum family. People have often said, "hmm, there must be something in the water in Gosling" when they read my writing. Whether I should take that as a compliment or criticism doesn't matter as long as I'm being read. A writer writes to be read. You can "quote" me on that. Yet despite my obvious talents, I can't keep a writing job very long because of my rather nonconforming attitude toward factual writing, as I've written about briefly earlier in these written pages.

Instead of wondering if there's something unusual in Gosling's water, those wonderers should really wonder if there's something unusual in Gosling's oil! Not the kind of oil that made "The Beverly Hillbillies" rich on the Reruns TV Channel (sing along: "♫ Black gold, Texas tea ♫". Well, the first thing you know Ole Jed's ♫...).

(Editors: I am excited about trying new ways to attract readers. Would you be up for experimenting with adding brief ♫ sing alongs ♫ like the one above? I would guess that would be another first in the history of novelling. Let's try it in this chapter and we can discuss it briefly before publication. JO)

The Odum hillbillies are hooked on a little family secret referred to within the family as The Family Secret or The Snake Oil, The Ointment, The Juice, The Cure-All, The Tonic, The Formula, The Recipe, The Fixer-Upper, The Miracle Drug, but most often, THE OIL.

Family legend has it that The Oil is a concoction conjured up by a woman who was my great, great, great-- maybe even one more great-- grandmother, Geraldine Odum. She and her husband, Jeramiah, lived in North Carolina when it was a British colony and Gosling was a one-horse town in the sticks. It still is a one-horse town in the sticks. My brother, JJ, owns an old grey mare (sing along: ♪ that ain't what she used to be ♪...) named Betty, the only horse in Gosling. Apparently, Grandma Geraldine was somewhat of a pharmacologist. Some say a sorceress. Some say a witch. Some say a druggie. Whatever, she made a mixture of liquids squeezed from the leaves and roots of plants around her backwoods farm, roughly where old Betty the grey mare is pastured today.

The Oil has been passed down through the generations and a big batch of it is made two or three times a year now by my brother, JJ, and his wife, Martha.

Everybody in the Odum family has The Oil running through their bloodstreams, hearts *and minds*. When someone gets sick, they drop a few drops of it. It tastes a tad tangy and it tingles the tongue when you take it. Read that last sentence fast three times. On the third try it comes out something like: "It tas tad tang ting tong tak." Ah, the simple joy of reading aloud. Anyway, almost immediately after dropping a drop of The Oil you feel better or, at least, different.

The Oil is part of our family's favorite food recipes. JJ's wife makes soap and adds The Oil to it. Several family members make their own beer, wine or 'shine and The Oil is among the ingredients.

I won't share here the recipe for The Oil-- because I don't know it-- but among the contents I've heard about are dandelions, rhubarb, teaberries, sumac, a certain kind of mushroom and ramps, which are wild mountain green onions. JJ and Martha know the exact ingredient amounts and preparation methods. Martha said it's alot easier to make

The Oil nowadays what with electric juicers and blenders. They're already teaching their oldest child how to make it. Of course, since it is hardly FDA approved, The Oil is made on the q-t as if it were moonshine whiskey. Alot of non-Odum Goslingers know about it, and use it, but don't tell anybody about it. It's as much a town secret as a family one. (sing along: "♫ We are fam-a-lee ♫...").

(Editors: I'm liking this sing-along concept so far. You? JO)

There are many Odums who are excellent artists and ♫musicians who show extraordinary talent at an early age-- farming to my brother JJ, architecture to my sister Bonnie, creative writing to me. We credit The Oil for enhancing those positive attributes.

There are also many Odums who exhibit an aptitude for committing crimes. It's a family embarrassment that we seldom talk about. The general consensus is that we may have a thief gene running through the family, as genes tend to do. There are several of we/us Odums who take things that aren't ours in the first place-- or the second or third. You may discover as you continue reading ahead-- and why read behind? -- that you may not necessarily like some of my crooked relatives. If so, I wish it wasn't so. Examples abound. There's my Uncle Phil and his son, Georgie. They served time in the state pen for stealing state highway equipment. And my cousin, Deputy Sheriff Doug Humphries, was arrested for possession of moonshine, which he stole from moonshiners he'd arrested. I'll probably expand on their crime capers in a later chapter. Our family tree's branches are hung (hanged?) with a horse thief, a bank robber and a couple of gas station bandits, according to some written information I managed to receive at the reunion from a reliable anonymous relative.

Question? Could extensive use of The Oil over the generations have mutated a gene that leads some of us, sadly and uncontrollably, to malfeasance? Answer. Nah! The Odum family is convinced, and don't tell us otherwise, that The Oil leads only to bonafeasance, the opposite of malfeasance, a Latin-based word I just made up, meaning good activities. I credit The Odum Oil for opening my mind and developing the creative writing skills I'm employing in this book-- and employed at the newspapers where I used to be employed.

That said, I used to suffer from a severely mild form of sticky finger syndrome. I've more or less beaten that problem thanks to modern pharmaceuticals. I haven't stolen something just to steal something for something like several months now. I say I'm more or less cured because, if I lift something, it's only because I feel I've been dissed or treated unfairly. To my mind, *you were UNFAIRLY fired from The Coastal Carolina Times, Jacko.* That's partly why their computer, tape recorder and stapler turned up missing, payback for my diss-missal.

Even before I was more or less cured, my thievery was petty and barely worth mentioning, mostly shoplifting and pickpocketing to have enough money to eat, drink, make merry and keep the lights and cable TV on. While it's certainly unacceptable behavior it is, perhaps, understandable when you know my history. I'm asking myself out loud right now as I type this, "Could my petty thievery be related to how poor we/us Odums were?"

We were definitely poor but I didn't realize it at the time. My sister Bonnie pointed this out to me about five years ago. "We were poorer than poop in a puddle," is exactly how she put it and that's why I put what she said in "quotation marks." Bonnie was under the assumption that I knew it. I told her that her assumption was all wrong. Besides, as the saying sort of goes: when you make an assumption, you just make an ASS out of U and, ah,

MPTION. I've been told that sometimes I don't comprehend obvious things. I do vaguely remember asking my mother once if there really was such a place as The Poor House because it seemed like we kids were always being told we were eating the family out of house and home and into The Poor House. She assured me, despite the risk of making an ASS out of U and somebody named RED, that there was such a place off Maynard Highway, but that we're okay thanks to government surplus food.

Once a month, we'd go to The Armory in Gosling to pick up our government rations. We'd get a large bag of flour, powdered eggs, powdered milk, a huge block of cheese, a bag of beans, a box of sugar, butter and a gallon of peanut butter. I'd manage to snatch some extra powdered eggs or a bag of beans from the stack and hide them in my coat. On the way home, we'd stop at a bakery and buy two and three-day-old white bread for a few cents a loaf. I always managed to pocket an extra loaf. Bread tastes just as good squished. We'd barter some of our government food with neighbors who weren't on welfare. I didn't know at the time that being on welfare meant we were poor. I thought it meant we were faring well. Of course, we grew and canned alot of vegetables and picked fruit to make jams and jellies. Our clothes were comfortable hand-me-downs from cousins and neighbors except for new things at Christmas and on birthdays. Socks and underwear were very common and expected-- if unappreciated.

Bonnie reminded me that many times the only thing in our refrigerator were ice cubes. Once, mom filled the fridge with cardboard cutouts of food. Our bellies hurt that day from laughter instead of hunger.

Our meals were quite unusual at times. There was a patch of dandelion weeds in the backyard that when sprinkled with vinegar served as salad on good days and our entire supper on bad days. For another meal, we'd put a slice of my mother's homemade bread on a plate, drench it with hot black coffee and spread sugar over it. We called it coffee cake and it was a favorite supper. A favorite dessert was sugar bread: a slice of mom's bread, preferably still warm from the oven, spread with butter and covered with sugar. The perfect supper to me was coffee cake and sugar bread.

My parents were always on the lookout for bill collectors. I recall one day when my mother heard a car pull up to the house and she knew by the sound of it that it was Jeff McGovern come for a life insurance policy payment. Mom would say, "Jack, you go tell Jeff there ain't none of us home raht now." I knew Jeff knew I was fibbing and said he'd come back another time. I honestly think Jeff wasn't really much better off than we were. My parents always paid their bills but not always when they were due.

I developed quite a skill for "finding" things.

"Jack, now where did you get that...?" box of cookies or bag of chips.

"I found them..." at the library or post office or school yard. "Somebody must not have wanted them and I figured I might as well not let them be wasted." To my great embarrassment, my parents made me return things with an apology and then a spanking, which made me realize I had to hide things from them.

I found lots of things as I grew up: toys (a really cool battery operated robot which was my favorite toy ever) ... then cigarettes... then a little money. I could pick a pocket like a pro. Probably still could. But I don't. Steal. Money. Anymore. Like I said.

To my credit, I didn't waste things I pinched. I used them, gave them away as gifts or sold them. If it was money I filched, or money I made by selling my filch, I put it into a kitty to go toward what I considered a good cause. Good causes included buying hair tonic for JJ to tame his cowlick so he didn't look so stupid in a school picture to the time I paid a neighbor kid to pull the porcupine quills out of our dog's nose. That was a sight and sound to behold.

As far as I know, I'm the only Odum who has ever tried to do something about a penchant to borrow things for keeps. The medical plan at *The Crimes* included mental health coverage and it seemed to surprise no one that I took full advantage of it by seeing a psychotherapist a half hour every other week. The first klepto control technique I tried was to hold my breath until it hurt when I felt the sudden urge to steal coming on. That method failed me at a WalMart cookie aisle a half hour later. Who in their right or dopamine-deprived mind can resist Moon Pies? It's easy to shove two or three of those delights into the waistband of your pants and they taste just as good squished. Next, the shrink tried a mind game where I would go into a state of Zen at the thought of stealing. I must say, and so I will say it right here, that I very much enjoyed the peace of mind yoga brought me. I also enjoyed the Nikes I walked out with at Dick's Sporting Goods. When meditation failed me, he put me on medication.

I've taken all the famous psych pills: Prozac, Paxil, Wellbutrin, Revia and others and cocktail mixes of each. One of them made me feel especially happy (high) but caused me to gain forty pounds in three months and didn't do anything whatsoever for whatever it is that causes the thrill to steal. The head doctor advised me that the cocktail I'm currently on might have the unusual side effects of causing me to ramble and digress in a stream of consciousness as well as foot-in-mouth-disease; that is, I might say whatever I'm thinking regardless of its correctness. So far I've experienced neither, and that particular med-mix seems to have cured me and I've had no need nor desire to pilfer or pocket other people's goods for many months now, except for the office supplies at the newspaper when I was fired for no good reason and to be honest there are alot of people who are so careless they're practically asking to be robbed but that's all in my past and thank you very much Pfizer and Naurex, Johnson and Johnson, Burroughs and Wellcome and all the other Stop-the-Crazies-and-Fruitcakes-Among-Us Big Pharma drug makers.

Now this could get a little deep, even philosophical. But here goes. Even in my currently medicated, mind altered state; my conceivable crime gene tells my kleptomaniacal brain to take something when I feel I'm being unduly wronged, treated poorly or unfairly. *Swipe something minor, Jacko. Not money. Just a little souvenir. For show.* I just noticed here that my conceivable crime gene, like my mind, speaks in *italics. Consider yourself a sort of modern day low-rent Robin Hood who takes from the disrespecting and gives to the worthy. It's wrong to be wronged, Jacko. Is it so wrong to fight a wrong with a wrong? You fight fire with fire. It's an eye for an eye... a tooth for a tooth. So, why not a bad for a bad?* (sing along: "♪ I'm b-b-b-bad to the bone ♫...")?

(Publisher: I can already picture, in the audio department of my mind, the soundtrack of this b-b-book when it b-b-b-becomes a movie. Maybe some of your Hollywood movie buds can set us up with some of their music producers and recording artists to work on the score. Speaking of score, maybe we could also score some free concert tickets and backstage passes. Worth a try! JO)

MANUSCRIPT CHAPTER FOUR

On the Road to Noveldom
Sunday Morning

I managed to get up bright and early at 10am. It was too late for church again, where I hadn't been since an Easter Sunday in the Nineties. Well, Christmas was coming up and I promised myself to go to church then.

After a hearty heart-damaging breakfast of three eggs, buttered grits, two sausage biscuits and four cups of coffee I was ready to take off on my first long vacation in more than three years.

Luggage? Check.

Full Gas Tank? Check.

Snacks? Rice Chex.

Money? Traveler's Checks.

Passport? Czech. Ha.

Weather? I checked. It was 69 degrees, bright sun and one little fluffy white cloud in the sky being pushed out to sea by a slight breeze. To Duckites, it was the definition of a crisp late autumn morning. Please don't call us Duckies. It ruffles our feathers. I was in an excellent mood. Feeling rather chipper (chirper?).

Passport? Czech! I repeated my joke to myself and repeated my laughing as I started up my Honda. "God," I said out loud to God who was in my car because, after all, He's everywhere. "I know I didn't make it to church again this morning but let me thank you again for the quickness of wit You have bestowed upon me. I hope to bestow it extensively in writing what promises to be a good book. Not as good as Your Good Book, of course, but Y'know, better than just okay good. Earthly good. Oh, by the way, God, it might get a little "earthy" if You-know-who is at the reunion: cousin Louis. But he is an Odum, try as we may to disown him (disOdum him?). I'm writing about my You-fearing family, which I'm sure You already know since You know everything. When the book sells-- and I pray You'll help me with that-- I'll try to give to my church the money I didn't put in the collection plate during my recent non-attendance. Amen and amen." God knows it won't be that much. And Jesus wept!

My seat adjusted, the radio on "99.9 The Wave," driver's side window down, rearview mirrors set, transmission in reverse, I was ready to hear the sweet gettin'-outta-town sound of tires on loose gravel when I hear, "Hey man." *Woah! Did God, after all these years of silence, just speak to me. He does exist and He's a man with a deep voice and southern accent,* I thought. But, it was just ole mortal Ray, my neighbor and landlord.

"Hey Ray, whatdayasay?"

That's whatIalwayssaywhenIseeRay.

He told me he noticed that I was talking to myself again. *Again? Do I talk out loud to myself (and God) often?* I asked myself, making sure I didn't just ask that question out loud. *No,* I mentally answered myself and nodded no with my head, for why would I think *no* but nod yes? I told Ray that since I didn't make it to church, the Honda was my cathedral this morning and that I was talking to The Man Above.

Ray looked to the sky and tightly closed his eyes. "Amen, brother. Amen."

I knew I owed Ray two month's rent but it turned out he wasn't there to collect. He just wanted to wish me "a raht good time" and to complain, as he often does about all the Damn Yankees living in Duck. We refer to visiting and vacationing northerners as Yankees. Northerners who come down here… and STAY… are DAMN Yankees. The Halfbacks especially annoy Ray. Halfbacks are northerners who move to Florida to escape the cold weather, decide Florida is too hot and then move half way back, to the Carolinas.

"You know what, Jack? I'm sure that when my time comes and I meet St. Pete at the Pearly Gates, he'll says to me, 'Ray, my man, I'd like to welcome y'all to Paradise where we all live and give, eat and greet and walk and talk SOUTHREN!' Northerners have a hard time adjustin' to the Hereafter. I'm sure of it, Jack. You jes wait and see."

"I hope you're right, Ray but I'm in no hurry to find out. Hey listen, I really gotta get a move on because…"

"I'm tellin' ya, Jack, if another person says to me 'youze guys' one more time, youze is gonna see meez a'wavin' the Stars and Bars in downtown Duck and beltin' out "Dixie." I mean, WTD?" (the Duck variation of WTF)," he grumped and groaned.

Ray looks like a disheveled Santa Claus. He scratched his tobacco-stained yellow beard with one hand and snapped worn-to-shreds red suspenders with the other and went on, "We're runnin' out of room 'round here. It's gittin' so you cain't piss off the back porch no more."

He does that. Piss off the porch. I live in a three-room apartment over his attached garage. Like many old people, Ray is set in his ways and on a set schedule. Every evening at 8:30, after his last shot of Southern Comfort and before turning in for the night, I hear Ray unlock his back door, walk onto the porch and pour his measly, swollen-prostate stream over the banister. The grass and weeds below are dead in a circle from his nightly urinations.

I finally escaped Ray but not until after a half hour or more of damning Damn Yankees. I didn't get the Honda on the highway until almost 11:45.

The reunion invitation and Ray's rant got me to thinking about my ex. I married one. A northerner. Susan. I said

I'd get around to telling you about her eventually. Well, now is eventually. Our pledge "to have and to hold till death do you part" fell apart in three years with neither of us dying. She left me just after I landed the journalling job at *The Crimes* newspaper. I thought our married life was going along just fine until Susan stated one night "there should have been alarm bells instead of church bells at our wedding." We agreed after an intense fifteen-minute discussion that, for whatever reasons, our attempt at living together in Holy matrimony was Holy Hell. There were numerous "whatever reasons" that led to our separation and divorce: communication problems, money problems, sex problems and in-law-problems. We didn't argue alot as a married couple. We just tried to out-sarcasm the other. Or, we ignored each other. We ate together without talking. Slept in the same bed at the same time but stopped wishing each other a good night or a good morning. Sex went from primo in year one, to so-so in year two to zero in year three.

Sue claimed I was "unaware of the obvious and self-obsessed." *Why would she ever think that*, I thought in my mind? So, I put the question to her this way: "I'm wondering Susan. Why do you think I'm unaware of the obvious and self-obsessed?" She said, "You're so into your own self, Jack. You're flippant, sarcastic, scramble-headed, non-ambitious and unserious." Sue made up words, too! She went on, "That job at the *PennySaver* was lousy but at least it paid the rent and you let it get away from you just because you want to write more cleverer. Mister Screw Around Smarty Pants Writer Man! You'll get fired at the Duck newspaper, too. You mark my words. Here we are stuck in this ridiculous apartment in this ridiculous town with a ridiculous name for God only knows how ridiculously long? Where's your head, Jack?"

"It's on my neck, Susan," I said.

"Oh, that's har har har hilarious, Jack. You oughta go on "The Tonight Show." They PAY their guests, y'know. We could use the money."

She won the sarcasm back-and-forth that time. I couldn't come up with a quick comeback. I did come up with one later -- in bed at 2am-- and I said it to her, but she was asleep and didn't hear me, "Yeah, well, why don't you go on "Oprah" and give her some of your amazing dieting tips." She sure was putting on the pounds. So was Sue! Ha. I'm kidding. I'm a laugh a minute at 2am. I'll be appearing Wednesday at the Funny Farm Club in… actually I'm glad Sue didn't hear me. That would have hurt her too much. She's always been plump and it was an unspoken off-limits issue.

The following are some Susan issues that were NOT off-limits and often discussed:

Her mommy and daddy. "It's obvious by your snarky comments that you don't like them very much, Jack."

True.

Cats. "I want a cat, Jack."

I don't like cats. I like dogs. She didn't want a dog.

Her job. "You're not interested in my career, Jack, are you?"

No, because I didn't understand what she did.

Susan was in financials. She kept trying to update me on something called MOB spreads. I'm not going to waste precious printer's ink-- courtesy *The Coastal Carolina Times*-- trying to explain MOB spreads in this book because I don't know what the hell they are and Susan couldn't adequately explain them either. I'm not sure anybody really knows what they are. And to hear them being explained is the height of boring. She had two clients (Mafia goons?) who were paying her peanuts to explain MOB spreads to them.

Her parents pretended they understood derivatives. I overhead her Reruns Channel Edith Bunker-like ditzy mother bragging to a friend on the phone how important and fascinating Susan's work was. "Well, Janet, she develops plans that rich people depend on to make them richer. How she does it is just so simple that we're surprised so few people understand derivatives and don't invest in them. What are they? Oh, my, Janet, I would much sooner let Suzie fill you in. She handles all our investments now and we totally understand what she's doing with our money. She has dozens of clients investing. It's so simple, rilly."

"Rilly." That is how Sue and her parents pronounce "really." They speak a peculiar form of English I'll call Area Code 814 Pennsylvanian. Susan grew up in Altoona, Pennsylvania and her parents still live there. If you're not from there, 814 Pennsylvanian is a dialect that takes several hearings before your brain registers what's being said. Like this 814-ism: "Didja red up yer room?" In regular everyday American English that means "did you straighten-up or "ready" your room. In North Carolina, if you asked someone if they red-up something, you'd be inquiring as to whether they had studied something, read up on it. They might also think you asked them if they'd tackied it up or red-necked it up.

Here's a brief glossary of 814 Pennsylvanian to help you when it shows up in this book, or if a native Altoonan accidentally calls you on the phone, or in case life should ever take you near or to Altoona:

814 Pennsylvanian: Correct English:
Chimley – Chimney
Crick – Creek
Eltoona – Altoona
Hain't – Ain't
Hows come? – Why?
Iggles – Eagles (Philadelphia)
Intrest – Interest
Mum – Mom

Nebby – Nosey
Red up – Straighten up
Rilly – Really
Slippy – Slippery
Smelt – Smelled
Stillers – Steelers
Sum-em – Something or some of them
Touwk – Talk
Worsh – Wash
Youns or Yinz – You or Y'all
Younses or Yinzes – Y'all or All Y'all

They don't use youse to say y'all like they do in many other predominately Yankee places up north.

(Editors: I think the above examination of a unique American dialect will draw the attention and readership of many linguists, English teachers, speech therapists and anthropologists. And Western Pennsylvanians, of which there are several hundred. JO)

Of course, many of us in the south talk funny, too what with "backer" and "baccy" (tobacco), "bidness" (business), "pert near" (pretty near) "ignert" (ignorant) and "I Swaneee" (well doggone). I only occasionally made fun of Sue's accent while she and her parents were constantly mocking my molasses-smooth southern dahrawlllllllllllll. "That there way youns touwk down here makes youns sound like youns hain't got no good sense," said my well-spoken sixth grade educated father-in-law.

It's a good thing Susan and I didn't have kids to raise in the South. I can hear them now speaking some kind of northern/southern hybrid language: "Hows comes all y'all hain't like all my fer-ends pay-rents? They don't make us red up evry thang when we are tha-ru pa-layin'."

And Susan's parents wouldn't stay out of our business and were relentless complainers.

Her mother, Phyllis: "When are we gonna be gramparents?" "How long do youns plan to live in this here little apartment?" "When is youns movin' back up near us?" "When are youns gonna have kids?" "Do you need tested or sum-em, Jack?"

Her father, Joe: "If you're such a good writer, hows come you hain't won no awards?" "Christ Almighty, hows come youns say y'all all the damn time?" "What kind of a name is Duck?" "Didjer landlord rilly piss off the porch last night?"

My in-laws visited us exactly once in three years. "How can youns stand it this damn hot down here?" old Joe asked me two minutes after arriving at our apartment. One day when we went out to eat, he sprinted to his car, turned on the a/c and quickly ran back to the apartment as if the pavement was on fire. The pavement might actually have been hot that day had the driveway actually been paved. Then, after five minutes or so, daddy-and-mommy-in-law hightailed it out and jumped into their cooled-off Buick tank. I moseyed on out, took in the hazy sky and droopy plants and pointed out what a perfectly beautiful southern day it was and that "the high humidity is why my skin is so moist and pliant. Unlike y'alls," I added. The snow white, splotchy faced couple and their daughter checked themselves out in the car mirrors and frowned in realized unison. I let out a mental Rebel Yell so loud I got a headache. "But you are right, Joe. It does get awfully hot down here. I'm awfully sorry about the discomfort y'all are experiencing. I'm used to it but understand how you must dislike it so hot. Your weather in Pennsylvania is so wonderful. The envy of the nation," I tell them. They smile and nod yes to the obviousness of what I just said. I go on and on about our terrible heat because I don't want them to move down here to be, as they once mentioned, "close to

Suzie." *Heavens no. Please no. I pray. Please no, no, no,* I said to God, not out loud, I'm fairly certain.

Susan had this habit of doing what so many Yankees do when they move down South. They're always telling us how superior things are done up North, "The way we do it in Rahchester or Bahston or Picksburgh, is so much better blah blah blah baloney..." I'd respond how we southerners always respond: "Then what the hell are y'all doing down here? Go back up there where all y'all do everything so raht." That didn't help our marriage either since Sue was down here because she married me. Now she's back up there probably bad-mounting our ways and me.

Also, Susan and I both have urinary problems.

Mine is understandable. I suffer from OMIGOD: Oh Man, I'm Getting Old Disease, enlarged prostate. What's a little penile dripping now and then, I say. Little Jacko is still my best friend.

Susan's is mental. She couldn't pass a restroom, fountain or body of water without having to pee. She'd see a bathroom sign and start squinting her eyes and walking knock-kneed. She'd hear Ray peeing off the back porch at night and head for the bathroom. She always announced her need to pee, "Ohhhh, I gotta pee so bad my back teeth are floating," or "Oh, mama. I gotta piss like a Russian race horse." Sue peed a dozen times a day. I spent a third of our married life waiting outside women's lavatories. I felt like a pervert standing there as other women entering the john sometimes gave me the evil eye. Sometimes she'd ask me to hold her purse while she went "potty." That brought looks of understanding and pity from fellow fellows-- a smile and a wink from a few.

Susan referred to her life in the South as being "stuck in Duck" and "banished to Birdland." Our apartment wasn't anything to brag about but I was, after all, making less than minimum wage at the *PennySaver* and Sue wanted to be a stay-at-home childless wife studying derivatives and petting a damn cat. The apartment was what we could afford on her derivative income (almost nothing!) and the money I managed to make at the *PennySaver* job-- and through, umm, other means. (See Chapter Two).

Duck is a beautiful, if too touristy town located near Kill Devil Hills on North Carolina's Outer Banks where the Wright Brothers figured out how to fly "like a duck," as I used to tell Sue. Somebody named it Duck because of all the wild ducks in the area, according to my extensive research. Ray told me.

As for my old hometown of Gosling, it isn't named Gosling because there are alot of baby geese in the area. It's named after the founder of the town, Admiral Alexander Geoffrey Gosling, according to more of my extensive research. My dad told me. Ole Alex was, in fact, British-born and was given a large chunk of land courtesy the British Crown.

The Odums aren't related to the Goslings. We often said we wished we were because they are loaded. We don't know any of them and have never met an actual Gosling. We never saw them around town. They never seemed to leave their gated mansion on Elizabeth Street, the only gated house in town; in fact, the only house on Elizabeth Street. Their house appeared empty all the time except for the occasional housekeeper, pool man or gardener coming or going. If we heard anything about them it was a newspaper story concerning some company they bought or their attendance at a social function in New York City or Palm Beach, Florida.

The current Gosling residing in Gosling Manor is Gregory Alexander Gosling the Second (Junior). We all call him "GAG," said with a choking sound. He is very old now but was some kind of business bigwig in the Big Apple who didn't like living up there but kept a place in Manhattan.

I grew up wishing I was/were a Gosling-- the rich man's son, not a baby goose. I wish I was/were a Gosling right now since I'm no longer getting a paycheck from the paper.

One night, my cousin Denny Roy and I climbed over GAG's high, sharp-pointed, wrought iron fence and walked all around their property as if we owned the place. Denny Roy, we all said, would wind-up in a 12x12 cell someday. He was always doing little things he shouldn't when he was little. Because we were together so often, I would get into trouble with him. We took a couple of souvenirs at GAG's to prove to everybody at school that we did, indeed, have brass balls. I swiped a bottle of cognac from the pool bar and Denny Roy broke the penis off a peeing fountain cherub. My school buddies and I worked on that cognac for weeks. We hated the taste of it but finished the bottle because we had it. Denny Roy flashed that concrete weenie around school for weeks until the metal shop teacher caught him soldering an aluminum condom for it.

Denny Roy and I made arrangements to get together at his place Wednesday night before the Thanksgiving eat-and-greet-and-drink-athon.

I managed to make it one mile from my driveway before I came to a dead stop that lasted half an hour or more. A Crash of the Tourons caused the tie-up. I'll tell all y'all all about our tourons in the next chapter.

(Editors: I just remembered an idea I came up with while stuck in Duck traffic that day. I would like to make this book double as a North Carolina Travelogue helping to make it even more unique in noveldom. I'll enlighten my readers on my adopted town of Duck, my hometown of Gosling and the character of the land and people between them as I traverse the Tarheel State reunion bound. What do you think? JO)

Don Ross

MANUSCRIPT CHAPTER FIVE

Tourons and Hineys
Sunday Afternoon

It is almost five hundred miles from Duck to Gosling-- as the crow flies. Duck, Gosling, Crow. I worked up that three-bird allegory (nice Roget word, allegory) to help set the stage for my trip back home to eat turkey-- now a four-bird allegory! It is, however, a five or six-hour drive because of some two-lane roads that are as crooked as a chicken's hind legs-- now a five-bird allegory! Add to that the pre-holiday traffic and "tourons." That's not one of my neologisms. It's what we locals call tourists in Duck: tourons or touridiots.

(Editors: An allegorical bird thought just crossed my mind. Perhaps my book needs a sub-sub-title: Adventures in Birdland. Thoughts?)

Getting out of the Outer Banks is enough to drive you out of (Outer?) your mind sometimes but especially during the summer months and holiday periods. Throngs of tourons-- mostly Yankees-- invade our barrier islands from June to September and they are dangerous, dangerous people. They are barely pay attention to the road as they search for restaurants, hotels, souvenir shops or parking spots. Hot and sweaty, tired and sunburn, unfamiliar and northern, they're reading "For Sale" and "For Rent" signs. The men are watching the pretty girls in bikinis. The women are watching the pretty girls in bikinis and judging how they might look in that same two piece. Duck is some kind of magnet for pretty girls in bikinis; Babes in Birdland, my ex, Susan, called them.

Everyone is also looking out for the wild ponies. We not only have wild ducks in Duck we also have wild horses in Duck. Why they named the place Duck rather than Pony is a mystery! An interesting quirk (quack?) about ducks: very few of them actually quack, according to Ray. They mostly grunt, groan or growl. Ray told me that most male ducks are silent and don't quack, groan, grunt or growl at all, letting the females make all the noise. Sue and my relationship became rather duck-like.

Keeping a close eye out for ponies, bikinis and tourons, I cruised down NC Route 2 in my Honda land yacht at 10 mph in a 35-mph zone. I rolled all my windows down-- because I had just remembered that something went wrong with the Civic's a/c several months ago. So, I enjoyed breathing in that healthy Outer Banks' fresh, sea, salty, fried fishy, car exhausty, suntan-lotiony air.

I finally made it to Whalebone where a right turn put me on the beginning of US Highway 64, which runs all the way to Arizona where no Odum has ever been as far as I know. Arizona would have to wait for this Odum, too. I had only to make it to Brevard, North Carolina and take the exit to Gosling. At Brevard, I zigzag my way through a series of mountainous back roads to good old Gosling, where I was born and reared (and fronted?).

It is a beautiful drive through that rugged country from Brevard to Gosling. Or so I hear. I know there are trees to see. And curves. Trees and curves are about all you see because the roads are so crooked and narrow that you can't take in the scenery or you'll scrape an oncoming car or, more likely, a pickup truck. In many spots, there's a high cliff on one side of the road and a deep drop off on the other. Some form of wildlife will almost surely jump out in front of you at the most dangerous places. I heard once of a six-point buck deer, attempting to cross the road at one such spot, leaping from the cliff into a convertible car carrying a newlywed couple on their honeymoon. You can imagine how that turned out. I don't know if that's a true story or not but it doesn't matter because this book is, you'll recall, a work of faction.

There can also be boulders on the road. Yellow bullet hole ridden caution signs warn: Watch for Fallen Rocks. I was probably nine or ten when I realized that my father was pulling my leg when he said Fallen Rocks was the name of a savage Indian still on the warpath against the white man.

I've gotten way ahead of myself. Let's back up five hundred miles to enjoy the drive through the eastern part of North Carolina first:

There are parts that are postcard pretty with stately white colonial houses surrounded by pink and purple rhododendron, azaleas and crepe myrtles, rivers and streams of dark black water, cedars and live oaks dripping with Spanish moss. Did you know that Spanish moss isn't from Spain and isn't even moss and that it's related to the pineapple? It's one of those botanical mysteries of plant life. I didn't know that either until Ray told me. The man's an encyclopedia and possibly a thesaurus, too.

There are also long stretches along 64 in the eastern part of the state that feature none of the above but rather mile after mile of field after field of tobacco or cotton or peanuts, dotted occasionally by abandoned barns or a chimney from a forgotten farmhouse or bakker barn. I'm "yawwwwwwwwwwwnnnniiinnngggggg" out loud right now as I remember that leg of the drive.

(Note to editor: Should I mention the odor of hog lagoons and all the dead possums on the road? It's a regular opossum omassacre out there. And the pig stink is terrible. I sprayed my Arid deodorant in the car in order to breathe in one spot. And Arid is not much better if you

want my opinion. I'm switching to Sure or Mennen. Probably Mennen because it's for Men. Let me know what you think about the pigs, possums and deodorants. JO)

My legs and arms and shoulders and neck and eyes needed a break. It was just about then that I noticed the largest American flag mine eyes had ever seen. Old Glory was the size of a semi and signaled the red, white and blue presence of "The US-64 Gas & Grits Truck Stop & Shop" just outside of Kinston.

Highway truck stops fascinate me. The aisles are packed tight with people looking over shelves of cheap cigarettes, perfume, stuffed animals, ceramic knickknacks and plastic wrapped snacks. I pick up things and pretend to be interested but I seldom buy. I pay close attention to the shoppers, watching how hard they concentrate on whether to buy a snow globe, belt buckle or trucker's hat and paying no attention, whatsoever, to their wallets and purses. In the old-days I could have robbed them blind. I must have spent an hour in the shop just watching shoppers shop and thinking about how easy the pickins would be. My medication was working.

Unknown to me, I was also being watched-- by a surveillance camera and the store manager.

Manager: "Can I hep you find somethin', sir?"

Me: "Nah, I'm just lookin'." I did rather fancy a rubber T-Rex dinosaur that cost $19.95. I knew someone who would love it. I'll tell you about him in a later chapter.

Manager: "You've been lookin' a long time, sir. Sure, I cain't hep ya?"

Me: "No. I'm good."

Manager: "Well, sir, I have a suspicious feelin' you're up to no good."

Me (thinking): *Jacko. You are being treated UNFAIRLY.*

Me (saying): "Why? Do I look like a crook, sir?" deciding to go sir to sir with him.

Manager: "I won't say that, sir. But I'm an ex-cop and I have a cop's gut instincts."

Me (thinking): *I don't know about instincts but that's quite a gut full of intestines you got there, Ossifer.*

Me (saying): "Well, sir, you're reading me wrong. I'm just resting up from a long drive and enjoying the amazing array of lovely merchandise you've made available for us road warriors, sir."

Manager: "I have to ask you to please move on, sir"

Me: "Sir. Yes sir." That's what Gomer Pyle says to authority figures on the Reruns Channel.

I moved on after "finding" a little something when Mister-Manager-Ex-Cop-Sir turned his head for a fraction of a second.

Back on the road, I started noticing people's yards. I don't have a yard so the ones in rural North Carolina fascinate me. Some are so large homeowners need full size farm tractors to keep the grass and weeds mowed down. Since many live in open fields with very few trees, I guess they must just stop mowing where they've apparently decided the yard looks good, or is large enough to keep snakes away from the house. For reasons I don't understand, they make yard mowing a royal pain in the gluteus assimus for themselves by littering the yard with numerous whirligigs, wind chimes, mirrored globes, bird houses, bird baths, pink plastic flamingos, ceramic deer, frogs, turtles, kissing gnomes and worn out truck tires painted white and filled with flowers. Then they have to spend more hours mowing around all those things with hand held trimmers.

Two kinds of lawn ornaments especially caught my eye on this trip. Alot of folks had black-painted plywood cutouts of people or animals. They look like silhouettes. There was a silhouette of a man smoking a pipe. Another of a little boy peeing. If Susan was with me and seen that one,

I would have had to pull over and let her weewee. There were also colorful painted plywood cutouts of people's butts, as if they're bent over working in the garden. They reminded me of the bent over shoppers in the crowded gift shop at the truck stop positioned pickpocket-ready.

I learned that the silhouettes were called "shadows" and the rear ends were called "hineys." I learned this at what must be the mother of all plywood art located in another town with a bird name, Turkey. There were hundreds of hineys and shadows for sale and more being cut out and painted by three men at a roadside store called "Wise Guys Yard Art."

I had taken a detour off NC 64 to visit my sister, Bonnie, who lives near Turkey. You'll meet her in the next chapter. The town of Turkey being named Turkey makes much more sense than calling my town of Duck, Duck. They raise trillions of turkeys in the Turkey area. Nobody in Duck raises ducks to the best of this former local reporter's knowledge. And if they did, Ray would have told me. They raise humongous amounts of hogs around Turkey, too. I suppose they could just as likely have named Turkey Hog as they could have named Duck Pony. It looked as if it had snowed along both sides of the roadway around Turkey from all the white feathers blown from trucks hauling loads of turkeys from local farms to slaughterhouses.

You know, since the turkey is the bird of choice to celebrate the all-American holiday of Thanksgiving, it really should be the national symbol as Ben Franklin proposed. I guess the other Founding Fathers told Ben it was another one of his bird-brained ideas, like electricity, and went with the eagle instead. Another reason the turkey should be the bird symbol of America is because the tom (Jefferson?) turkey can change the color of its head and neck to red, white or blue when trying to attract a mate. On the other hand, there are good reasons for not having the turkey symbolize us (the US of A us). Farm turkeys are so dumb that when it rains it's not unusual for them to look up, open their mouths and drown. Wikipedia provides a wealth of turkey trivia, which I looked up and studied in case I needed something clever to say at the Thanksgiving reunion. Sometimes a conversation will come to an abrupt end and everyone stands there uncomfortably trying to think up something to break the silence. That's why I was ready just in case with, "Hey, um, did you know that farmed turkeys are bred now to have such huge breasts that they can't have sex. No? Not only that. They're also so dumb that…"

But I digress which I seldom do. So, back to the Wise Guys Yard Art roadside shop in Turkey, North Carolina:

"Why do you call this place Wise Guys?" I asked the three guys running the place. All three had run out to greet me and were obviously glad to see me because there were no other customers.

"Us three is in this business here together. We has us three of these stores in Norf Carolina," one of the guys answered. "This-un here in Turkey, another-un in Goldsboro and another-un up in our hometown of Wise. We from Wise, Norf Carolina up near Virginia where we begun the bidness."

"So, you are The Three Wise Men?" I asked smart-assly.

Pause. Stares.

I figured they might have found that blasphemous rather than funny so I didn't ask which one kept a stash of myrrh. But they had good senses of humor (sense of humors?).

"Ya wanna assess the inventory?" asked Wise man number one.

They had a whole comedy routine worked up to sell their works of arts (arse?).

"We just caught up wif demand," said Wise man number two. "Now we're not behind no mo'."

Wise man number three added, "We got a million of 'em. Hineys and hiney jokes."

The two most popular posteriors are of a bent over woman in a bikini and a plumber's vertical smile.

"That'un really cracks everybody up," one of them said wisely.

Funny stuff. The four of us were heartily laughing out loud and having a good time. But then a white church bus filled with white haired passengers pulled in and The Three Wise Guys stumbled over each other to get away from me-- just one person who might buy one hiney-- to greet them -- many people who will likely buy several hinies. There was no, "please browse, sir, we'll be right back after we welcome the others." There were three of them. Couldn't one have stayed to help me? My mind told me *Jacko, you are being treated UNFAIRLY!*

As I stood there abandoned and alone among the wooden asses, I wondered if the Wise men would deliver their repertoire of rear-end one-liners to the church group. I listened closely. They did. "Y'all need any ass-istance?" The group loved it. Laughed out loud. One old guy even bent over to mimic the bent over plumber hiney. Huge laugh. Two of the other old men had to help him straighten back up. More laughter when he said, "I thought for a moment I had my head up my ass." *Gutter language so soon after words from the Gospel?* I thought.

I noticed a nice plywood hiney of a woman in a red and white polka dot dress with her blue bloomers showing. It was displayed next to the cash register. In hindsight, I was surprised they'd leave the cash register, and me, unattended like that. No, I did not get into the cash register. I do not steal money anymore as I keep pointing out, not even when being unfairly neglected by the Wise guys in favor of the others.

Once the churchgoers left with their hineys stacked in the backend of the bus, the Wise guys suddenly remembered I was still there. I told them I wanted the red, white and blue bloomered lady beside the cash register.

"You're takin' our Betsy Ross Bloomer home witcha?"

"Yes sirs, Wisemen."

Betsy Ross cost me twenty-two George Washingtons.

I thought *JJ would like a piece of ass art as a gift for holding the Thanksgiving reunion at his farm, Jacko. But I see a hiney he'll like even more.* I put Betsy Ross and another hiney I, ah, found near my Honda of a cow's backside with her prominently featured udders displayed. I threw the two plywood assterpieces in the trunk and headed off toward my sister Bonnie's place a few miles away.

MANUSCRIPT CHAPTER SIX

Bombshell Bonnie's Bombshell
Sunday Night

My sister lives out in the country near Turkey in the crossroad town of Spivey's Corner, known far and wide as The Hollerin' Capital of the World. They hold a festival every year there where people from around the world compete in a hollering contest. Some of the hollerer's hollers are hysterical while others are historical.

Before there were telephones in eastern North Carolina, hollering was how neighbors in far apart farms communicated with each other. And it was how mountainfolk communicated across the hills and hollows of Appalachia. There was an agreed upon kind of 911 holler. It wasn't just "HEEEELLLLLLLLLPPPPPPP!!!," although I'm sure that was hollered on occasion and would have been quite effective. From what I hear, and I heard it very LOUD and clear at the Hollerin' Festival one year, it was a high pitched, rapid, pulsing holler that you just felt it in your gut when you heard it in your ears that something was terribly wrong. There was a standard holler question that asked "hey, how're y'all doin' way over yonder there? All is well here abouts." It was sing-songy and bordered on being a yodel. I don't quite know how to write how it sounded but maybe something like this:

"HeOOOOOyyaaaHHHHoooYYYYYYeeeeAHH!"

Of course, there was also the kind of holler you would

expect from the kitchen to the field workers: "COME'N'GIT ITTTTTTT. FOOD'S ON."

And, hollers to call in the animals: "SOOOOOOOOOOOOOOOOOOOOOEEEYYYYY."

SOME OF THE... I mean... some of the participants in the festival can holler a beautiful melody while others sound like they're barking like a dog. My sister Bonnie came in third one year with a holler that was a cross between a grunt and a screech owl's screech.

Bonnie is the Odum family star-- unless or until this book makes me an acclaimed author. She's an architect in New York City but returns to this quiet little town when she can, except during Hollerin' weekend when the noise is almost unbearable, to do her serious thinking and drafting. My little sister was into architecture even when she was literally little. You should have seen the buildings she made out of Lincoln Logs, Legos, toothpicks and Popsickle sticks. She is 38, very pretty, very intelligent and very unmarried. When you see her she's always on the arm of a different very handsome man.

There was no man, handsome or otherwise, when I visited Bonnie at her small farmhouse this time. I did, however, notice a picture of her with a tall, dark complexioned very handsome man prominently displayed in her living room. I couldn't tell from the photo if he was African-American or Arab-American or Indian-American or Some-Other-Dark-Skinned-Place-in-the-World-American. She informed me, when I asked her for information, that he is a Floridian-American.

"He's very tanned, Jack. Jeez."

"Where is he, sis?"

"Greg's in Florida right now. Palm Beach. His family has a house down there."

"Where did you meet him?"

"At an art and architecture exhibit in New York. His family also has a place up there."

"In New York City?"

"Yeah, Park Avenue."

"Okay. Wow. Little Sis hits pay dirt."

"Stop it. Jack. We've been together for almost a year."

"Okay, are you two going to JJ's for Thanksgiving?"

"No, Greg and I are off to Punta Arenas and we leave Wednesday morning."

Bonnie is likely the most travelled resident in Spivey's Corner and definitely the most traveled Goslinger. She's been everywhere. I joked about having a Czech passport a few pages back but my sister has likely been to the Czech Republic, although I've neither Czeched nor Slovakiaed that. (Yet another Czech joke from yours truly, yours author). Paris, London, Rome are old hat to Bonnie. So are Tokyo, New Delhi, Nairobi or JustNameSomeOtherFarFlungPlace.

I love her dearly but her extensive travel makes it hard to hold up your end of a conversation with her sometimes. If you say something like, "holy cow, it's hot this summer," she'll tell you where she's been where it really gets hot: "I'll never forget the time it reached 123 in Kuranda."

When we greeted each other, she kissed me foreign-style, on both cheeks. That was a new experience for me and I wasn't sure how to respond. I wondered if I should bow and kiss her hand. I just hugged her. American-style.

"You're looking good, Jacko. What's up with you?"

"I'm pretty good. I'm glad I could work out seeing you during my little one week vacay."

"I'm glad, too. You never take vacations. How's the newspaper biz?"

"Good," I lied because it would disappoint her to learn of my present unemployment. And why embarrass myself needlessly? "But I needed to get away from that daily deadline, y'know, Bon? Oh, and I'm also novelling now."

"You're what?"

"I'm novelling. I'm writing a novel."

"That's not a word, Jack. Are you still making up words? Remember how well that worked for you writing essays in school?"

"Hey. I'm a neologer. A maker-upper of words. What can I say?"

"I'm looking up neologer as we speak," she said as she double-thumb-Googled her cell phone. "Ah, Jacko, the word is neologist not neologer."

"I know, Bonnie, but I prefer the -er ending to the –ist ending. You know why?"

"Okay, I'll bite. Why do you like the -er ending to the –ist ending, Jack?"

"Because to -er is human!"

Pause by Bonnie. Longer pause by reader.

"C'mon, Bonnie (and reader), you know that's a good one! At least, a moaner."

Bonnie moaned. "Okay. That actually wasn't a bad pun, Jack. You're getting better at it."

"Thank you, Sis." And thank you, reader, for whatever your reaction was, whether a moan or groan or chuckle. I couldn't see you.

(Editors: When are we ever going to finally get around to having two way visual books? JO)

"So, I see you're off and running again?" I asked because she was running around packing her suitcase. "Does all that traveling help your architecturing career somehow?"

"Architecturing? Stop already. But yes, for inspiration. You should see some of the incredible structures made of bamboo in Yangon."

Where the hell is Yangon? I didn't ask because I didn't want to come off as geographically ignorant to my travel seasoned sister.

"What about this new guy, Greg. Is he an architecter, too?" I asked.

"Stop it! No. He works for the Secretary of State. So his job requires alot of travel. He's arriving tomorrow night from Punakha. You know how much I enjoy traveling abroad so I try to coordinate my trips with his whenever possible. We recently had a wonderful four days in Borgarnes."

Borgnine? That's an actor not a place? I almost said but thankfully didn't. Instead I said, "That's interesting. When was the last time you visited exotic Gosling, North Carolina?"

"I was in Gosling last year. But I never managed to get around to seeing any of the family," she said.

"Well, then, what did you do there?"

"Okay, ah, Jack, well, listen, the guy I'm going with is originally from Gosling, too."

"What? Do I know him?"

"Well, you know of him."

OF him? I thought and then said, "OF him?"

"Yeah, Greg is another reason I'm not going to JJ's Thanksgiving. We're not ready to meet the Odum family just yet. Jack, he's not only from Gosling. He is a Gosling."

"A baby goose?"

"Stop it! He's Mr. Gosling's son from his first marriage, okay."

"You're dating GAG's son?" I gagged questioningly.

"Yes. I'm currently living with Gregory Alexander Gosling the Third." She laughed. "I love him thoroughly, Jack, and I think I'll probably become Mrs. Gosling if and when he asks me, which I think is going to happen soon. He threw some hints when we were in Ostuni last month."

"I. DO. NOT. BE. LIEVE. IT," I. said. loud. ly.

"That's right Jack. The Odums and Goslings unite."

"Wow. I'll try not to let word of that get out at the reunion," I wowed. And bowed. And kissed her hand. "Has he sampled the Family Recipe yet?"

"Oh yeah. I slipped a few drops of The Oil into his mojitos in Camaguey. If it affected him at all it was, as we all claim, in a good way. Right? Let's just leave it at that," she smiled and turned away after turning dark red. *Hmm, baby sis is having sex with a rich GAG.*

I spent the night at Bonnie's and we relived the many good and bad moments of our youth. I reminded her how Denny Roy and I had jumped the Gosling's fence and stole a bottle of expensive cognac and the swimming pool cherub's little penis.

"I mentioned that to Greg once," she said, "He said he knew about the penis thieves. When his father discovered the cherub was missing its member, Mr. GAG told Mrs. GAG something like, 'I suppose we need to let the Odums know that we don't appreciate the kids invading our privacy, destroying property and stealing. But, you know what, Lucille, honey? I hate that damn sissy statue. If you don't mind, I'm going to put something nicer in there.'"

Mrs. GAG apparently didn't mind. He replaced the emasculated cherub with a very well endowed mermaid.

I got a good night's sleep at Bonnie's. I dreamt about a well endowed... rather, I enjoyed the newness, freshness and lushness of the high thread count Egyptian cotton (more than likely from Egypt) she put on her guest room beds. She even scented the room and linen with a French lavender mist (more than likely from France). Breakfast was yogurt, fresh fruits and muesli (more than likely from Muesli).

"Invite me to your wedding, Bonnie, unless it's in some hot hut in tropical Zaniguma."

"No such place, Jack, but I'll let you know where and when if Greg asks me. But he's going to ask me. I can feel it. Probably in New York or Palm Beach."

"Okay. Bye Sis. Love you. Jury is still out on your Greggy."

"Kwaheri, Jack. Ninakupenda."

"Say what?"

"Swahili. Good Bye and I love you, too." Kiss on each cheek from her. American hug from me.

The rest of the drive to my hometown of Gosling isn't worth writing home about but I'll write a few things about it anyway since I have a whole book to fill:

--The bedroom boomtown of Cary, southwest of Raleigh, is impossible to negotiate. I wanted to see up close and personal Damn-Yankeedom-Gone-Mad because a running North Carolina joke is that C-A-R-Y stands for Containment Area for Relocated Yankees. I somehow ended up on a Parkway or Loop and looped around Cary twice and into Morrisville and Inner Looped and Outer Looped Raleigh's Beltline at the required speed of about ninety miles per hour and finally into Loop-free Durham. Thanks to my handy guidance system-- an outdated, poorly folded and coffee stained AAA map-- I found my way back to US-64 somewhere around Chapel Hill. I did, by the way, see a ton of Yankees.

--The farther west and closer to Gosling I got the fewer cars with northern license plates honked and zoomed past me. No Yankees at all on the snaky mountain roads to Gosling.

--Statewide, the road is littered with run over possums. It's a regular opossum omassacre out there.

(Editors: I decided to go ahead and mention all the dead possums. It seems important. I also really like the term "opossum omassacre." JO)

--I'm extremely sad to report here that I ran over and killed a squirrel in Brevard. Not just any squirrel. A white squirrel. Brevard is known for its white squirrels. My dad told me about them while I was skinning a squirrel I killed on the first day of small game hunting season when I was twelve. He said a circus truck wrecked there in the 1940's and two freak white squirrels escaped and bred with the local grays and now there are lots of white squirrels in Brevard. There's one less now because it ran right out in front of me and then... fump fump... I looked in my rear-view mirror and saw a white and red smear on the road. I didn't hang around because dad said the white squirrels are revered in Brevard. Sorry Brevardians. Accidents happen. I wondered if the white squirrel tasted the same as the grey one I killed as a kid.

--There was a trace of snow on the ground north of Brevard. I tried to enjoy the scenery but couldn't because the narrow roads are so crooked, the turns so sharp and so many pickups coming the other way. I kept thinking a deer might jump off the bank onto the roof of my Honda at any moment.

MANUSCRIPT CHAPTER SEVEN

Aunt Minnie: My Novelling Mentor
Just after 1:00 Monday Afternoon

I entered Gosling town limits just after 1:00 Monday afternoon, as vaguely indicated above. I wanted to take a gander at Gosling by cruising uptown. The Gosling Chamber of Commerce calls downtown "uptown" in all its literature in an attempt to add a little class. There are no buildings in uptown Gosling over two stories high but, through the visual trickery of its facade, The Dimeling Department Store looks larger and taller and looms over Main Street. Unfortunately, the Dimeling went out of business several years ago and now the first floor is a bizarre bazaar of junk and antiques (read: more junk). The former A&P was now a J&S Market, a grocery store where the prices are low because the products aren't shelved but displayed in their cardboard shipping boxes. What was once a corner service station, was now an inconvenience store selling Smiley Face Gas, lottery tickets and some kind of awful falafel thing. Bob's Gun Shop appeared to be the most successful business in town with seven or eight people rifling through a sidewalk clothes rack hunting for the latest in camo comfy.

Then who(m) did I see walking down uptown's main street but Minnie Crane, my mama's youngest sister, the only one of her six siblings to graduate from college. Aunt Minnie rather resembles the wicked witch in "The Wonderful Wizard of Oz," but instead of a nose wart, hers is under her right eye and she is always playing with it. It looked cancerous to me but I'm not exactly Doctor Oz (not to be confused with The Wonderful Wizard). She has a mustache. And, she dresses in bright colors that, to my fashion sense, don't make sense, although I'm not exactly Doctor Dior de la Renta, either. This day she was wearing an orange top with neon pink pants and topped it off with a yellowish straw hat that matched her shoes and belt.

Aunt Minnie was a fourth-grade teacher at Jefferson County Elementary. Students called her Crane the Pain. She was the meanest teacher in the school. She would have been an excellent Catholic School nun and probably a good Catholic if she weren't a Baptist. She gave Denny Roy three hard smacks across the butt one afternoon in front of the entire class with a long paddle that had holes in it. She swung it hard and Denny Roy howled after each whack and went back to his desk with tears in his eyes and rubbing his behind. All he did to deserve that was to be overheard by asking Bobby Jeffries something that Denny Roy's older brother always asked his buddies, "Hey, you gettin' any?" To which they'd reply, "More than I can handle." Bobby Jeffries shook his head no because he didn't know what exactly "any" was. Neither did I. Nor did Denny Roy.

Crane the Pain loved making us write essays. I'm glad she did, now that I'm a professional writer, but there has never ever been a fourth-grade boy who liked to write essays. Fourth grade girls, yes. They live for them. Teacher's pets. The best essay grade I ever managed in my aunt's class was a C+. She said my essays, while creative, lacked attention to detail and accuracy. Not that different from what I'd hear from a newspaper editor many years later: "We report the news as it is, Jack, not as we want it to be." Live and don't learn, huh?

I'll never forget the giant red "F" she gave me for an assignment we were given to write about something we loved very much. I very much loved our Zenith TV so I wrote an essay I thought was good and practically memorized it from the satisfaction of reading it over and over again before handing it in.

"How TV Pictures Fly Through the Air to Your TV Set at Your House" by Jack Odum
Much is made of how TV pictures leave the TV station and fly through the air to your TV set at your house. It almost seems like magic but it's actually science. Based on information in a World Book Encyclopedia, the most accepted theory is that TV pictures get to your house the same way radio music does.
The picture on TV rides piggyback on radio waves which have been around for many more years than TV waves. That is why it is a good idea to place a television set near the radio in your house. The TV picture, called the reception, will be stronger with less snow.
We have a Zenith TV console at our house with a radio built in and it gets a good reception. My friends Denny Roy and Clyde Hicks will agree with this.
How voices and music travel on radio waves is much more difficult to explain but the TV channels have it very easy.
The End

Getting that F at that early age could have disillusioned me but I didn't allow that to happen. As I aged my writings improved to the quality of what you're reading now. Somewhere between an A and an A+.

I decided to get this reunion in Gosling with my family off to an early start and stopped to say hi to Aunt Minnie.

"Jack. Help me with these groceries, will you, and give me a ride home?" No smile or hug or any indication that she was glad to see me. We hadn't seen each other or talked since my parent's funerals six years ago.

Nice to see you, too, Aunt Minnie. Hope you're doing well. I am. Thanks for asking, I wish I had said. Instead: "Are you shopping for the Thanksgiving meal, Aunt Minnie?" I pronounced her name Meany. Everyone in the family does.

"Yes, I had to get the ingredients at the J&S for what, I'm proud to say, is the meanest potato salad in the northern hemisphere, Jack." *Meany used the word "meanest." Interesting. She must know we call her that.*

Her house was five blocks away. I carried in the groceries and we covered the basics about the weather, how the town isn't growing and who'll be at the reunion. Over sweet cake and sweeter tea, Aunt Minnie brought me up to date on her life as a widow, retired teacher and grandmother.

Her son Frank is a marine biologist, married with two grown kids in California. Her daughter, Darlene, is a high school English teacher, married and lives in Dallas, Texas.

"English teacher, huh? Do they still speak English in Texas, Aunt Minnie?"

"Si, Jacko." She pronounced Jacko in Spanish: "Whacko." *Very funny,* I thought in English because I didn't know the Spanish word for funny. I'll Google it and change this paragraph before I send it to the publisher.

"Any of your side of the Odum fam going to the reunion, Aunt Meany?"

"No. None of the others is able to make it this time."

"Woah. Don't you mean 'none ARE able to make it this time?'" I asked, saying ARE loudly as if in capital letters.

"OH, JACK. I never got THROUGH to you, did I?" she groaned in English, loudly and capital lettersly.

"You did, in a way. I write for a living. Well, I wrote. Past tense, I'm afraid. I was recently let go at a newspaper in Duck where I live. But I'm working on a manuscript now, Aunt Meany. So, if it ever becomes a book you were somewhat instrumental in my success as a noveller." I confessed my joblessness to her because, well, she's getting up there and there's a will to consider.

"Noveller? That's not a word unless you're into neologism, Jack*?" Figures she would know the word. Damn. I was hoping to teach the teacher a word.*

"Yeah. I am. But it cost me my job as a reporter. I discovered journallers have to use real words"

"Journallers, huh? Well, you sure weren't much of an ESSAYER in the fourth grade, Jack." *She's quick. Gotta give that to her.*

"You didn't care much for me as a student, did you? But you love me as a nephew, right?"

"Not really, no."

She's blunt and to the point. Gotta give her that, too.

"You know," she continued "when you get as old as I am, Jack, you've earned the right to speak freely. We've had our problems through the years, haven't we? It just seems that you never worked at your full potential, Jack. You seemed more interested in working at your FOOL potential." *Ditto, Jacko, about quickness, bluntness and having to give it to her.* Two funny lines in a row delivered without the slightest smile.

"You were always looking for an easy way out," she went on but with a slight smile on her face. "And stealing that essay out of my desk did not endear me to you."

Right. That didn't turn out so well. I was simply looking for a pen in her desk but noticed a paper with a B+ in one of the drawers. I borrowed it and used it as the basis for my own paper and returned it the next day. Obviously, I didn't re-work it enough and Aunt Minnie knew what I had done.

"Sorry about that, Aunt Minnie. I was a stupid lazy kid and I deserved the F and the reprimand." There was no "that's okay Jack, kids will be kids" or even "thieves will be thieves." But then I didn't really expect it because she put me through the ringer for that episode. My parents were called in and I was forbidden to leave the house or see friends for a week. I had to complete the original writing assignment and a second one as well. I received a D on one and another F on the other.

The phone thankfully and loudly interrupted our discussion and my thoughts about my poor essay writing abilities a thousand years ago. Minnie pounced on it as if it would bite her if she didn't make it stop ringing immediately. The ringer had to be set on LOUD because the ring seemed to bounce around the kitchen. She had the phone mounted on the wall and the spiral cord was all twisted into a knot that she had to untangle before she could say hello.

"Hello," Aunt Minnie said sweetly. I never thought I would ever write "sweet" and "Aunt Minnie" in the same sentence but there it is!

I wandered into her living room/office and looked at pictures and such. There were many pictures on her mantel including a black and white of my parents with we/us three kids. We looked like a family in the Great Depression. Only mom was smiling. Dad wasn't even looking into the camera. JJ and I looked like we had dirty faces and had just eaten a popsicle or something chocolate. Our hair was cut close to the scalp. Maybe that picture was taken after we had our heads sheared and deloused. JJ and I had a lice infestation we caught from a neighbor boy we were told not to play with, Lynnie Odell, the kid I paid to pull porcupine quills out of our dog's nose. Bonnie was a baby in the picture. She was in mom's arms and crying. Bonnie, as mom often told us, was a colicky baby and, until she was four or five years old, was rather melancholy. I looked up "colicky" and "melancholy" in the dictionary at school and came up with the word "melancolicky," one of my first forays into the world of neologism. On a desk, next to the mantel laid several print outs of a manuscript Minnie was working on entitled "There Must Be Something in the Water." Leafing through it, I saw that it was an Odum family history. Interesting! I thought, *I could use some of this information to add a few family facts to my book.* She wrote about The Secret Odum Oil and The Gosling Water Theory and I decided to include that in my book, as you probably recall my mentioning in Chapter Three.

(Editors: We should probably credit my Aunt Minnie when we publish because, as it turns out, she helped me very much in my research for this book. Especially Chapter Three. JO)

Aunt Minnie was on the phone a very long time and sounded thrilled by what she was hearing on the other end. When she hung up she told me, "Sorry, but that was a very important call I've been waiting for. I may get a book published, Jack! My life's dream may come true. I'm so excited." I don't believe I had ever seen Aunt Minnie excited and I had never heard her actually say the word "sorry" to me or anyone else.

"Wow. Congratulations. That's great, Aunt Minnie." *You're jealous, Jacko.*

"Look, I'm sorry but I'd better get going. I've made arrangements to meet some buddies uptown." I hadn't. But I was jealous, as my mind pointedly pointed out.

She asked, "Where are you staying?"

I thought to myself, *I hope she isn't going to invite me to stay at her house.* And then I thought, *are you kidding me, Jacko. She can't wait for to you to leave.* And then I also thought, *now that's mind boggling. My mind considers itself separate from me because it just said, "are you kidding ME."* My mind has a mind of its own!

I told her, "Thanks. But I've made reservations at the Americana Motel," adding, "I wouldn't want to inconvenience anyone," in case she did ask me. She didn't. *I told you she wouldn't, Jacko,"* my mind told me.

She said, "Say hi to Jeffrey. He runs the Americana now."

"Will do. Love ya, Aunt Minnie." I don't.

"Adios, Whacko."

No hugs or kisses or even a wave goodbye.

***

I checked into The Americana Motel, which bragged about being "American Owned and Operated" and offered free breakfast, air conditioning and Color TV. It cost thirty-five dollars a night but Jeffrey Patel, the owner and operator, checked me in for thirty dollars if I paid in cash, which I did and understood why, because then he wouldn't have to claim it for taxes. If I didn't know better I'd think Mr. Patel was an Odum.

The TV in the Patel Motel room received exactly no good channels. The antenna brought in six or seven stations but they were all too snowy to watch. The snow was, however, in color. The air conditioner in the window was so loud I couldn't have heard the TV anyway. When it thumped on or off the lights flickered. I gave the mattress the once over-- twice over—thrice over--for bed bugs as we're all advised to do now. No bugs. A couple of tears in the sheets but my sheets at home are in worse shape. I'm glad I brought soap and shampoo I saved from previous hotels because the Americana didn't provide such extravagances. The towel (one) was thin, grey and small. I wished I had brought one of the many towels and robes I've borrowed over the years from better sleeperies. There was one of those beer bottle openers on the bathroom doorway that had been painted over so many times there was no room to insert the bottle top. I didn't have a bottle of beer to open anyway. *What? No minibar?* A print of marigolds, which I must admit I liked very much for all its orangeness, helped to brighten up the room. The ten watt bulbs made it impossible to read or write. So, I fell into the lumpy bed and with one hand on my stomach and the other on my heart, mindfully *started drifting off to sleep*, yoga inhaling and exhaling the room's strong aroma of curry and incense.

Still, it's better than staying at mean ole Aunt Meanie's.

Namaste, y'all.
Namaste, Jacko.

MANUSCRIPT CHAPTER EIGHT
Grits and Co-cola

Tuesday Morning

The next morning, I decided to have a further look-see around downtown uptown Gosling.

The Americana Motel's free breakfast was instant coffee and rock hard powdered donuts in the manager's office. I wanted more than that for breakfast. There was no sugar or non-dairy creamer to claim for future use. *Come on, Mr. Patel*, my groggy uncaffeinated mind complained, *would it kill you to offer some amenities, like say, sugar and non-dairy creamer? A washcloth in the bathroom. Or a TV with a picture? I missed "Bonanza" on the Rerun Channel last night.* My mind apparently enjoys watching TV! *$35.00 a night for a room the size of a jail cell? I think you're being kinda chintzy, Jeff, and not treating your guests fairly. I think you're being treated UNFAIRLY, Jacko!* "Well, perhaps," I told my mind, "but the marigold print over the bed is nice." My mother would have loved it. I walked a few blocks and discovered a diner-- in the former 5&10-- called Pearl's Diner. A handwritten sign advertised "2 Fryed Eggs, Grits, Country Ham and Coffee. $2.00." They could use some of my *PennySaver* advertising expertise.

I took a table at the window and started pocketing, as I always do at restaurants, several packets of sugar, saccharin and creamer to use them at the Americana's breakfast layout tomorrow morning. I'm really paying for them anyway, I reason, since diner owners have worked the costs into their prices. I live on the coast, remember, and if a hurricane or tornado should hit I could live for weeks on my stash of condiments. I've copped enough mayo and relish from Chic-Fil-A, hot sauce from Taco Bell and ketchup from McDonald's to survive a tsunami.

I picked up that habit from my mother. A child of the Great Depression, she saved everything in anticipation of the next Big Crash. She hid money all over the house. Quarters fit perfectly into prescription pill bottles. As long as it was clean, she saved and reused aluminum foil. She stored thousands of paper clips and scores of rolls of Scotch tape. One time I told her I needed a little bit of masking tape for something. She dug up a roll of tape that must have been twenty years old. The tape was all stuck together and wouldn't come off. She took a butcher knife and cut deep into the roll and threw away the stuck-together part and handed me the still usable tiny section near the center that remained. I looked in the drawer later and there were at least ten other new unopened rolls of masking tape. My mother had bagsful of plastic bags. Paper sacksful of paper sacks. Boxes and boxes of plastic zip lock storage bags. Before she'd use one, she'd wash the inside of it. "We don't know what kinda person mighta touched what with what at the factry, Jack." She said she was keeping bags to store stuff in when she "got old." She was 81 when she told me that. And bobby pins. Mom's bobby pins were everywhere. On tables, the couch, chairs, the floor. But that was okay because bobby pins were always useful for more than just holding hair in place. They work as substitute paper clips. Bite off the plastic tips on the end and they're good for picking locks or your teeth or using as a little knife to cut cheese or hotdogs.

Just as I was about to slip a breakfast packet of cinnamon apple jelly into my shirt pocket, the woman working the breakfast counter came over and very loudly called me, by name, and began pouring on coffee and love.

"JACK. Why, you looking right HUNGRY there, darlin'," she said and everyone turned to look at right hungry ole me. "Let me getcha some EGGS AND GRITS, SWEETIE," and poured steaming hot non-instant coffee in my cup. She's my Aunt Ruth, my mom's younger sister, next up in age from Minnie.

Ruth is the physical opposite of my mother and Minnie. She's tall and large with big hair and a bigger voice.

"How ya like yer EGGS, HON?" she boomed.

"Scrambled," I said relatively quiet to my relative who was practically in my face.

"How MANY you wantin', Love? Two or four or MORE?"

"Two, Aunt Ruth. Two eggs'll be fine."

She screamed my order at the cook on the other side of the restaurant: "TWO EGGS. WRECK'EM. Want some SAUSAGE, BABY?"

"Ah, no. I'll have bacon, please," I said.

"TRIPLE SLICE A HOG BELLY," she yelled.

"Oh, and make the bacon very crispy, please."

"BURN 'EM IN HELL. Want TOAST?"

"I'd rather have a biscuit, Aunt Ruth, if you got 'em."

"Got BISCUITS? Where you think you AT, boy? TWO HARDTACKS," she yelled.

She told me to put back that pack of jelly and began to bring me up to date on scores of people I don't think I know or ever knew or am related to.

"How's MARRIED life been treatin' ya? I ain't seen your WIFE since I don't KNOW WHEN." Aunt Ruth never met Susan.

"Well, I ain't seen her in a while neither 'cause Susan and I are divorced." I heard myself using English I can't believe I heard myself using.

"REALLY? Hmm. Y'know, I don't reckon I can THINK of any other DE-VORCED Odums. Can you?"

"Nope. I'm the first Odum to de-marry."

"Well, guess someone has to be first, RAHT? Believe you me, I thought 'bout quittin' Charlie more times than you can count but he went and DIED on me before I could get AROUND TO IT." Very loud belly laugh. "Say, did you happen to see HENRIETTA outside?" surprising me by changing the subject before I could.

"I don't know Henrietta, Aunt Ruth."

"Henrietta is a CHICKEN that ROOSTS on the STOOP out there," she practically crowed.

"Oh, well, no, I didn't see any STOOPID rooster outside."

"GOOD ONE JACKO! We LIKE 'EM Henrietta jokes around here. But y'know what? SHE'S A SHE CHICKEN, JACK, and she provides the diner with FRESH EGGS now and agin. Hows 'bout I scramble you up TWO of Henrietta's ALMOST baby chicks?"

"Hmmmm, when said that way, eggs don't sound very appetizing right now, Aunt Ruth. I think I'll pass on the scrambled eggs."

"OSCAR," she screamed at Oscar the cook who looked frantic with beads of his sweat sizzling as they hit the hot grill. "KILL THEM WRECKED EGGS!"

"ARE YOU GOING TO THE…" I practically yelled and then caught myself, "I mean, are you going to the reunion tomorrow, Aunt Ruth?"

"I wouldn't MISS it," she said. "Gonna bring my world-famous CHICKEN SALAD. Best chicken salad in the NORTHERN hemisphere." Aunts Minnie and Ruth apparently talk.

"After you eat, let's go HEN HUNTIN', HON. Find Henrietta."

Oscar rang the bell that my food was ready. Ruth was over there and back with my meal before the peal of the bell had rung out. *She is one fast fat woman, Jacko.* The breakfast wasn't what I ordered, which seems to always happen to me. Instead, I got the advertised special of two fried eggs, grits, a slice of country ham (on a biscuit, at least) and coffee (which was not being regularly refilled). Oscar must cook on automatic. Aunt Ruth loudly explained that "OSCAR'S 'BOUT DEAF, JACKO. That's why I TEND to talk SO LOUD." Aunt Ruth has always talked loud.

"Can you eat that instead? Or I can yell at him and try agin?" she said rather quietly.

"No, no," I told her, just as rather quietly. "No, this is fine. Thanks anyway. This looks good, Aunt Ruth." It looked awful and tasted terrible.

"OKAY THEN." Then, in what to her was a whisper so the other breakfasters couldn't hear, "breakfast on me, Jacko."

That'll set the diner back two whole dollars! I ate the grits and ham, tried unsuccessfully to get her attention for a coffee refill, stashed some packets of Texas Pete in my jeans for future use, put two bucks under my empty coffee cup and joined the search outside for the stoopid chicken preoccupying my aunt's attention.

We found Henrietta perched in a nearby Bradford pear tree. "Lookee thar now. POULTRY in a PEAR tree. MERRY CHRISTMAS Y'ALL," howled Aunt Ruth to us all. "KNOW WHAT JACK? Y'all might arta (ought to) wander on down and see Ole Miss Sarah at her store. She ain't got long for this world. And she's ALMOST BLOOD. She won't be at the reunion. Sarah's yer daddy's aunt on his mama's SECOND husband's side." I thought hard on that for a sec-- possibly an entire min-- and concluded that Sarah, at most, was an aunt-in-law.

Across the street and two blocks down is one of those classic Southern shotgun houses built with a door on the front and a door on the back with rooms off to either side. If you opened both doors you could shoot a shotgun through it and not hit a thing. It had a deeply weathered grey dilapidated front porch. There was a crinkled, stained and faded cardboard "Open" sign hanging on the rusty screen door knob and an old metal Royal Crown soda advertisement nailed above the doorway. I remembered it being there when I was a kid but it looked new then because it was. A room off to the left served as a store. Miss Sarah lived in the other rooms.

I could use a soft drink since Aunt Ruth only poured me one cup of the diner's coffee and, by the general look of things, Miss Sarah could use some business. So, Henrietta chicken-like, I crossed the road.

Inside still sat Miss Sarah who looked as old and beaten as the store. She looked old and beaten when I was a kid. In front of her was an ancient crank cash register that registered $0.00. The till was wide open and not a bill in it. On the floor beside her was a rusty, dented Chock Full O Nuts Coffee can for spitting tobacco juice into. It was chock full o gross.

"Can I hep you?" she said (patooey).

"Ah, yep. I'd like a grape Nehi, Miss Sarah."

"Ain't had no Nehi of any kind in ages."

"Oh, well, how about Cheerwine. Got any Cheerwine?" Cheerwine is a North Carolina soft drink that's somewhat like Dr. Pepper, only better.

"None of that neither." (patooey).

"RC?"

"Don't have RC neither, jes Co-cola. Hep yerself over yonder there."

"Co-cola" is how everybody pronounces Coca Cola in these parts. Sometimes store clerks have to ask customers what kind of Co-cola they want when they ask for a Co-cola because many people in North Carolina consider 7-Up, Mountain Dew, even Pepsi Cola, as Co-cola. The marketers at PepsiCo must hate that, if they know it, because Pepsi Cola was actually invented in North Carolina, according to my always reliable historical source, my landlord Ray.

Where Sarah pointed over yonder sat a prehistoric Pepsi machine placed on cement blocks because two of the cooler's legs had rusted off. The machine was old but the Co-cola was cold.

I gave her a dollar. She said it was fifty cents.

"Mighta 'swell git 'nother 'cause I ain't got no change."

"That's okay," I said because there weren't any more Co-colas or any other brand in the Pepsi cooler.

Miss Sarah obviously didn't remember me despite my being a nephew-in-law.

"Things kinda slow, Miss Sarah?" I asked the obvious.

"Ain't that obvious, son? Dollar Store done me in. But that's no never mind. Jes a place to pass the time now. If I sell something, 'at's okay, I reckon. Don't matter none. I sell some crackers and some canned goods and quite alot of them shoes."

Them shoes was (were?) Wolverines (Werewol-verines?). She sold a pair to me for fifteen-dollars cash, since she doesn't, never has and couldn't if she wanted to, take plastic. Fifteen dollars plus a buck for the Co-cola had to be a big sales day for Miss Sarah. She put the money in her dress pocket. The till remained bill free. "It don't add up right no how," she said.

Miss Sarah said work shoes sell but not dress shoes. A pair of dull black loafers from the Fifties sat where they have since the Fifties and probably never will sell. "But they might too," she adds with a patooey that missed the coffee can and further stained the wood floor around it a darker shade of tobacco brown.

A Sanforized shirt, its plastic cover covered in dust, is still available at its original price of $2.59.

"Mosta this stuff ain't for sale no more no how." Miss Sarah said she would part with the Fab Detergent and the Punch and Judy Diaper Wash but not the hand water pump and a rubber spring-looking thing.

"I don't know what that is. And the man who brung it in don't know neither. But it's a good un."

There was also a peanut warmer, a notched police nightstick, a petrified potato with spikes sticking out of it and a wooden leg for a mule.

"Are any of these for sale, Miss Sarah?"

"No. They's there jes for gawkin' at."

"But what if I offered to buy, say, this. Whatever this is."

"If I sell it then it's gone and then I don't have it no more. The man what gave it to me said he found it under an undertaker's house. Don't know what it might have been used for."

When she was younger, Miss Sarah snapped Polaroids of any new people who came in and she kept them in an old green album she pulled out from under a stack of yellowed newspapers. The album wanted very much to disintegrate. We managed to find a picture of me as a twelve-year-old. What a local yokel dorkal I was! Even then she didn't recall me, despite my being a non-blood relative. There's one picture of a man who rode his horse into the store and a snapshot of a pair of Siamese twins who stopped en route to the Jefferson County Fair where they were appearing that week. Now them, she remembered. "They bought two pairs of Wolverines," she recalled.

The screen door screeched open and then loudly slammed shut to announce the arrival of Billy Holmes. Good ole Billy Holmes. He's related to me but I don't know how. He's old now but when I was a kid my friends and I teased him unmercifully about his hiccupping. We called him Wild Bill Hiccup.

Billy told Miss Sarah he came in to get a Co-cola. Of course, when he opened the lid to the cooler and saw it was empty, he hiccuppingly complained. "Whar's the (hiccup) Co-cola, Miss Sarah?"

She told him that if there weren't any more Co-colas in the Pepsi cooler than I had just drunk the last one.

"Well then I'll have (hiccup) a bag of them root beer barrels."

Wild Billy is tall and lanky with a very ruddy complexion from his pimply youth. He dresses as if it's 1950 with tight blue jeans, rolled up cuffs and a white tee shirt with rolled up sleeves holding a pack of Winstons. He wore his hair in a flat top that stood straight and stiff thanks to a liberal application of Butch Hair Paste, original tubes still available at Miss Sarah's. On his feet were Wolverines.

Billy didn't remember me either. He sucked on the candy, stared at me awhile and eventually asked where I was from and going. I told him about being from Duck and staying in Gosling. He asked me if I noticed he had the hiccups. I said I had. He felt he had to explain. "I've been (hiccup) hiccupping long as I can re (hiccup) member." Billy said he accidentally swallowed a toothpick as a child. "I used to suck on a (hiccup) toothpick all the time and I swallered it and (hiccup) it stuck inside my craw. I tried to git it out and I started hiccupping real fast. I just got used to it. I talk slow 'cause I hiccup (hiccup) less when I talk slow." He was talking soooo slowwww.

He said when he gets anxious or nervous the hiccupping gets worse. His wife assured him that he doesn't hiccup in his sleep. He had a surgeon clip a nerve thirty years ago but that didn't help. He'd tried all the home remedies like blowing in a paper sack or having someone scare him. Billy said he hoped they'd just stop someday but said he's not holding his breath. He actually said that. So, I didn't laugh. I swear I didn't. Okay, I did laugh, but coughed to cover it up and then, to my utter surprise, hiccupped once. It made me wonder if hiccupping, like yawning, is contagious.

As you can imagine, that conversation took about an hour. I picked up the tab as the three of us finished off Billy's root beer barrels and a stale bag of Wise potato chips-- best sold before 11-10-2002 it said on the package.

"Thanks for the tater (hiccup) chips, Jake."

"It's Jack. You're welcome, Billy. See you, Miss Sarah."

"Patooey." Hit the side of the coffee can that time.

Sarah began closing the store as Wild Billy and I started leaving. It was half past noon. Sarah seemed plenty pleased to have sold some Wolverines, a Co-cola and some root beer candy in a single day.

On the way out, I noticed a very old apparently well used toilet plunger. "Miss Sarah, is this plunger just for gawkin' at or can I buy it?"

"One dollar and it's yourn (patooey)."

I had a great need for that plunger which I'll explain later on-- and not for the reason you're probably thinking.

MANUSCRIPT CHAPTER NINE

The Stoop Twins
Tuesday Afternoon

Later that day, I almost had to rub my eyes in disbelief when they (my eyes) saw that Johnny and Stella were still around. Like Miss Sarah, they also seemed old when I was a kid and there they were looking exactly as they did back then.

Johnny and Stella wander into town, at most, nine or ten times a year. They're pretty much avoided by the townspeople. Nobody in Gosling claims a kinship with them, but I took the time to get to know them when I was young and liked them very much.

(Editors: I want to include them in my book because I want the reader to see my positive and sensitive sides which are not being adequately expressed in this book so far despite the fact that I'm writing it myself. You will see those sides of me when we eventually meet in person to discuss publication, promotion and compensation. JO)

When I pulled over to say hello and told them who I was they broke into wide grins. Ah, it's always nice to be remembered, I remembered somebody once reminded me upon my remembering them.

Johnny and Stella are both small and dainty with deeply creased faces, high cheekbones and long, dark grey hair. They're thought to be brother and sister and live as hermits in an abandoned stone quarry about a mile out of Gosling.

They are poorer than poor and disheveler than disheveled. They never make eye contact. Local gossip is that they are the result of inbreeding and people whisper their suspicion that they are still inbreeding. They're derogatorily called The Stoop Twins, not only because they are mentally challenged, but also because when you see them they're often stooped over picking up things along the highway. They walk the roadways, most often just after dawn or just before dusk, searching for anything that might have some value or use to them. I used to help them pick up Co-cola bottles in ditches for the two cents per bottle refund. I once stole an entire crate of empty soda bottles from Steven's Mini Mart and gave them to Johnny and Stella to turn in. They took my advice to wait about six months before returning them and then only two or three bottles at a time. We/us Odums are a crafty bunch and willing to share such knowledge.

I would visit their shack in a far corner of the quarry once or twice a year. I used to wonder if I was their only visitor. I liked them because they would listen to me when I was of the age when it seemed nobody else would. And I would listen to them. Nobody would want their lifestyle but they seemed perfectly happy with their circumstances.

They had a pet possum back then. Now, possums are actually quite cute even though they're alot like a rat (raht?). They're related to the panda bear and you can probably see that now that I've pointed it out. I learned that from my landlord, Ray. You might remember him from Chapter Four. The man knows everything. Johnny and Stella would get a big laugh when I held their possum, which they named Possum, because possums have this nasty saliva thing going for them. After a few minutes your hands are covered in slimy marsupial spit. It's almost as disgusting as old Miss Sarah's coffee spit can but I'd hold the possum just to see Johnny and Stella smile. Possum the possum quit playing dead and did the real thing many years ago, the result, of course, of a road accident.

(Editors: It hit me just this minute that Possum the possum is probably why I felt it important to mention all the dead possums on US 64. I must have a fondness for possums buried deep in my psyche going back to my youthful encounter with Possum. I also think mentioning my sympathy for a fellow creature of the animal kingdom will further my intentions of showing readers my positive sensitive side as a counter to what they might perceive as an occasional negative indifference to things. JO)

While they liked possums, they despised snakes and skunks and killed them every chance they had. They liked to tell me how stupid skunks are. Yes, skunks are stoops! When a skunk invades their space they simply walk up as close to it as possible without getting sprayed and bonk it on the back of the head with a rock. The skunk dies instantly. Who knew? They knew! Ray probably knows.

I almost had to rub my ears in disbelief when they (my ears) heard them inviting me to stay for supper. They (not my ears. Johnny and Stella) had never done that before. I considered telling them *Thanks, but I'm in a hurry and have to go* but instead my ears heard my voice saying "sure, why not, Stella? Thanks."

We sat on upside down bright orange five gallon buckets from Home Depot. The table was an ironing board. Stella served a meal of lima beans she had boiled over an open fire. There was a meat in the beans which I think (hoped) was ham but I didn't ask, and honestly, didn't want to know for sure (possum? snake? skunk?). They poured on a little vinegar, which added zest to the beans. They were delicious. We drank water. They're not the alkies some people in Gosling presume they are.

Johnny mentioned some of the interesting things he

and Stella had seen recently. Last week, he said, they watched a deer fawn suckling a farmer's milk cow. Another day they saw a young blue heron eating a dragonfly while a turtle was trying to eat the heron. He said it seemed like the heron and the dragonfly had accepted their fates and were not struggling to survive and the turtle seemed in no hurry to finish the job.

"Know what? Not everything makes sense," Johnny said.

"Well, Johnny, maybe there was a big ole cottonmouth under the water trying to eat the turtle," I offered. We all quietly thought about the possibility or unlikelihood of that. *You know, you can't think noisily, Jacko.*

I got a good laugh out of them when I gave them the Betsy Ross ass-art I bought at The Three Wise Men's Hiney Stand in Turkey. I told Stella that the bent-over-bloomers-flashing-hiney-woman is how people in town see her all the time, "stooped over showing your underwear."

"I don't never got no undies on, Jack."

I fought off that very disturbing mental image. *Woah!!*

It began to rain and was getting thunderous and lightningous so I bid farewell to Johnny and Stella. I don't know their last name(s). I wondered what their Thanksgiving dinner would be.

***

Let me jump ahead of myself, narratively here, because physically doing so is impossible, and tell you right now what they had for their Thanksgiving dinner, in case you were wondering. They had barbecued pork, turkey and stuffing, mashed potatoes, mac and cheese, candied yams, green beans, cranberry sauce and pecan pie. Everybody at the reunion was so busy stuffing their faces they never noticed my making three plates for myself. I spent an hour on Thanksgiving Day at Johnny and Stella's camp enjoying the feast I'd brought them and rinsing it down with their real coffee brewed over an open fire.

"I gotta get back to the reunion. Happy Thanksgiving, Stella. Johnny," I said.

"Happy Thanksgiving-- brother," Johnny replied. A toothless smile from Stella.

Now don't go getting all teary-eyed on me like I am on me right now.

MANUSCRIPT CHAPTER TEN

Mom the Artiste and Dad the Plumber's Helper
Tuesday Night

Back at The Americana, I tried to hear the last five minutes of a noisy, snowy "CBS Evening News" on the motel's 1970's TV set. The story of great national importance had something to do with tryptophan, the snooze-inducing amino acid in turkey that we'd all be ingesting on Thanksgiving. I think the reporter said that it's a myth and that chicken actually has more tryptophan than turkey. I don't know if it was the reporter's slow delivery or the never-ending talking head with a nutritionist but I became drowsy and almost fell asleep. The loud "Wheel of Fortune" intro that followed the newscast shocked me awake. Pat Sajak and Vanna White were in The Bahamas, I think, and they smiled at me through the heavy TV snowstorm. Vanna still looks fantastic after all these years despite her difficult job of turning letters five nights a week. Ray, my landlord, is crazy in love with Vanna. He said she's a South Carolina girl and nightly walking proof of southern women's superior beauty and poise. I watched her turn three vowels but still couldn't figure out the hidden phrase. My mind, which was just sitting there in my head doing nothing, unable even to solve a simple game show puzzle, suddenly switched to thinking about my family in Gosling, *I don't know why JJ called his Thanksgiving gathering the Odum "annual" reunion, Jacko!?*

Gosling is home to almost my entire family but the Odums only manage a big get-together about every four or five years. The last reunion was four years ago, which I didn't attend. I did make it to the one eight years ago. JJ hosted those two, too. Our annual reunions started to die when Great Grandpa Orrin Odum died, dad's grandfather and master moonshiner and beer brewer. I never knew him. Great Grandma Clara lived as a widow for a decade and it was for her that the family kept trying to hold annual reunions but it soon became every other year, then every third. After she died at the ripe old age of 97, of old age, the reunions died with her.

Grandma Clara Odum was an odd old bird. She was a big-boned, heavyset German who could somehow disappear in a room. You might not even know she was there if you didn't seek her out. She had her chair and her knitting in one corner of the living room and sometimes a bottle of her homebrewed beer on the coffee (beer?) table. She spent the better part of every day there. About every half hour she'd take out a pouch of loose tobacco and rolling paper and make a cigarette. Her hands were shaky and some of the tobacco would spill out onto her lap and chair. Grandma Clara would slowly, lovingly lick the paper's edge and roll a cigarette that Phillip Morris, who(m) ever he is, would envy, strike a match, light the twisted end, take in the nicotine in a big inhalation, blow the smoke into the air and let out a series of coughs that would scare small children and animals. We treated her like a Mafia don. When we visited, it was customary to approach her chair one at a time, give her a hug, wish her well and go elsewhere. Our feeling toward Grandma Clara was one of respect more than love. We may have even feared her. She'd acknowledge us with a nod. She wouldn't say a word. I can't tell you what Grandma Clara's voice sounded like. Wait, yes, I can. That's because when I was about ten, I hugged her, wished her well and asked if I could have a swig of her beer. A deep German-sounding guttural grunt accompanied a swat.

Now, when a rare-honest-to-Betsy-come-one-come-all-Odum-family-reunion is planned, it's always held in Gosling because my family doesn't travel very much or far. I have relatives who've never ventured farther than Charlotte, about a hundred miles away. They'll go to Charlotte to see a NASCAR race or fine dine at a Sonny's BBQ joint. A rare trip all the way to Raleigh would include driving by the YMCA because there's an "Andy Griffith Show" rerun where Deputy Barney Fife says he always stays in a corner room at the Y when he leaves Mayberry for the big city.

Getting out of the house to many of my kinfolk, and many of our neighbors, usually meant going to someone else's house in town for a few hours. My parent's house was apparently an especially inviting getaway because we seemed always to have guests on weekends for lunch or dinner or both. Uninvited guests. They'd just show up. Not so much as a phone call to tell us they "might could" come over. My mother would roll her eyes and groan something along the lines of "Oh Christ. It's Beth and them again," yet welcome them like long lost friends. By coincidence or not, and I'm sure it's by not, the uninvited would show up around noon or five. Those are the times we ate. Somehow or other my mother could manage to whip up a gourmet government surplus extravaganza. I don't know how she did it. All of a sudden out of nowhere there was a table set with, say, leftover mashed potatoes formed into cakes and fried, warmed up leftover navy beans, maybe some warmed up leftover country ham or slices of a kind of lunch meat I despised (still do) that has olives and red peppers mixed in it, slices of surplus cheese, scrambled surplus powdered eggs, sliced cukes, tomatoes and beets from the garden, a stack of week-old white bread (fresh homemade bread on a good day), butter, peanut butter, ketchup, mustard and mayonnaise. Sweet iced tea. For dessert, Jell-O with fruit cocktail in it, which I hated (still do) even more than the olive/pepper lunch meat. Everyone would just dig in and make do creating some unlikely combinations. I'm here to highly recommend tossing chunks of cheddar cheese in your navy beans. And you haven't eaten until you've experienced a mayo, mustard, country ham and scrambled egg sandwich on white bread.

Beth Graham and her brood were especially strange house/meal guests. They would arrive by car from their house half a mile away. The six of them would sit on our front porch or in the living room and hardly say a word depending, I guess, on my parents to entertain and feed them. They'd smile and nod but not offer anything to discuss or lift a finger to help with supper. They would sit and watch our TV for hours, which, I understood because they didn't own a television set. Come to think of it, maybe they didn't have a telephone either. In that case, no wonder they never called. *Maybe you're being too harsh, Jacko.* I can be harsh, I just thought, as indicated by the *italics*. Still, they seemed to always make it to any of our family's gatherings, saying nothing and eating plenty. So did the Sommervilles.

The Sommervilles were the opposite of Beth's gang. They didn't know how to not talk. When they'd come calling, the five of them would talk over each other; telling jokes, spreading rumors, or relating in great detail some recent event. I remember an especially excited conversation about how a real estate agent wanted them to invest in a planned development. They would receive a free toaster oven by touring a planned mobile home luxury resort near Weaverton, eight miles north of Gosling. The realtor inquired as to what they liked to do in their spare time, "play a little golf, tennis, boating, fine dining, or travel somewhere?" They told him they liked to "sit on the porch and watch their Bug Whacker zap insects." He gave the Sommervilles the nickel tour and the fifteen-dollar toaster oven but never followed up with them. "But them trailers was raht nice," Neal Sommerville said, "and we asked the real-a-tor if we might could have a Bug Whacker instead of a toaster oven 'cause we already have a good toaster oven and our Bug Whacker is about shot. He said he'd ask his manager but we knowed he was jes tryin' to get rid a us 'cause he knowed we wasn't interested." They were our favorite drop-ins. They always brought a goodie, usually a fresh baked loaf of bread or something from their bug free garden.

Mom and Dad are gone. They died six months apart six years ago next year. I can easily picture the two of them all these years later, like it's yesterday, because I carry a photo of them in my wallet.

When they married after the War, Ralph and Faye Odum set-up housekeeping in Gosling where they were both born and raised. They never moved from that first house.

They didn't want us to call them Mama and Daddy, as is common in the South. I'm not sure why because that's what they called their parents? So, it was Mom and Dad in our house and I have to admit that I do find it strange hearing a grown man call his father Daddy. "Tell you what," Dad told JJ and me once, "y'all don't call me Daddy and I won't call you Bubba, Bo, Skeeter or Geyser." I think maybe Dad and his Daddy had issues but we never went there.

Mom was somewhat of an artist. Dad was somewhat of a plumber. My mother's works of art filled the kitchen. My father's plumbing fixtures filled the living room.

Our kitchen was part real and part art. There was a real stove, refrigerator, table and chairs. But many other things were painted on the walls. There was only one cabinet but it looked like there were more because mom had painted the wall to look like there were cabinets all around. There appeared to be an herb rack and ceramic cookie jars that were just paintings on the wall. The Cheerios and coffee pot were real but not the sugar bowl. There was just enough real stuff that it functioned as a kitchen. Faye Odum had a wonderful sense of humor. She painted spilled milk on the floor and a hole in the baseboard with a little mouse peeking out. There were three windows in the kitchen. Only one was real. On it, she painted an alternative, nicer outdoor scene than was our real outdoors. My mother was actually quite a good artist. Visitors were cautious before they picked up anything because they weren't sure at first. She kept real and plastic fruit, vegetables and sweets in the fridge. Her art was restricted to the kitchen and a little bit in their bedroom. What appeared as a bench at the bottom of their double bed was actually a painting on the footboard. The painting over the bed was a framed picture of a lightning storm painted by somebody else.

We spent most of our family time in dad's living room, which looked something like a big bathroom. He had the hobby of turning old bathroom items into living room furniture. We had a curio cabinet flush against the wall that was made out of stainless steel sinks. Two old commodes were made comfy enough to serve as chairs. "Go ahead and sit yerself down," he'd invite visitors.

My ex, Susan, was especially affected by dad's toilet-themed living room because it sent her urinary tract into spasms.

Dad turned an old claw leg bathtub into a sofa by cutting out one side of the tub and then fitting it with cushions and pillows. "I always like to do something that nobody else ain't never done before," I remember him saying. Dad would have loved that plywood hiney of the bent over plumber the Wise Men had on display.

I recall many evenings sitting on a toilet in the living room watching TV. I also recall in vivid color how our family had to watch the black-and-white Moon Landing on a neighbor's set. That's because on the day of the broadcast our brand-new Zenith Color TV Console was repossessed.

Mom and dad were as proud as the NBC peacock of having a color television. We were late getting into color because of my father's on-again-off-again job at the brick company.

A quick side note here: I worked at the brickyard myself one summer after high school. I hesitate to even mention that part of my life experience because it was even more boring than working at the *PennySaver* and had nothing to do with writing, which is what this book is all about. If you've seen one brick you've seen a wall of them. My back is still killing me from moving bricks. That's another reason I decided to let them fire me at the brickyard. It's painful right now in fact-- down near my vertical smile-- as I sit here writing about it. Now back to what I was writing about before I broke away to write this paragraph:

Since dad's job was mostly off-again we were among the last families in Gosling to get a color television. But in 1969, when our old black and white Zenith finally went kaput, my parents made a down payment on a brand-new Zenith at Sears and Roebuck. It was a fine piece of furniture. Large. Not just a color TV but also an AM/FM radio and a stereo record player for 78s, 33&1/3s and 45s built into it. We may have been among the last in Gosling to get a TV but we now had the finest and newest and largest entertainment console on the block.

A telephone call from Jim Thompson down at Sears ended our chance of seeing Armstrong's black and white giant moon leap in living color. It went something like this:

Mom: "JJ, Jack, turn down the TV a minute. Hello."

JJ and I: "What?" "Huh?"

Mom: "Turn down the Zenith. I'm trying to talk on the phone."

Mom again: "Hello. I'm sorry. I couldn't hear who you said this is."

Man on Phone: "Ah. Hello. Is this Faye? This here is Jim down at Sears."

Mom: "Well, hey, Jim. We're jest a-lovin' our new

Zenith."

Jim: "Um, well, that's why I'm calling, Faye. I was going through our accounts and I see that you haven't made any payments in over four months on that TV."

Mom: "Well, we was going to make another payment on that next week when Ralph gets paid. He's workin' again now. The brickyard laid him off but he's back and we'll be down to the store next week."

Jim: "Y'know, you're four months overdue?"

Mom: "I think it's only two but…"

Jim: "I'm terrible sorry Faye but we're going to have to have the TV returned since you're so far behind on your payments."

Me: "Mom, are you off the phone yet? We can't hear the TV."

Mom: "No."

Jim: "Huh?"

Me: "What?"

Mom: "I said no."

Jim: Faye, I can't take no as an answ…"

Mom: "No, Jim, I didn't say no. Well, I said no but I said no to my kids who are, ah, but not to you… but did you say y'all want the Zenith back?"

Jim: "Well, Faye, we'll do y'all a favor and reimburse y'all half of the down payment y'all made. Five dollars, as a gesture of goodwill, you know. But, yes, we'll have a truck there tomorrow morning."

Me as narrator/author now and not part of the phone conversation: Upset about this development and the likelihood of missing the Moon Landing, my mother told Jim that a week sure would be more convenient.

Jim again: "No, no, tomorrow, Faye. That's the best I can do. I'll have a truck their tomorrow at ten. I'm sorry. Say hey to Ralph. Bye."

Now back to my regular narration: The truth was my

father had no work the week ahead. We awaited the visit from the Repo Man by watching that TV and playing that radio and phonograph non-stop until then. The Repo Man didn't show up until four o'clock with a truck full of other repoed appliances from around the county. He was in a bad mood because his partner failed to show up. As a result, he was a one-man band, driver and loader-upper.

When he saw the size of the Zenith TV/radio/stereo console he knew it was a two-man job. Rather than putting it off for another day he offered my father a twenty-dollar bill to help him haul the set out of the house and into the truck. Dad wasn't happy, of course, about losing the TV but gave in when the Repo Guy showed him the twenty. That was alot of quick easy money.

With my dad on one side and the Repo Man on the other, they slowly lifted the console, carefully guided it from the living room to the hallway and onto the front porch. As they were taking it down the front steps toward the truck, the TV somehow slipped from my father's hands. The wooden legs broke off and the TV tubes and screen splintered spreading glass all over the street.

Dad said he was "raht sorry about his sweaty hands slipping and all" and offered to return the twenty. The two men looked at each other for a while and then both cracked up laughing. We think maybe the Repo Man had been repoed himself at some point.

My father eventually went back to work at the brick-yard and a couple of months later we got another Zenith color TV/Stereo for our bathroom/living room.

The décor de tub of our living room made us stand up (sit down?) comics at bathroom humor.

Me: "I think 'The Howdy Doodoo Show' is on now."

Dad: "I'd rather watch 'Flush Gordon.'"

Bonnie: "No, let's watch 'The Pissidon Adventure.'"
Bonnie laughed so hard at her own joke she peed her pants.

Me, as a present day grown up and your current author: Dad's love of the lav worked to Bonnie's benefit much later at college. She volunteered at Raleigh's Botanical Garden while studying architecture at North Carolina State. She applied for and got a small grant to redesign the park's bathroom. Bonnie argued successfully on how the odors from the toilets were dramatically interfering with the flowergarden's bouquet and received the go-ahead to design a new WC for visitor's nature calls. Her toilet was a thing of beauty. *"Architectural Digest"* got wind of her project and named it "the prettiest pooper in America." She was "quoted" in the article saying that a bathroom is "the one place where we're by ourselves and enjoying ourselves physically and psychologically. It should be a beautiful and inspirational place to sit for a while." The magazine also did a sidebar on dad's living room and mom's kitchen. I hadn't seen my parents that proud since we got the first Zenith.

My parent's house was sold shortly after they died to Paul Cramer, Gosling's one and only plumber. He always loved my Dad's laving room.

I flicked off "Wheel of Fortune" before the contestants or I could solve the puzzle:

_ AVE _ _ Y T_ E _ELL.

I wanted to hit the sack early because I had to get up early Wednesday morning and drive to my cousin Denny Roy's house for a day of fishing. I was in the mood for some fish. Since moving to the coast I had grown accustomed to the custom in some homes of serving seafood on Thanksgiving. My ex, Susan, and I enjoyed several Thanksgiving dinners with my landlord, Ray. The night before and the morning of Thanksgiving, Ray would go fishing for flounder. One especially memorable year he caught a flounder the size of a doormat and two others almost as big. The three of us ate all three of them plus some oysters and shrimp, yams and greens.

I fell asleep just as I remembered Ray cutting into a warm pecan pie. I dreamt about The Bahamas where Sue and I honeymooned. Except in my dream, Ray was with us and he was with Vanna White. I woke up briefly at about 3am with the answer to The Wheel of Fortune puzzle, which I'll reveal in the next chapter. Like Pat Sajak says, "Stay tuned. We'll be right back."

I went right back to sleep.

MANUSCRIPT CHAPTER ELEVEN

Copping Copper
Wednesday Morning

I'd called my closest cousin and best childhood friend, Denny Roy Rogers, about spending some time with him during my vacation. Yes, his name is Denny Roy Rogers. My uncle-by-marriage, Buddy Rogers, was a big fan of the singing cowboy and Roy's wife, Dale, and Roy's horse, Trigger and of course, Dale's horse, Buttermilk. I wish the Rerun Channel would rerun the old "Roy Rogers Show." Denny Roy's (and my's?) favorite character on that show was Pat Brady, who rode the range in Nellybelle, his Jeep. Denny Roy joked that if he ever had a daughter, he was going to name her Nellie Belle Rogers and if a boy, Pat Brady Rogers. He never had any kids. His marriage was worse than mine.

Denny Roy doesn't live in Gosling but about fifty miles farther west on the outskirts of Murphy, North Carolina. We'd made arrangements to meet Wednesday morning. I followed the directions he emailed to me. I didn't have a GPS but he said, even if I did, it would never find him.

"It's easy. 'Bout ten or twelve miles 'fore you get to Murphy on 64 look for a beaten-up ole trailer park called 'Glory Estates' on your left. Right after you see that, make the first right onto a gravel road that ain't marked but there's a big mailbox right there that says Wilson. They was the people who lived in the house there when it were livable. Then follow the road about a mile or a mile and a half or two miles or more and cross over a bridge and go up the next hill. If you see a very old dead oak tree on the right then you've gone too far. Turn around as soon as you can and be careful and go back about an eighth of a mile and make a right and follow that path down a while and you're there. Easy. White house with green shutters and my red truck out front. Cain't miss it."

Of course, I missed it. It's a fact of life that once someone says, "you can't miss it" you'll miss it. I failed to see the trailer park or the dead tree. But after four passes I noticed the "path" -- a dirt road with weeds growing between the tire tracks. That fifty or so miles from Gosling to Denny Roy's took me almost two hours because of the winding mountain roads and the getting lost. When I arrived he already had his pickup packed with camping and fishing gear. Denny Roy didn't mind. He and I had been best buds since the first grade in Gosling and all through high school. But we lost track of each other for ten years or more, re-united at a class reunion and have stayed in touch by phone and email ever since. We're now as thick as thieves. I hope you remember me mentioning Denny Roy several chapters back as the cherub penis thief at GAG's swimming pool when we were about eleven or twelve.

He came up with a great plan to go fishing and camping Wednesday night at a construction site where a lake was being expanded. A valley and a small crossroads town were to be flooded in the near future.

"Let's go on up 'ere and look around. The town's a ghost now but the river in the valley 'ere has some good trout jes waitin' for us to eat 'em."

He talked me right into it. I hadn't fished nor camped in many years so it sounded perfect. It also sounded inexpensive since I was currently cash challenged being unemployed, as I think I mentioned earlier.

"How're ya comin' along as a novelist, Jacko?"

"Still working on it, Denny Roy. I'm going to write a book about my family now. It'll be kind of like a novel only with alot of true stuff in it. I might even write about you some. And, Denny Roy, I told you on the phone that I was thinking about being a noveller not a novelist."

"That's raht. I remember now you sayin' that but I didn't understand that."

"Well, let me ask you. Are you a reader or a readist?"

"I'm a reader when I read, which ain't much." Pause, furrowed brow, squinted eyes, light bulb appears above head. "Well, I'll be damned. Now that I think about yer question 'ere, I see yer point. Hell, calling yerself that noveller crap makes sense, Jacko."

Denny Roy is in business for himself. He's a jack-of-all-trades but his specialty is plumbing and electrical work. "So, I reckon that's why I'm a plumber instead of a plumbist," he reckoned. "And I'll start calling myself an electricianer from now on, too." Ah, we're blood.

Denny Roy appeared to be doing okay because his modular home --no wheels that I could see-- looked new and sat on at least an acre. Everything inside and out, from the siding to the paneling to the rugs had a plastic look and feel, appeared indestructible and plastically comfortable.

The lake expansion construction site was an hour away. During the drive there, I told him about my joblessness and he told me about his businessless.

"I ain't had a good year, Jacko. I been living off last year."

"How are you keeping that nice house up?" probably sticking my nose in where it shouldn't be but curiosity was killing me.

"You can't say nothin' about this to Janice 'kay?"

Janice was his long-time girlfriend of two months. Janice was no beauty queen but pretty enough in a hard living, redneck kind of way and sweeter than sugar. She sported a most joyous tattoo. It was of a string of red and green Christmas lights that began at her left ankle and wound around her leg and pelvic area, *I imagined*, stomach, breasts, *also imagined*, neck and ended at her right ear. I couldn't stop myself from repeatedly following it with my eyes from ankle to ear and back down to ankle. Both she and Denny Roy noticed and smiled after I brought my bobbing head under control. Janice feminized Denny Roy's house in many ways by spraying perfume all around and placing plastic flowers on just about every table and counter. She showed alot of leg and played with her hair and giggled at everything Denny Roy or I said whether it was funny or not. "You boys is nuttier than nutmeg," she said when we told her about some of our high school hijinks. I couldn't determine her accent. It was south of my southern. I meant to look up where nutmeg comes from for this book but forgot to do it.

"Sure. I won't say nothing to Janice," I said double negatively. "Why? What?" I asked double W-ly.

"About ten years ago I bought a truck load of copper wire and pipes from a guy who came around and told me he'd sell it cheap 'cause he had to get rid of it 'cause it was hot. I buried it out back of the house and figured I would dig it up and sell it someday when it weren't hot no more. I dug it up last fall and sold the copper and some of them iron manhole covers you know I had, Jack. 'Member them manhole covers?"

"Yes," I said and nodded in the appropriate direction.

"And I made some right smart money on it. But don't tell no one, 'specially Janice 'cause it would severely upset her."

"Who'd you sell it to?" I asked since my curiosity hadn't killed me yet.

"Scrap yards over in Tennessee."

"Did they wonder where you got so much copper or manhole covers?"

"Never asked. So, I never said. And I sold some of it at different scrappers. That way it didn't seem so much to them, y'know. Besides, them manhole covers was three years old and the wires and pipes was over ten years old. With my bidness bad right now, that copper and them manhole covers is keepin' me and Janice goin'. So, don't tell Janice."

"I won't. But be careful, Denny Roy. And to think your life of crime started way back at GAG's house when you broke off that statue's penis."

"I still have that thing in a box somewheres, Jacko. Mama threw it away but I found it in the garbage and got alot more laughing miles out of it in school. Mama was royally pissed 'bout that, y'know. She went over to the Gosling's house, practically on her hands and knees, and returned the pecker to Mr. Gosling and offered to pay for the damage. GAG told mama to just keep her kids on a leash and keep the pecker. Mama tried not to, but she was laughin' good when she told daddy about her handing over that baby weenie to Old Man Gosling. She told daddy she always thought GAG was a little prick and now she knew it for sure."

I started but then stopped myself from telling him about my sister Bonnie's likelihood of marrying GAG the Third. He'd gag at that news.

"Yeah, well, you won't be laughing if you get caught," I said more motherly than cousinly.

"I won't get caught. And here you are, an Odum, lecturing me about the hazards of stealing." Point well taken.

We caught some nice trout and with chips, dip and beer we enjoyed an amazing campfire dinner. Afterwards, we hopped in the pickup and did what we did when we always got together; we went out howling, which means we do whatever we feel like doing at the moment.

It started at a bar and proceeded to another bar and another and then another, et cetera... and then to more et ceteras. I don't recall everything that happened that night and overnight as I was (another Gosling cliché alert!) loose as a goose. I do recall going into several abandoned houses in the lake construction zone that were to be demolished and spent some time looking through them and drinking beer. Denny Roy was especially interested in how the old houses were plumbed and wired with copper.

Well, some of them were now no longer plumbed or wired with copper. I recall laughing myself silly when Denny Roy said something like "what a' awesome coppertunity this is, Jacko." It seemed funny at the time.

It was almost noon when we woke up back at Denny Roy's house. After a quick shower I felt pretty good, considering. Janice can't cook and Denny Roy was in no condition to try, so we ate cold cereal with a bottle of the hair of the dog and coffee (instant). Janice boiled the water. We laughed about the good time we'd had and promised each other we'd do it again sometime.

Denny Roy had to move his truck before I could leave. It was blocking my car. He could hardly see to backup because the truck bed was so full of stuff we found at the dam site that it blocked the rear window. A blue tarp covered it all. That was just half of it. He'd put the other half in the trunk and backseat of my Honda when we got back early that morning. Denny Roy said he'd bury his share like he did before, and in a couple of years, he would sell the copper at Tennessee, Georgia or South Carolina scrap yards.

"Don't tell Janice. It ain't a serious crime no how, Jacko, 'cause all they was gonna do was bulldoze them houses anyways," he said. "Hey. Take care, cuz, and don't do nothin' that I wouldn't have nothin' to do with."

"I already didn't do it, Denny Roy. Bye." I waved goodbye to Janice who(m) was standing on the porch in her nightgown showing alot of Christmas leg and twirling her hair.

I drove squinty eyed back to Gosling, checked into the Americana and hit the head to shit, shower, shave and shampoo before heading over to JJ's for the Odum family Thanksgiving Reunion Feast I've been telling y'all about.

Oh, and before I forget and start writing the next chapter, the "Wheel of Fortune" answer was SAVED BY THE BELL which is also a very funny old TV show on the Rerun Channel.

MANUSCRIPT CHAPTER TWELVE

Rock'n'Roll Chickens and Spic'n'Span Pigs
Thanksgiving Day

Since this book is about my family's Thanksgiving re-union, I suppose I ought to get into that since I'm already up to Chapter Twelve.

Most Odum family gatherings are outside affairs because so many Odums will show up when free food and drink are available. There's not a house in Gosling big enough to handle them except for GAG's mansion and they're not Odums... yet. The weather often cooperates for Thanksgiving in western North Carolina. It's been known to be very pleasant in late November with temperatures in the high sixties and many trees still in full fall color, or surrounded by fallen leaves in need of raking or piled high and ready for jumping into. It wasn't quite that nice this Thanksgiving. It was overcast, a little windy, the trees bare and the temperature in the high fifties. No snow in the forecast and for that I was thankful because the heater in the Honda is out and you can see the steel in my radial tires.

I arrived just as JJ was saying grace and people were telling everyone what they were thankful for this Thanksgiving:

"I'm thankful not to be no more sicker than I was before," said a relative-by-marriage I didn't know. Applause all around.

"I'm thankful I didn't win the lottery 'cause all y'all would be after me to pay all y'all's bills," joked an apparent relative I had never seen before but liked his sense of humor, honesty and correct insight. Some smiles. Some frowns. One person applauding. Me.

"I'm thankful to have reached the ripe old age of fifty-two without dying first," said somebody who looked seventy-two.

"I'm thankful I came here 'cause that food over yonder is calling my name," said my obese cousin Bobby Dean Odum. "Bobbbbby Deannnnn. Bobbbby Deannnn. Come and git me," he said vertical head nodding all around and simultaneous head turns to the left to look and whiff at the food being set out over yonder.

After six or seven more thankfuls, I joined the kumbayaing and quipped the quip I quip every Thanksgiving, "I'm just thankful I'm not a turkey at this time of year." Quizzical looks, horizontal head nodding and furrowed brows. Then, finally: "THAT'S A GOOD'UN JACK," screamed Aunt Ruth, who(m) I wrote about a couple of chapters ago and has a loud voice and works at the diner. She had also just arrived and was holding her "best in the northern hemisphere chicken salad." My father used to say, "That Ruth is ALOT of woman." I still can't decide if that's a compliment or a criticism.

"I hope that's not Henrietta from the diner in that dish there, Aunt Ruth."

"No, no. Not HENRIETTA, Jack. But I'll bet a close RELATIVE OR TWO of hers is in there. A family reunion is all about RELATIVES, RAHT?" Laughter from her and one other person. Me.

The reunion setup was much better than I had expected. JJ outdid himself. People were playing badminton and horseshoes; there were dogs and cats and rabbits to pet; there were four long tables overflowing with food and drink.

It may be Thanksgiving but the star of JJ's show was not a turkey but a pig. When Odums put on a big doin', we do it over roasted pig flesh. A "hog autopsy" is how a vegan friend of mine once described a southern pig pickin'. The carcass is laid out in the cooker with its skin folded back so that picnickers can easily pick at the meat on all parts of its body.

"Remember bro', the meat's best in the rib area and the shoulders," JJ reminded me needlessly as I stood ready to stab a fork in the porker.

"I haven't been to a real pig pickin' in years, JJ. That's a right beautiful thing right there."

"I'm not cookin' him. Georgie there did all the work," he said. "And Uncle Phil provided the pig."

I asked him where Phil got the pig. He advised me not to visit the Farley farm anytime soon because this particular hog was hot in more ways than one.

"What's the punishment for pig theft in North Carolina, JJ?"

"I don't know but the Farley's also provided the two turkeys and a chicken Uncle Phil is frying."

I hope you remember from way back when when I mentioned how my Uncle Phil and his son Georgie served a year behind bars for stealing state highway department equipment. As I understand it, it was after a Friday night of boilermakers that they decided it would be a profitable idea to break into a state transportation facility next county over and permanently borrow a forklift and several thousand dollars worth of truck parts. By not hiding the hot forklift well enough; that is, in high weeds behind their garage, they were arrested two months later. The forklift and some of the truck parts were returned to the state. Father and son asked and were granted the right to share a jail cell during their nine-month incarceration. "It might could be cheaper, Judge, for the state that way and we're used to each other, Your Honor sir, please," pleaded Phil guiltily.

Still, you need to know that my uncle and cousin are great fun to be around. Phil can play any musical instrument known to man and Georgie is an excellent cook. They run a truck repair and parts business in Gosling now.

Every Memorial Day, Phil and Georgie turn their garage into a little café for the afternoon. The grease pit becomes a greasy spoon. They invite all their customers over for lunch. They'll have a hundred-people sitting on tool chests and leaning against pegboards chowing down on ham hocks, pinto beans and biscuits and guzzling sweet tea. Every Christmas, they stack a huge pile of blown out threadbare tires in a giant heap outside the garage, string hundreds of blinking lights over it, put a blow-up Santa Claus on top and call it a "treaditional" Christmas tree.

"With them lights on at night that there tire tree looks right sharp," say they.

"But it's gawd awful ugly in the daylight and it's a fire hazard and it violates the town ordinance on heights," says the long-time mayor of Gosling who(m) the Odums never vote for and ignore.

I knew I would see them at Thanksgiving; Phil playing violin, guitar, mandolin, banjo, juice harp, jug and spoons and Georgie burning hog flesh.

Now, one table was just booze, everything from store-bought and homemade beer to store-bought and homemade liquor. A second table was all munchies; chips and pretzels, dips and salsas and my favorite, cheese puffs, which kind of smell like throw-up but are delicious anyway. A third table was all desserts: homemade cakes, cobblers, cookies and, my personal weakness, pies. How to decide between pumpkin, lemon meringue, blueberry, coconut cream, peanut butter, sweet potato, mince meat, pecan or chocolate chess. The fourth table contained all the fixins you'd need at a pig-pickin'-turkey-jerkin'chicken-lickin'-pic-nicin'-reunion: butter beans, macaroni and cheese, new potatoes, collard greens, corn on the cob and corn bread and paté. Actually, no way, Paté! I wrote in paté as a jab at Aunt Minnié who actually brought paté to a picnic once when I was a kid. Everybody hated it. Nobody ate it. We don't even eat goose in Gosling let alone their liver. Why? That's a good question I asked myself on your behalf. Answer: I don't know. *You don't know, Jack?* I don't, but I'll extensively research it someday by asking JJ. Maybe goose liver is good fried. What isn't?

It was so ironic that the meat at the reunion was from other farms because JJ has hundreds of farm animals. But he doesn't slaughter them. They're pets. JJ is the sensible and most sensitive one in the family. His goodness is probably the way his brain processes The Oil.

He raises cows and goats for their milk but farm animals of all ilk roam his little ranch. That's because he has a big heart and has opened up his place to allow aging farm animals to live out their final years in peace. It's rather like an old folks' home for aged goats, chickens, cows and that old grey mare, Betty, I mentioned, many pages ago. None will ever be sold for slaughter. They're there until they die a natural death.

He has four young cows and four young goats to provide his family with an income and their daily dairy requirements. When the cows and goats get old and milked-out, he retires them and replaces them. He said the death and replacement rate equals out and so he always has roughly the same number of animals.

Most of his animals have names. The goats are named for female singers. The current four are Madonna, Cher, Janis Joplin and Dolly Parton. To watch him milking the especially well endowed Dolly is a laugh-a-squirt.

JJ owns about nine acres and farms every square inch of it. The soil on the farm is as fertile as his wife, Martha. They have five kids.

"This land'll produce all kindsa produce. All she needs is a good dose of chicken manure once a year. You know don't you, Jacko, that chickens give you the best shit?"

I did, actually, because he'd told me this several times before. JJ repeats himself alot. Maybe it's because his name is Jay Jay.

"Pig dung's good, too. But I prefer chicken," he went on despite knowing that I knew that, too.

He told me about a trip he took once to Asheville when the circus was in town. "They was givin' elephant dung away. They can't get rid of it fast enough. They told me elephants shit three hundred pounds a day. I brought home a shitload of shit and put it in the rhubarb patch. I had rhubarb as big as trees. A forest of rhubarb, Jacko! You believe that?"

"If anyone can grow uber rhubarb it's you, brother."

"Urban rhubarb?"

"No. Uber. It's a word I just rememebered. It means super in German."

"Do you speak German, Jack?"

"No. That's the only German word I know. Susan's from Pennsylvania and she told me that word. There are alot of Germans in Pennsylvania."

"Why didn't you just say super instead of suber?"

"It's uber not suber. I guess I said you grew uber rhubarb because uber and rhubarb sounded kinda good together. Y'know, uber… rhuber."

"It's rhu-barb, Jack, not rhuber."

"I know." *Sometimes JJ's an uber goober, Jacko.*

"I guess you must know what you're sayin'. You're the word sayer in the family, Jack."

Well, JJ claims the chickens that provide him with his favorite manure lay more than the average amount of eggs. He says it's because he pumps music into his coops twenty-four hours a day. The music playlist is chicken appropriate. He plays a reel-to-reel tape I made for him years ago of country, rock and jazz birdy music, y'know, like The Everly Brothers' "Bird Dog," "Rockin' Robin" by Bobby Day and "Everybody Knows that the Bird is a Word" by the The Trashmen. I also put on two whole albums by The Eagles, The Byrds and Charlie Byrd.

(Editors: Another idea just occurred to me to make this book stand out from the others: a book soundtrack! Let's attach to the back cover a cd, or whatever is new and exciting, of appropriate music. We could place this ♫ wherever we want on pages to alert the reader when to play the music. We could charge more and make more money. It would also thicken the book. JO)

JJ's cows get pedicures in an experiment to make them more contented and, therefore, give more milk. A farrier comes by once a year to clip and polish their hooves. His most contented and pedied milker, Molly, will come to him when he calls her name, and she follows him around the pasture like a dog. He experiments with milk flavors by feeding his cows kudzu, cotton or sweet clover to see how different plants affect the taste. Interestingly, something as pleasant sounding as sweet clover gave the milk a yucky taste.

JJ sometimes adds beer or a few drops of The Oil to his pet's watering troughs. "Makes 'em smile, brother. Ever seen a pig grin?"

He's gained a statewide reputation for his unusual farming techniques. The county agriculture agent gets JJ media coverage every so often by convincing newspaper and TV reporters into doing stories on his music loving chickens, cows with pedis and especially his clean, nice smelling hogs. WLOS-TV's Todd Grisson did a live report on JJ's pigs last month. He mailed me a DVD of the story. I wish I could show the video in this book but here's roughly how it sounded, so try to picture it in your mind, but then where else in your body could you picture it?

Todd the Reporter says: "JJ Odum's pigs aren't spic

and span clean. They are, after all, hogs and they do what hogs like to do... root and roll in mud. But these three piglets are the cleanest porkers Jefferson County agriculture agent Bo Jackson has ever seen."

Bo the Ag Agent as a TV talking head: "It's an interesting way to not only raise clean hogs but better smelling hogs. His secret is sawdust and potatoes."

Todd the Reporter: "Odum rotates the use of his pig pens. One year he uses his hog pens for hogs, and the following year to grow potatoes. Every other year, he covers the ground in the pens in two feet of sawdust... sawdust that includes pleasant smelling cedar chips. He plants potatoes in the sawdust which benefit from the pig manure in the soil below it."

Now JJ as a talking head: "When the potatoes are ready to pick in the fall I can just pull 'em right out of the sawdust by hand. Don't have to dig 'em up. Pull 'em right out and the taters are hanging there on the roots of the plant with nary a speck of dirt on 'em."

Todd the Reporter: "Then the following year he'll put his three pigs in the sawdust pens and they, too, stay clean... as hogs go... and smell of cedar wood."

JJ: "They're in there raht now rootin' around in the sawdust and fertilizing them pens for next year's tater crop."

Pigs: "Oink" "Grunt" "Oink"

Bo the Ag Agent again: "When JJ told me he was raising clean hogs, I said 'Yeah, sure, when pigs fly!' but you can see for yourself there that his hogs are pink and pretty. And they smell right good. Go ahead and sniff one of them, Todd."

Todd the Reporter: "So, I took a good whiff..."

Sound of Todd smelling a pig: "Sniff sniff."

Todd again: "...and I'll confirm it... that pig smells a bit like a cedar chest... although a cedar chest that could use a little airing out!"

Pig Sounds again: "Oink "Grunt" "Snort"
Todd: "Todd Grisson Action News, Gosling, back to you Dave and Michelle."

Me, not as a talking head or on the video but as the author of this book: JJ had only three pigs when that aired. Todd failed to report the nice little tidbit that JJ named them Straw, Wood and Brick after the houses in "The Three Little Pigs" fairytale.

I asked him once why he doesn't butcher at least some of his farm animals.

"I just like havin' 'em 'round here," he said. "They're real easy goin' when they get old. They ain't like some of us people who get old and mean, know what I mean?"

He told me that, as a young boy, he saw a neighbor pull a bull out of a barn and tie it up to a post to be shot and then butchered. The farmer pointed a .22 between the bull's eyes and pulled the trigger. The bull's eyes bulged and he stood there in shock for about five seconds before his front legs gave in and then his body fell to the side. In less than thirty seconds that huge, strong creature died of a shot from a small .22 bullet. It shocked JJ how fragile life is and how easily it can be taken away.

He also reminded me of the time we watched a mass chicken slaughter at a neighbor's farm. The farmer had pounded two nails into a tree stump. The birds seemed to stupidly comply with their assassin when he held them to the stump by stretching their neck between the two nails. The chickens were beheaded with one hack from the farmer's hatchet. Their heads would fall into a bucket at the foot of the stump and their headless bodies would flap around, spurting blood and eventually falling over after thirty seconds or so. With helpers handing him chickens, the farmer was chopping off a head about every ten seconds. The bucket filled up with hundreds of identical wide eyed chicken heads staring up as their bodies piled up in the barnyard. I'd forgotten about that. But that neighbor shooting the bull and the image of chickens running around with their heads cut off would never leave JJ's mind.

JJ is a bit younger than me. His name is Jesse James Odum but he's always been called Jesse Jim or JJ. I don't know what my parents were thinking giving him the name of the famous outlaw with that alleged thievery gene running in the family.

He's won North Carolina's Largest Watermelon Contest three years in a row. Last year he entered and won with a melon that weighed in at 258 pounds. It took a forklift to get it out of the field and onto a trailer truck for transport to the Jefferson County Fair. JJ credits four things to his monster melons: Chicken crap as fertilizer, seeds from previous monster melons, planting only when the soil is warm and his singing to them. He'll sit right down in the watermelon patch and belt out a Johnny Cash or Willie Nelson song. Once the baby melons appear on the vine, JJ makes it a Sunday morning after-church ritual to grab his guitar and sing to them. When a certain melon shows exceptional growth, he entertains it daily until harvest time and the County Fair.

He's taken to serenading pumpkins now and pointed to a three hundred pounder serving as the centerpiece of a giant cornucopia in his front yard. I immediately pictured how nicely the ass-and-udder hiney of a cow I, um, found for JJ in Turkey would look there. He claims that, like chickens, watermelons and probably other fruits and vegetables are sensitive to music. "My singing penetrates that melon and satisfies it. Watermelons got a sense of feel. Not like human feelings. They got fruity feelings."

I'm a sensitive guy, as you know by now, but JJ puts me to sensitivity shame. And so might his uber melons and squash.

MANUSCRIPT CHAPTER THIRTEEN

Gunslingers, Geezers, Geetars and GM
Thanksgiving Day

As you've likely noticed by now, we're a musical family and by 2pm there was already a full-fledged, beer-soaked C&W&G concert going on at the picnic area beside the creek. I was disappointed to see that the Odum family's most gifted guitarist, my father's brother, Tony, wasn't among the music makers. His wife, Laura, was there singing and swigging. Laura and Tony are my family's most talked about couple which I'll talk about later on.

My cousin Louis, who immediately handed me a brew, enthusiastically greeted me as a long lost cuz. Louis likes his beer and it shows at his waist. He's short and fat and bald and always smiling. He likes to shake hands and pat you on the back. We also call Louis "Luey-loo-way" after the old rock'n'roll song lyrics. Louis greeting you can be somewhat uncomfortable until you get used to him. That's because he's a roaring swearaholic. He's the only one in the family who uses foul language. He said he learned to do it in "juvie." We have all gotten so used to it we hardly notice anymore.

(Editors: I think it would be wise to put a disclaimer *right here for educators should this book wind up in* *school libraries as I hope and expect. This chapter de-* *serves at least a PG and possibly an R rating. Example:* **Teachers, the following chapter contains some (implied)** **rough words that may not be suitable for children of**

certain ages. Parental guidance is suggested. *What do you think? JO)*

"Son of a (gun). Look who the (devil) showed up. (Darn), Jack, how the (heck) have you been." I cleaned up that "quote" for print. Just insert a cuss word where the parenthesized words are and you'll know how Louis talks when he's drunk, which is almost always.

(Editors: I don't think parenthesizing and substituting words like gee, gosh, darn, dang, heck and freakin effectively reflect Louis' personality. He would never talk like that. This is difficult for me because I speak out loud what I'm writing and I never swear. Well, I have but it's rare. I have to be extremely upset about something. Writing and saying out loud Louis' "quotes" is uncomfortable and probably unwise. I don't want this book to get banned in public schools. In fact, I hope to see it become required reading someday. On the other hand, if I used the actual swear words, many more kids would probably seek it out to read it. Hmmm. Let me think. Let... me... think. Hmmm. My mind is telling me one thing but my conscience is telling me another.

Conscience: *Keep it tasteful, Jack.*

Mind: *C'mon, Jacko, every kid in America has heard the F word by kindergarten and used it by third grade.*

Conscience: *Do the right thing here, Jack.*

Mind: *Jacko, you know I'm smart because I am, after all, a brain. Show some cojones and quote Louis the way he talks-- and the way I've heard you talk when you're really upset about something. I remember-- and I remember alot because I'm a brain, mind you-- that the last time you swore was when Susan told you that you should..."*

Me: *Be quiet mind and conscience. I've decided that for this manuscript I'm going to go with _____ and* *let the readers and the editors fill in the* _____ *s however they want.*

Conscience: *Good plan, Jack. You're a good and decent man.*

Mind: _____ *woose.*

Emotions and Intuition: *Would you like to hear from us, Jacko?*

Me: *No. Stay out of this.*

Good luck editors. I'm _____ *flummoxed. JO)*

Dear reader: I've given it a great deal of thought for a minute and have decided to go with my conscience and not precisely "quote" my cousin Louis. What I'll do is leave a blank line (_____) and you can insert whatever cuss word you're comfortable reading.

So...

There were six guitars being played at one time, a mandolin and a fiddle. Two of my aunt-in-laws were belting out how Hank Williams was so lonesome he could cry.

Louis and I took our lonesome selves and two beers each to the driveway where four men, smoking hand rolled cigarettes, were looking under the hood of Louis' 1957 Chevy and studying it like it was Detroit-new. The car is blue but the hood, roof, trunk and parts of the fenders, door and bumpers are rust colored. That's because they're rusty.

The odometer is broken at 122,538 miles but Louis claims it's actually 322,000-plus miles since the odometer has been broken for fifteen years. The speedometer, dome light, clock, horn and radio don't work either. "But, _____, I don't _____ care nothin' about that," Louis said. "The _____ engine and transmission and rear end are all _____ original... and what _____ great paint there is. I'm telling you this _____ car hasn't _____ me. Know what I'm _____ saying? It's just been a no-breakdown _____ automobile. I put nothing into her but oral (oil) and gas and some _____ duct tape in a few

spots. I can't go into a _____ service station but someone asking me if I want to _____ sell 'er. I'd have to be
dead or dead drunk to _____ sell 'er."

Louis said he has been offered three thousand dollars,
which is about what the car cost in 1957.

"You arda write a _____ news story on her, Jacko,
for that _____ rag you call a _____ newspaper in
Duck." He mispronounced Duck.

I said, "Louis, I'm writing a book about the Odum
family and I'll mention you and your Chevy in it."

"That'll be the _____ day when you write a _____
book. What crazy _____ would wanna read anything
about our _____ fam damly?"

"I think you're getting wasted, Louis."

"I ain't as thunkin frunk as you drink I am."

Two Eighties-era cars also had their hoods up, discussed in depth and dismissed as being inferior to Louis'
antique (read: junky) Chevy.

"What're you driving these days, Jackoff?"

"I have a Honda."

Everybody paused. Stared at me. Nodded yes and then
no and then went back to studying the engine.

"Any _____ good?"

"It got me here," I said.

Long pause. Long stare.

"Ain't never had a _____ Jap car. Cain't beat GM."

With that, the car talk came to a screeching halt. Louis
ambled (stumbled) over to the other car guys studying the
engine of a beat-up Buick and asked if anyone wanted to
"shrow shum _____ shoes."

Now, you don't have to beg Aunt Ruth's brand new
(her fourth) husband, Claire, to play horseshoes. Like a
pool shark, he carries a shiny expensive set of "throwing
shoes" with him in a fancy felt lined box. He was wearing
his favorite shirt that sported a National Horseshoe Pitch-
er's Association pocket patch. "I throwed thirty out of thir-

ty last time there," he bragged and then threw another ringer.

"Holy Christ, Claire, you _____ bashard. I hate shur _____ guts," belched Louis.

What sounded like a bomb going off caught my attention but was ignored by all the engine studiers. JJ had set-up a target practice area in a wooded area beyond a bunch of junked cars and some of the men were over there shooting guns.

You need to know that when you grow-up in Gosling you will-- YOU WILL-- shoot guns. You cannot be twelve or older and male and not hunt. You will have a rifle and a shotgun. We may not have had diddly squat when I was a teenager but I had a 12-gauge shotgun and a .22 rifle. Now that I'm an adult, I will admit right here on this page, that I was never much of a hunter. Not from the first time I fired a shotgun at the age of eight was I a gun guy. I'm the only Odum who doesn't hunt. But all male Odums and male Goslingers are required by birthright to get up hours before sunrise to join the heavily armed manly masses heading for the kills. We hunted deer, bear, wild boar, rabbits, squirrels, turkey-- whatever was in season. It seemed like there was always some meat in season.

Deer season starts at sunrise. That means getting up in the dead of night, downing the preferred hunter's breakfast of sausage biscuits, grits and coffee and claiming a spot in the woods to await daylight. At the first streak of light, there's a thunderous roar as scores of rifles herald the dawn and frightened deer dart through the trees. By 7am there are dead deer all over the forest floor and then all over the fenders of four wheel drives. Alot of hunters are home by 9 and eat a second fried breakfast.

I was never able to bag a buck or a doe and today live in near shame of it since I am, after all, a Goslinger/Odum. I did, however, manage to bring supper home sometimes. My first prize was that grey squirrel I told you about which my mother cooked but refused to eat. "Skirrel ain't nothing but a fancy rat," she complained while frying-up the small chunks of meat from the critter's hindquarters. Most of the squirrel and rabbit meat we brought home ended up in a stew and was quite tasty, if gamey. Deer meat was eaten as steaks by we/us men or mixed with hamburger meat for mom and Bonnie. They hated the wild taste of venison. I hated it, too, (still do) but didn't dare admit it because I'm a male Goslinger/Odum.

I also killed a ringed-neck pheasant once. Walking through a cornfield during small game season, I saw the bird about twenty feet away, blasted it with my shotgun and proudly announced to fellow hunters that I had just killed a turkey. When we ate it the next night everyone agreed that pheasant is even tastier than turkey. On my next outing, a grouse practically let me step on it before it flew. It scared me so much I nearly dropped the gun. But I managed to open fire, wounded it seriously enough that it couldn't fly. As it flapped its wings on the ground, I shot it two more times until it quit. Unfortunately, there was so much buck-shot in her she was inedible. So, I don't know if grouse is better than pheasant or turkey.

I hunted bear armed with "punkin balls" in my 12 gauge. Punkin balls turn a shotgun into a pseudo-rifle. They're a shotgun shell that sends a ball out the barrel in-stead of spraying beebees. I honestly hoped I wouldn't see a bear-- and thankfully never did-- because I'm sure I'd have done in my pants what bears famously do in the woods.

We also hunted deer and wild boar with bow and ar-row. I never got close to either. We hunted big game ille-gally by what's called "road hunting." We'd just drive the country roads and when anyone saw a deer or boar, we'd all jump out and hurl an arrow at it. There are North Caro-lina trees that shake in fear of me today because of all the arrows I sunk into them during archery season.

There's a hunting technique we used that perplexed me but seemed to make sense to everybody else. It's called "driving." Hunters split into two groups. One group walks through the woods side-by-side making noise to chase any deer in front of them toward the second group of hunters standing side-by-side about half a mile away. As a result, one group is shooting toward the other group, which is fine as long as the deer or the trees stop the bullets or arrows.

My uncles Bob and Rob, Mom's identically similar twin sibs, used to hunt with slingshots. The brothers make slingshots out of inner tube rubber and a fork of wood. As slingshot sharpshooters, they can knock a can off your head or a corncob out of your hand at fifty feet. Throw a quarter in the air and they can hit it with a bean shot from their sling. They're incredible to watch. I've seen it. They shot a cigarette out of my mouth once when I was a kid stupid enough to let them.

They make their slings in four sizes, mini to magnum. Over the years, they've made thousands of them and autograph them. I have two of them, a Bob-Mini-Sling and a Rob-Maxi-Sling. At the reunion, I asked Uncle Bob if he'd make me a mini. Sure, he said. At least I think that's what he answered, "Preacher came here one day, Jacko, and asked if I had time to make one. I said, 'Mister, if I was that busy, I'd quit and go fishing.'"

I noticed that Rob and Bob's older brother, Jeb, was also at the reunion. He's a Civil War nut although he refers to it as The Late Unpleasantness or The War of Northern Aggression. He was named after Jeb Stuart, the Confederate General. Jeb is known around Gosling as The Cannon Blaster. He can be seen, or more likely heard, at all the Jefferson County High School football games. He's a seventy-five-year-old cheerleader who keeps the fans fired up by blasting a Civil War era cannon each time the Jefferson County Falcons score a touchdown.

"When I was in high school," he said, "I tried out for football but I only weighed ninety-five pounds and I got rejected and that hurt my feelings."

So, he drags a cannon around now that weighs more than he does to all the home games. It began as his approach to parental involvement when his son played for the Falcons. Jeb's a Korean War vet and flies both the Stars and Stripes and the Confederate flag at his home. We call him a Southern Hindu Baptist because he believes in reincarnation. Uncle Jeb claims he served in the Civil War in a former life, as well as at The Alamo, Waterloo and Troy. Jeb is of concern.

Jeb's cannon's kaboom can be heard two miles away and neighbors often complain when he blasts it at home for the fun of it. He loads it with a four-ounce bag of powder to propel an eight-ounce pack of sand. "Not a bit more or less. I weigh it out on scales 'cause I wanna know exactly what I'm rammin' down that barrel there."

SHOOT, I shouted to myself in my head when Jeb's son, Clint, called me over to do some "shootin'." They were not shooting slingshots or rifles or shotguns but a large pistol that looked meaner than the gun another Clint carries in the "Dirty Harry" movies. The fifty-caliber pistol was so big and heavy that Clint placed it on a "gun stick" that looked like a metal crutch with a V on top and a strap; not unlike one of Bob and Rob's slingshots but five feet tall.

Clint asked me what I hoped he wouldn't: "Wanner far'er?" (Do you want to fire her?). Clint might stand five feet tall on a good day and a hundred pounds after a big meal. There is nothing to him but you could tell he felt mighty holding that pistol. The gun looked like a cannon in his hands. I believe father and son may suffer from a Napoleon complex. Maybe Jeb really was at Waterloo.

"You bet," I said enthusiastically, because I had to, because I was born here, but didn't want to. I rested the big gun on the V and strapped on the strap and sighted in on a beer bottle a hundred yards away. When I pulled the trigger the bullet missed the bottle. I don't know where it went. I worry about where it went. I remember hearing a branch of a tree fall down somewhere. My arm hurt from the kick of the pistol. My ego was as bruised as my arm became the next day. I had to face the laughter and kidding the rest of my visit.

Meantime, Louey-loo-way staggered over and said, _____ Jacko never was much at guns or _____ huntin', were he?"

I had almost forgotten until my mind reminded me to *give Louis the gift I found.* I figured he would be at the reunion and I'd seen something I knew he'd enjoy at the Gas & Grits Truck Stop in Kinston on the way there. There was an old beat-up and broken "Welcome Truckers" sign on the door at the truck stop's souvenir shop that I knew Cousin Louis would just, in his words, "_____ love."

MANUSCRIPT CHAPTER FOURTEEN

Smooshed Snakes and Snake Oral
Thanksgiving Day

I heard in the distance the pleasing, joyful sound of children loudly giggling. There were about fifteen of them loudly splashing around in JJ's swimming pool. But as I got closer to the pool, I discovered they were playing Marco _____ Polo. Oh, sorry. This is a new chapter. Ignore that. Start again:

I heard... children... in a pool... playing that swimming game Marco Polo. In case you're fortunate enough never to have heard of, or heard, this game, it requires the poor sucker who is "it" to close his eyes and say "Marco" while the others must respond by saying "Polo" as a hint to their location. The problem is kids don't "say" Marco and then Polo. They yell it.

"MARCO... POLO..."

I like loud as the very subtitle of this book indicates (The Journaller: My Novel: Written and to be Read Out Loud) but not fifteen or more kids screaming at the top of their lungs...

"...MARCO... POLO..."

... over and over and over again...

"MARCO... POLO..."

JJ built his own in-ground swimming pool. It looks more like a small pond. He took a front-end loader and dug a ditch five feet deep, thirty feet wide and seventy feet long. He covered the whole hole in six mil black plastic and pumped forty thousand gallons of well water into it. He got the idea from his two young boys who'd dug a hole in the backyard's hard yellow clay, filled it with water and jumped in.

"MARCO..."

"POLO..."

"They came in the house muddy as hell," JJ told me. "But I looked at their hole and my imagination ran wild."

"Interesting but tell me something, brother. Does that Marco Polo game ever get on your nerves?"

"Huh?" he huhed. I guess he couldn't hear me over all the Marco-Poloing.

The plastic he used is strong enough to keep holes from being punched in it and the black color helps heat the water. The plastic, pool chemicals and electricity to pump the water cost him all of ninety-five dollars.

"MARCO..."

"POLO..."

"Dirt cheap," he said, "And I didn't have to float a loan and drown in debt."

I would have laughed at his punning but I was running out of patience and was ready to drown some kids.

"MARCO..."

"DUCK..."

Marco Duck?

Then some of the kids jumped out of the pool and started playing the Duck Duck Goose game nearby. I live in a town called Duck and I'm from a town called Gosling but if I could I would put a hex on who(m)ever's bird brained idea Duck Duck Goose was. A variation on Tag, the "it" person calls everybody a Duck until he decides someone is a Goose and the Goose chases the "it" person who tries to take the Goose's seat. Like Marco Polo, Duck Duck Goose is a noisy game. Now it sounded like the Marco Polos were trying to drown out the Duck Goosers.

"DUCK..."

"DUCK…"
"POLO…"
"GOOSE…"
"MARCO…"

So, I excused myself before committing mass childricide. "Excuse me, JJ, but I gotta piss like a Russian racehorse." *Did I just channel my ex-wife and her ever-bloated bladder?* "Mind if I go in the house?" I asked because I didn't want to use his outhouse.

He asked, "Why not visit the outhouse?" just as I expected he would.

JJ's outhouse is a classic, complete with a crescent moon cutout in the door. It's a three holer; sizes large, medium and small. Each seat is rounded off and sanded down for the pooper's pleasure. JJ put a roll of toilet paper in there but it's always too damp to use. Apparently, the Sears magazine was all used up (wiped out?). It's a terrible place to do your duty. It's just a hole in the ground and you don't want to look down into it. And stink! Even though JJ sprinkles lime down there it still smells to high Heaven (low Hell?).

"Why don't you tear that thing down and fill in the hole, JJ. That's a public health hazard," I complained.

"It's historical, Jack. That outhouse is over a hundred years old," he complained back to me. "It's a original. They're disappearing, Jack."

"As they should," I said.

"The kids and me still use it sometimes when we're outside and don't wanna traipse things inside the house. Martha won't go near it. Says there are probably spiders in there. There are. Lots of 'em. Part of the charm, Jack. Wasps, too. I kill 'em though when I go in there to dump (pause) lime. Never seen a snake in there yet."

"Well, if you don't mind, my indoor plumbing would prefer using your indoor plumbing."

"Sure, go ahead. Martha's in there cooking. See how she's doin'."

"Why is Martha cooking in the bathroom, JJ?"

"Very funny, Jacko. The bathroom humor from dad's living room days live on! Go, will ya? And see how the food's comin' along... in the kitchen. I'm gonna stay here and enjoy watchin' the kids swim and play."

"Huh?" I huhed. *Oh, yeah, right. Enjoy... kids... playing... Marco... Polo... Duck... Duck... Goose. Must be a parent thing.* "I'll talk to you more later, JJ."

(Editors: You know, I just brought to my own attention the fact that things having to do with the bathroom are playing a prominent role in this manuscript: Sue and my urinary problems, my neighbor Ray Clegg's nightly back porch drain, dad's living room furniture, Russian horses, hineys and JJ's outhouse. Perhaps your promotion people could play that up and advertise this as good bathroom reading material. Readers are readers whether in a chair or on the crapper. I won't be offended. JO)

JJ and his wife-of-forever, Martha, make alot of their own things besides kids.

As I walked through the kitchen I saw that Martha was, indeed, busy cooking potatoes, corn, and greens-- and soap. In JJ and Martha's house, the household soap bars are huge, off white chunks of homemade soap. She was also making another batch of The Oil.

Outside: "POLO...."

"Hi, Martha. Talk you in a few minutes. I gotta..."

But she saw me in her peripheral vision and yelled at me, "Jacko, hold yer horses a minute." My Russian horses didn't really want to be held but I reined them in.

"I just put a brand-new bar of lye soap in there, Jack. I'm spearamintin (experimenting) with scents. Tell me whatcha think. I just mixed me up a brand-new batch 'cause there were a full moon."

Martha claims you can only make soap three days before, during, and three days after a full moon. "Every time the full moon comes round I'm a cookin' up soap."

"C'mon, Martha, that's just an Old Wives' Tale," I said while walking in place and squeezing in my groin and its urinary associated parts. Now I wished I had gone to the outhouse.

"No, it ain't, Jacko. That's a lye." (My spelling. Too good to pass up). "It'll fall flat. The full moon makes the soap harden up and get whiter."

All of a sudden, I'm being lectured on Lye Soap Making 101: "All you need is water, lye, grease and a full moon," she continued. All I needed was bladder relief.

"First off, I boirl (boil) the water."

Oh, water? I thought, stomped and squeezed and wished she wouldn't mention water. "Then I pour a can of lye into the boirling water real careful-like 'cause it can flare up on you. That happened to me once. It went swoosh."

She had some nasty swoosh scars to prove it. "Look at my arm here. And my hand. And it burned my neck here, too. See that?"

She said she gives free soap to her neighbors in exchange for them giving her their kitchen scrap grease. "Chicken, pork, beef, fish, I don't care. Just gimmee grease."

The mix sits overnight and the next morning she cuts the hardened soap into squares.

"Jack. You need to pee or something?"

I nodded loudly in the affirmative.

"Go on. I'll wait."

She waited-- outside the bathroom door.

Outside: "GOOSE..."

I closed the bathroom door and barely got my zipper down. Actually, a couple of drops couldn't wait. I tried to be quiet but I couldn't help myself and moaned "Ooohhhhhhhhhhoooohhhhhhhooooooo"-- she surely heard my relief on the other side of the door so I went-- "ooooooooooooooooohhhhhooooo-wow-this soap smells wooooonderful."

"You like that soap smell in there?" Martha yelled through the door.

"Yes," I said. "It's very nice. What is that fragrance?"

"Confederate jasmine. I don't want my soap stinkin' of grease. And it smells much better than store bought Ivry, don't it?" Ivry being Ivory Soap.

I noticed a hairdryer so I dried off the front of my pants where the Russian horses couldn't wait to leave the gate.

"Were you blow dryin' your hair in there?" Martha asked when I came out.

"No. Well, yes. I got my hair wet when I washed my face so I thought I'd, y'know, dry my hair where I got it wet, y'know, when I washed my face. So how are you doin', Martha?"

"I'm as happy as a bee in a bonnet," she buzzed.

I followed her to the kitchen where she checked the soap and stirred The Oil, which was boirling in a large pot on another burner.

Outside: "DUCK... MARCO... GOOSE... POLO..."

"Got me a good dose of The Famly Snake Oral (how she pronounces oil) cookin' up, too, Jacko. Fourth batch this year. You likin' The Oral ain't ya?"

"Yeah, I guess. I think maybe it helps my brain think. *Thanks.* But sometimes I get mental blocks and can't write. And, you know, I'm the family writer."

"Well, that ain't much good for a writer now, is it?"

"No, it ain't," I said, noticing that my English was deteriorating by the second. My English goes north when I go home. North not South! Some of us southerners don't cotton much to the term that if something is "going south" it means it's getting worse.

"The Oral is right good, Jacko. Do you know it can cure itches, borals (boils), warts, fungus and hemorrhoids?"

"I did not know that," I said trying not to sound skeptical.

"It does. I been spearamintin and it does. It'll help cure roomytism, gout, arthur-itis and poison ivory (not to be confused with Ivry Soap)."

"Then I'm going to start rubbing The Oil on my right hand, Martha. I have some AUTHOR-itis in my novel writing right hand," I joked, but it went nowhere.

"You got corns on yer feet, Jack?"

"No. Why?"

"The Oral'll is good against corns. Don't even have to take yer shoes off. Rub it on the side of your shoe and it penetrates and fixes that corn."

"Wow," I said un-wow-like.

"You ain't convinced are ya?" she said convinced that I wasn't, which I wasn't.

Outside: "POLO... GOOSE... MARCO..."

"Got anything for a headache, Marco, I mean, Martha?" I didn't know if all the loud kids or the lye soap cooking brought it on.

"Surely do. My last batch of The Oral. I been spearamintin' with adding a new herb or weed I found out back in the horse pasture. Jes rub a dab of this in yer temples and it'll cure that migraine in no time flat. It goes right to the brain, Jacko. It's a miracle."

We'll see.

***

Later, as Martha was laying out some devilled eggs on a picnic table, I heard her brother Rusty say, "They taste raht good with snake."

That's exactly what he said: "They taste raht good with snake!" I know because I asked him to repeat that.

"They taste raht good with snake," he repeated upon my suggestion.

Rusty is an ex-Green Beret who has the habit of keeping the local roadways clear of road kill to fill his freezer. If he sees a deer, squirrel, rabbit or snake or something that was recently run over, still bloody, not flattened, he takes the dead critter home to grill or fry. My mind brought up the image of the bloody white squirrel I ran over in Brevard. He doesn't reclaim squashed raccoons, skunks and possums.

I asked him if the meat didn't have just a slight hint of diesel fuel and radial tires.

"Perfectly good food," he insisted and politely laughed. "If you're eating a squirrel or a deer off the road then that's one less animal shot or bought at a grocery store. So, it's kind of ecological." Not to mention, free.

"Snakes is delicious. Tastes like, well, you know what it tastes like, right?" Yet another white meat.

Rusty said he likes to cut a snake into nugget-sized pieces, boil them in a smidge of The Oil and when ready, slither on some barbecue sauce. He said the only bad thing about snake is that it takes alot of time to eat it. "You have to dig your canines in between all them back bones to get to the meat. But it's worth it."

He brought to the reunion a freshly road-killed rabbit. He skinned it as I watched, threw the carcass on the cooker beside the hog and tossed the fur, head and feet into the woods nearby. He actually rubbed one of the rabbit's feet first for (fur?) good luck.

After shedding Uncle Rusty, I looked for a comfortable place to sit and rub more of Martha's latest experimental batch of The Oral into my temples. It helped my headache. *Thank you, Martha*, my head said. I didn't know what Martha's new ingredient was but her Oral had an interesting new side effect. *A nice little buzz.* And my stomach, which like my mind, conscience, emotions and intuition also talks to me in *italics*, was growling that it was *hungry. Feed me, Jacko, feed me now.*

MANUSCRIPT CHAPTER FIFTEEN

Aaron the Hemo and Deppity Doug
Thanksgiving Day

JJ is forever on the brink of losing his farm. His income is low, his mortgage is high and his medicals bills, he says, "are eatin' me alive." His youngest son, twelve-year-old Aaron, is a hemophiliac who's always scaring the daylights out of everyone because he's so active and forever getting bumped and bruised and, as a result, bloodied and bedfast.

Small, thin and pale, Aaron looks like a weakling but he's a dynamo. He has an excellent attitude and a super sense of humor. "They always put me in a room on the first, second or third floors of the hospital, Uncle Jack, because the fourth floor is considered too high up for us hemos. It's the nosebleed section." See what I mean? He's my favorite nephew.

His medical costs are enough to make you sick. JJ's and Martha's sales of lye soap, eggs, milk, cheese, melons, herbs and vegetables bring in enough to handle the family's regular living expenses but the hospital bills are, as Aaron puts it in his hemo-humor, "bleeding daddy dry."

Except for Aaron, JJ's kids were all Marco-Poloing or Duck Duck Goosing. Where was Aaron? Sitting high up in a pecan tree-- exactly the kind of place he shouldn't be, taking the chance of falling or cutting himself on the bark or a limb.

"Hey. Uncle Jack. C'mon up?"

"I think my tree climbing days are over, Aaron. How

are you doing?"

"Bloody good," he said, putting a British accent to his southern one.

"That's funny Aaron but be careful up there."

"I'm always careful, Uncle Jack. I know what can happen," he said as he slowly wiggled his way to the ground.

"I know you do. Why aren't you swimming or something like the other kids?"

"I was swimming but I got tired playing that dumb Marco Polo game." See why I like this kid?

Aaron has always been fascinated with dinosaurs and I got a huge smile when I handed him the rubber T-Rex I, ah, picked up at the truck stop on the way here. We talked for a while about his school and my important newspaper job-- he doesn't have to know my employment status-- and he said he has thought about becoming a reporter like me.

"I thought you wanted to be a farmer like your daddy?" Unlike our dad, JJ wants his kids to call him daddy.

"Mrs. Rogers, my teacher, said all newspaper reporters are bleeders so I figured that's what I should be. Are you a hemo too, Uncle Jack?"

I almost said, *no, Aaron, I'm not a hemo but I used to be a klepto,* but what I said was "No, Aaron, I'm not a hemo and all reporters aren't bleeders. I don't know what she meant by that."

"She said reporters have bleeding hearts and livers."

"What? That's crazy." I kept rolling that around in my mind (*hmmm, ah, well, hmmm, what? no! if, well, but, hmmm*) until it finally hit me. "Wait. I know what she said, Aaron. She said all reporters are 'bleeding heart liberals.' Well, I'm sure there are plenty of left-wingers in the news but your teacher never met my boss Bernie the Hernia or Awesome Sam Cooke at *The Carolina Times.* They're so far to the right their yellow journalism is red. The only change they want is clean underwear twice a month. But trust me, Aaron, there are plenty of reporters who are blood-red, redneck conservatives. I'm probably one myself. The only liberal bone in my body is...ah, well never mind. Anyway, if you want to be a reporter someday than be a reporter someday and I'll help you if I can when someday comes."

"Thanks, Uncle Jack, but I don't really want to be a reporter. I just said I thought about it once. I already told daddy I'm gonna be a farmer like he is."

"What did he say about that?"

"He said being a farmer takes 'alot of blood, sweat, blood, tears and blood' and then we both laughed real good on a count of my hemophoolishness." A word maker-upper just like his favorite uncle.

The sound of a police siren caught our attention (attentions?). We joined all the kids at the party running toward the road to see what was going on. Nothing gets the adrenaline of a professional newsman going more than the sound of a siren. There was, however, no news breaking. It was just Deputy Sheriff Doug Humphries, a third cousin, letting everyone know he'd arrived. Apparently, his county cop car is his calling card.

Doug is truly a good ole boy. The county deputy sheriff de-fined! Southern to the bone. Countrifried and overweight, his brown uniform is overly snug and his police belt overly loaded down with an arsenal of emergency crime fighting hardware including a club, cuffs, long black flashlight and a gun. It's doubtful any of them have ever seen action.

We love him to death, "bless his heart," as we southerners say when we often mean we're concerned in a smug way. That's because Deputy Sheriff Humphries has had some trouble-- with the law.

In junior high school, he stole a car in the town nextover and took it for a weekend joy ride that cost his parents a hefty fine. In high school, he was the guy with the muscle car who challenged any and all to drag races. He was charged at least twice for dragging. And speeding. And drunk driving.

But Gosling is a small town, and things pass and are forgotten, and ten years after graduation he somehow managed to get hired on as a policeman in that very same next-town-over. Go figure. The family figured he'd finally grown up and straightened up. He made the local news for some big moonshine busts and was up for chief of police for a while. There were newspaper pictures of him and other officers breaking up stills and pouring gallons of the whiskey onto the ground.

However, not all the white lightning was destroyed. A few (many) gallons made it to Doug's house. A fellow officer snitched and the would-be chief was arrested, fined, and dismissed.

Alot of my family found this especially regrettable because Doug's moonshine stash was a holiday tradition. Many a holiday, birthday or anniversary we'd venture over to his house for a shot or two or three of moonshine. He'd reach way back in under his kitchen sink and pull out a jug and we'd all take a big ole swig. I'm here to tell you it was always a fine drink. Soooo smoooooth you'd barely make a face as it warmed up your innards allllll the way downnnn. *Ummmmm*. Innards apparently also speak in *italics*.

If I've written it once then I'll write it again, Gosling is a very small town and things pass and get forgotten. Somehow Doug managed to get on at the Jefferson County Sheriffs Department where he's been patrolling the mean streets now for at least a decade.

"Jacko, is 'at you?"

"Sure is, Dougy. I see you're back in uniform."

"Yeah, man. I'm like a bad penny-- but good a quarter of the time. Ha."

"Are you staying out of trouble, Doug?"

"Me? Who you talking at? Trouble follows me. But I jes look behind me and arrest it. Ha. That's what makes me such a good depitty. What about you, Jacko? You still got them itchy fingers?"

"Not as itchy as when I was young."

"Ha. You stole my bike that time. 'Member? Why you reckon you did that?"

"I don't know. Klepto or something I guess, Dougy. I'm taking medicine for it now."

"Ha," he haed. "Hold on a sec. I gotta entertain the citizens of tomorrow."

He took time to show the kids the police radio, the things on his belt and let Aaron blow the siren. Doug was a hit with the kids and answered all their questions. But the siren blowing was the big finale and kids rushed back to the pool. Aaron ran back to... well, I don't know where Aaron went because I lost track of him when Doug reproached me.

"I like doin' a little po-lice P-R now and agin, Jacko."

We talked a good while about mutual acquaintances, particularly Denny Roy.

"Y'know, Jacko, he's gonna wind up in a jail cell someday. He's worser than I ever was."

"I know. I just saw him and he's doing some things he shouldn't." My mind visualized the hot copper in my Honda just three cars away at that very moment. *I wish Denny Roy would've kept it all. Now I have to figure out what to do with all that stolen copper he ripped out of those dam (damn?) houses. I don't think I actually helped Denny Roy tear it out. Maybe I helped carry it out of the houses and to his truck. I don't know for sure exactly what I did or didn't do. Except, I do know I over drank. I won't share any of this with Doug, although it did cross me (me, being Jacko's mind) that maybe, since we're family, and what with his background, that he would know how to get rid of ...* but then Doug interrupted my thought processes:

"Say, Jacko. You still got a taste fer corn?"

"Don't tell me that you...?"

"Oh, I got me the finest jug of corn this side of the Missisip."

I thought for a moment he was going to say "northern hemisphere."

"Doug, you're going to get busted again, man?"

"No I ain't. The sheriff's in on it, too. Me and Reggie, Sheriff Moore, we bust this moonshiner over in Culver about every two years and keep some of it and he jes fixes up the still again. We're fixin' to bust him next month and he knows it 'cause we're running out. Thirsty?"

"Well, sure. Why not?"

We went to his place and he reached far in under the sink and retrieved a Ball jar of the clearest, whitest white lightning I'd ever seen. It was a beautiful thing. I must say that it went down sooo smoooo... well, like I said a few paragraphs ago.

He drove us back to the reunion in the squad car, our innards whiskey-warm, our eyes having trouble adjusting to daylight and our heads reeling. We headed for the liquids table and Doug poured half a pint of hooch into the lemonade bowl and the other half into the punch.

Everyone was having a good ole time; especially the teetotalers, although Doug did worry and kept a close, if bleary eye on the guys, Louis especially, shooting target practice with a gigantic pistol.

(Editors: I'm curious. What makes a novel a novel and not a novella? Is it the number of pages? Its thickness? I can expand on the making and enjoying of moonshine if you think I'm coming up light. I think I also mentioned using **large print** *once. Let me know. JO)*

MANUSCRIPT CHAPTER SIXTEEN

Kissin' Cuzin
Thanksgiving Day

I noticed Peggy Lou Odum sitting all by herself at the dessert table.

My heart skipped a beat when I saw her because Peggy Lou is special to me. She's a cousin. A third cousin! That's an important point because our relationship-- other than the fact that she's my third cousin-- was sexual in nature. Literally, "in nature." She's the girl in my life who decided to show me hers if I showed her mine. Twice.

The first time was in the first grade at recess in the coatroom. I remember being disappointed because I had a little something to show but there appeared to be nothing down there for me to see on her.

Then when we were fifteen, almost sixteen, the two of us went for a long walk in Poole's Woods near her house outside Gosling. It was the early Seventies and Peggy Lou was a blossoming flower child. I used to sing a slightly altered version of Buddy Holly's "Peggy Sue" to Peggy Lou.

She was very pretty with long red hair, freckled nose and light blue eyes. I always thought, *now why did she have to be my cousin*? I've always understood that third cousinship is acceptable. In fact, I may be wrong, because I was wrong once before, but I think first cousins can legally marry in North Carolina, but don't hold me to it. Just as long they're not first cousins on both sides of the family is what I've been led to believe. I Wikipediaed it once and that was what it said. But can you trust Wikipedia enough to take a genetic gamble? We've all seen the banjo playing kid in the movie "Deliverance." If we took a chance and got married, Peggy Lou Odum's married name would be Peggy Lou Odum.

Anyway, Peggy Lou was still pretty but as round as the pie she brought to the dessert table. Pushing two hundred pounds, she was. But, hey, I've put on a few ounces myself.

Well, that day in the woods, I reached down to pick a wild flower and when I looked up to give it to her, I saw she had pulled the top of her sundress down to her waist and was walking along the path as nonchalant as if she wasn't walking along that path topless. She looked perfectly comfortable walking around breasts-free picking flowers and tossing them into the wind. I wondered at the time if The Oil in her brain was causing this behavior.

Oh My God! Thank you, Heavenly Father, I thought out loud, in my head as usual, to myself. I didn't say it out loud because I couldn't speak. So I did my best acting as if it was an everyday occurrence for me to walk around with a half-naked girl.

It was the early Seventies, I'll remind you; free love and all that. One of the "all thats" turned out to be marijuana. She fired up a joint, took a long deep hit and passed it to me as if we'd done this a million times before. So I acted like I'd smoked marijuana a million times before with half-naked girls. After a long coughing fit, I took a smaller toke and only coughed twice. No coughing at all on the third, fourth, fifth and sixth inhales.

And then... *Oh Wow!!...* I suddenly realized just how beautiful Poole's Woods was and how bright the sun was and how cool that I was there with topless Peggy Lou. At the same time, I became paranoid about being seen by family, friends or the police with her half dressed and both of us smoking pot. Just when I was absolutely sure I heard police sirens coming to get us, Peggy Lou told me to go ahead and touch them. She even told me to go ahead and kiss her. And them!

Jesus, Joseph, Mary and all the Apostles, I thought out even louder to myself.

So, I did. Touched and kissed them. The afternoon sun was setting on a warm summer day and I'm in the woods kissing and fondling the breasts of my beautiful red-headed, freckled, blue eyed, third (legit, remember!) cousin. Stoned. *Grooooovy, Baby!* She, in turn, was tapping her fingers on the front of my pants. Right there before the eyes of God, under a clear blue sunny sky among the trees and the birds and the bees, I was about to lose my virginity. *I'm gonna take my chances. I like banjo music!*

(Editors: I could expand on this if you want because I remember it like it was yesterday. I mean, I gotta tell ya it was an amazing day. But I don't want things to get corny or porny. Let me know. I'm flexible... and so was Peggy Lou. JO)

Things progressed to the point where I was about to scream "Hallelujah" when Peggy Lou screamed "Holy Hell" instead. That's because a long black snake slithered across the path in front of us. In a millisecond, she had her dress top up and her dress bottom down and was heading home. It was an abrupt end to my Adam and Eve evening in the Garden of Eden. *Serpentus Interruptus!*

"I hear you got divorced?" she said at the dessert table, bringing me back to the present. *Bummer!*

"Yep. Red hot redneck bachelor on the warpath," I said. "Look out female America. This bod is on the market again." No reaction whatsoever.

"I hear tell you're a newspaperman somewheres."

"Yeah, I write for an award-winning paper on the Outer Banks," I lied. Not only was I not working, the paper had never won an award.

"I'll bet you're glad you went into newspapers instead of TV News because of what happened in seventh grade, huh?"

What happened in the seventh grade has haunted me my entire life and did, in fact, keep me from pursuing a television journalism career despite my being somewhat photogenic. That is to say, I have a good head of hair. Everybody points that out. Sue said she married me for my hair. I auditioned for a job once at the TV station in Manteo. They needed a talk show host for a morning show. A producer told me that when the red light came on to smile, welcome an imagined audience and then tell them my name and a little bit about myself. When the light came on I said something to the effect of "Ah, Hi. Hello out there. Um, ah, I'm Jack. And I'm in here..." and could think of nothing else to say. I stared at the red light until it went out. A producer came out from behind the camera and asked me if I would like a glass of water or something. I nodded no and she thanked me for trying out and wished me well in my pursuit of a TV career. "Thanks," I think I said. "You're welcome," I think she said. "By the way, Jack, you have gorgeous hair," I know she said.

But about the incident in the seventh grade: I had to give a book report in front of the class on "Ali Baba and the Forty Thieves." I thought I'd like it based on the title and my family's thieving ways. I read two or three chapters and feared I was going to yawn to death. I began by telling the class how the book began since that's all I knew about it and then defended Ali Baba for being one of the thieves. I happened to notice the teacher's pained expression at my commentary and realized that I probably should have also read some of the last chapters. My forehead began to sweat but my mouth kept talking. That's when I passed out cold. When I came to the whole class was looking down on me. Some of them were smiling. My head hurt where it hit the linoleum floor. I also discovered to my horror that I had wet my pants.

Gosling Junior High School is small and so the humiliation followed me through several more grades; "Hey Ali Baba Bladder!" "Next time, don't hurt your head. Pass out on your magic carpet, Ali." *Juvenile humor, but not too bad now that I think about it.*

"You passed out and peed your pants right there in front of the whole class, 'member?" Peggy Lou said too loudly.

"How could I forget? Hey, remember when we almost had sex in Poole's Woods..." I said even louder. I figured, hey, what's good for the goose is good for the gander" -- another cliché we like in Birdland-West Gosling.

"Shhh, cripes Jacko. Keep it down. Jim's right over there. I hope he didn't hear-- here he comes..."

She married fellow schoolmate Jim Logan. I was shocked and, yes, amazed beyond belief and wonder when I heard they'd hitched. I was invited to the wedding but couldn't make it because I couldn't stand the thought that Jim Logan was going to marry the once very-lovely-and-very-thin and now not-so-hot-and-rather-fat Peggy Lou. He's a heavyweight, too, and I'll bet he's responsible for Peggy Lou letting herself go. *Damn you, Jim Logan!*

"Jacko," said Jimbo.

"Hey, man," said Jacko back to Jimbo.

"What are you two talkin' 'bout?"

"Hendrix," I answered.

I said that because Jim had two annoying habits when we were in school. He was always playing air guitar to the music in his head, usually a Jimi Hendrix song. We even called him Jimi instead of Jim for years. He would also walk up to you and hit you hard in the arm in some sort of male show of affection. Jim is short and wiry. His hair is straight and jet black. The name Logan may be Irish but Jim's complexion was dark. He looked Hispanic. *Me thinks*

Mrs. Logan had been down Mehico way! He always has a forced grin on his face that makes you wince. Except when he was in school or the weather was cold, Jim would walk around shirtless to show off his muscles and wiriness. He was not popular in school because he was hard to like. I couldn't believe it when I heard he and Peggy Lou were dating. I pictured him shirtless and her topless kissing and it made me cringe.

"I hear you're a newspaperman, Jacko?" he stated as a question.

"Yeah, I work for a prize-winning paper on the Outer Banks," I lied again.

"Ever faint writing news for the paper?" he said while grinning that grin.

Hahahas with all three of us faking grins.

"What kind of work are you doing, Jimi?" I asked to stop the hahaing.

"A little of this, a little of that. Mostly alot of a little..."

Aha! Ha ha. Apparently, I'm not the only one presently out of work...

"...ah, hey, ah, Jacko, if you're in town for a while why don't we three get together?"

"Sounds great," I said, although I wondered, *why do we need to get together later since we are together right now and that's what reunions are for.*

Peggy Lou adjusted her bra and Jim strummed air guitar as they walked away.

Back to the present: I rubbed some more of that excellent experimental Oil Martha gave me for my headache and sang some Hendrix in my head to myself

(Editors: I'm liking, more and more, the idea of a soundtrack for this book. JO)

and had a piece of Peggy Lou's pie. I. Scarfed. It. Down!

Jimi knew about Peggy Lou and my teenage sex and pot experience in Poole's Woods. I told him all about it at school the day after. And several days after that. I knew Jimi had a crush on his future wife way back then and I also knew he was getting nowhere with her. My arm was bruised purple (haze?) for a week but it was worth every punch.

MANUSCRIPT CHAPTER SEVENTEEN

The Boyles, The Coles, The Guvmint and Clyde
Thanksgiving Day

No sooner had Peggy Lou and Jimi Hendrix left than Clyde sat down beside me. Clyde Hicks isn't family but he might as well be. He lived next door to us but was hardly ever at his own home. He was always at our house. He ate three meals a day with my family and would sometimes even sleep in the bathtub my dad had turned into a couch in our living room. The Hicks didn't have a television so our Zenith was a major reason he liked to hang out at our house. Clyde had the run of the place and was treated by my family as if he were another son. And he was like a brother to me.

Clyde is bound and determined to get his name in the Guinness Book of World Records.

He has this preoccupation with making a paperclip chain, a nervous habit that he began as a junior high school student. He's in his sixties now.

"Are you still working on that paperclip chain, Clyde?"

"George Damn Strait I am, Jacko. I cain't quit. I'm addicted. It's relaxin'. I forget my problems."

"What problems?"

"You know. The morgue."

Clyde runs a motorcycle junkyard. He calls it a motorcycle morgue. There are probably five hundred motorcycles on his property in various states of disrepair. Harleys and Hondas half gone, Yamahas and Suzukis cannibalized to skeletons.

I asked, "You mean people ain't buying motorcycle parts no more?" slipping easily into localese now. I notice that when I speak, in what I consider newspaperman English in Gosling, I am often misunderstood and then have to repeat myself and then have to say it a third time in the local lingo. So, sometimes I just talk local right off the bat. I straightened up my quotes for this book to make it easier for you to read.

"They's wantin' parts. But they ain't got the cash money to pay for them like they ardah."

"Hmm. I talked to my cousin Denny Roy the other day and he said business is slow for him, too. You remember Denny Roy?"

"Sure as Shootin', Annie Oakley. I'm surprised he ain't in jail somewheres. Say 'Howdy Doody' to him next time ya see 'im, will ya?"

"I Shirley Temple will," I said, getting into the groove of Clyde's name dropping. "Say, Clyde, how long is that paperclip chain of yourn now?" actually saying "yourn" for the first time in years.

"It damn near takes up a raht much of mah livin' room, Jacko. Let's go on over to mah place a tad and getcha a cold one and I'll show you and let ya read the letter I wrote to the Guinness folks. You bein' a writer and all maybe you can make it read better."

Clyde lives in a double wide mobile home and that's as it should be because, at five foot four, two hundred fifty plus pounds, Clyde is double wide. We both had to turn sideways and breathe in to get past a huge pile of chained paper clips in his living room. The pile was at least ten feet wide and six feet high. It took up so much room that the only furniture he had was a Lazy Boy and a fifty-inch TV. He said he guesstimates it would stretch eight miles and weighs at least two tons. It was so heavy that Clyde built cement pillars under the trailer to keep the floor from falling in.

"I 'spect it'll touch the ceiling 'fore I die."

Clyde buys paper clips about every time he goes to a store and picks them up anytime he sees them on someone's desk. Sneaks them if he has to. You'd think he was an Odum.

Plastic paper clips of many colors are mixed in with the metal ones.

"Them colored plastic paper clips make the chain look more perty."

"If the Guinness people or a museum wants the pile someday," I asked "just how will you get it out of here, Clyde?"

"Well, the way I figure it, the only way to git it outer the house would be to knock out a wall. And it ain't worth knockin' out no wall, y'know, 'cause it ain't worth nothin' but the wall is."

"That's too bad, Leroy Brown. You're at about the retiring age ain't ya, Clyde?"

"You betcha, Betty Boop. I'm gonna re-tire perty soon, Jacko, and live off what I got. It ain't much. But I can make it. I plan to build me a Harley out of my parts and hit the road for a time. Maybe go to Raleigh. Check in at Barney Fife's 'Y' for a spell."

"That sounds like a good plan, Superman. Listen, I'm going back to the party now, Clyde. You comin'?"

"No. I've had 'bout all the visitin' I can take. I gotta git hoppin' into gittin' that Harley up an' runnin'."

"Okay, Hoppalong Cassidy," I said. "Nice seein' ya again, Clyde."

"So long, John Silver."

Clyde has spent far too many years watching the Rerun TV Channel.

***

Back at the reunion, The Boyles and the Coles took over my spot at the main picnic table. The Coles aren't related but the Boyles are, on my dad's side somehow. The two families have always lived next door to each other a few blocks down the street from us.

If you see a Boyle somewhere you're likely to also see a Cole. The two families get along as if they are one. Even though the Coles are much better off financially than the Boyles they act and talk as if the Boyles are richer than they are. When the Boyles laid down new linoleum in the kitchen, the Coles complained for weeks that they'd like new linoleum, too, but just couldn't afford it. "We'll just have to do without for a few years, Betty," Mr. Cole told his wife. A few months later the Coles redid their kitchen floor in tile.

One time, the Boyles got a brand new five-year-old Chevy. "Oh my, I wish we could afford a new car," grieved Mrs. Cole to Mrs. Boyle. "But we just can't afford that kind of splurge right now." A few months later, they traded in their five-year-old Ford for a two-year-old Chevy.

If a Boyle boy got a bike, a Cole boy would get a motor scooter. If a Boyle girl got a cloth doll, a Cole daughter soon had a Barbie. And so, it went and probably still goes.

Frank Boyle was unemployed more than employed over the years and picked up any work he could around town. Much of the food in the Boyle household was, and probably still is, government funded. Tom Cole had a steady, good paying job at the brick plant. Tom complained nightly and mightily about how the Boyles ate better than the Coles and that he wished he was on government assistance instead of "working so damned hard every day for 'piddlin' pay'."

The two families usually ate Sunday supper together. Tom Cole would give the blessing and while thanking God for providing the food they were about to receive he'd damn the government for providing some of it through surplus food and food stamps.

The Boyle's brought a nice three bean salad to the reunion. The Cole's brought a nice five bean salad.

I talked to Frank Boyle a bit. He was telling me how his water and sewer bill had gone through the roof.

"I'm sure the Coles are just as upset about that as you are," I said.

"No, they're not affected," he answered.

"Why is yours so high and not theirs?"

"Well, y'know, the same guy who built my house forty years ago built Tom's right after he built mine. He saved them some money by running a spur off my water and sewer lines to Tom's house instead of a whole nother line. The meter is on my house and I get the bill each month."

"Tom doesn't get a water and sewer bill?"

"No. Never has."

"In forty years?"

"No."

"Well, doesn't he pay half, or at least part, of your bill?"

"Well, no. They was on real hard times raht after they bought that house and we helped them make due by paying the water bill and not sayin' nothin'. Time went by and Tom and Betty never offered and we never asked."

"Jeez, Frank, that doesn't seem fair. Do the Coles have dirt or something on the Boyles?"

"Now that's a raht good one," he laughed. "We're clean livers, Jack."

"Did you just say you and Darlene have clean livers, Frank? Then drink up!"

We were laughing when Tom Cole came over and shook my hand. "Jack. Long time. Howzit hangin'?"

"Low," I said, which is the expected answer to that question. "How are you, Tom?"

"Fair to middlin'. Alot of good eats here. Try Betty's five bean salad. It'll make you toot The Star-Spangled Banner in five fart harmony."

The three of us laughed pretty hard at that. Nothing like a good fart joke.

"I'll do just that," I said and put a scoop of it on my plate since Tom's body language was saying to try it that very minute.

"Ooo. That's so good," I said what he wanted and expected to hear through a mouthful of five bean salad. I swallowed and asked, "What have you been up to lately, Tom?" in hopes he'd stop watching me eat. It worked.

"Well, Jack, I'm old. Okay. I'm lucky to get up at all. Gettin' old's a real bitch. Right, Frank?" Frank nodded and smiled in agreement.

I said, "I'm not exactly a spring chicken. I'm pushin' sixty, Tom."

"Yeah, well things start breaking down in your seventies and Frank and I are in our eighties. We're falling apart before your eyes. Jack, I'm tellin' ya, the highlight of my day now is a bowel movement."

More and louder laughing. In fact, I take it back. A b-m joke is better than a fart joke. The three of us empty our glasses and look over the table to decide which of the forty or more dishes to put on our plates.

"You bought any food lately, Jack?"

"Well, yeah, man's gotta eat," I said and took a bite of beans.

He said, "It's nuts. I wish I was on welfare to get them guvmint food stamps they's givin' out."

"Frank was just telling me how expensive Gosling's water and sewer is getting, Tom."

"Really? Didn't know that. Too bad they don't hand out water and sewer stamps, huh? Hey, Betty's pointing at me. Better get on over there to see what I done wrong. Nice seein' ya again, Jack. Say hi to Susan."

"We're no longer togeth... see ya, Tom." He waved over his back as he walked away.

I made a point of eating and complimenting Betty Cole on her five-bean salad. "That was right good eatin', Mrs. Cole," I told Mrs. Cole.

I also ate and complimented Darlene Boyle on her three-bean salad. "Your bean salad was a de-lish dish, Mrs. B. Best beans on the table."

"Thank you, Jack. You're the best fibber in North Carolina." *What? Not the northern hemisphere?* And then she added, "But have you tried Betty's?"

MANUSCRIPT CHAPTER EIGHTEEN

My Rich Polack Uncle
Thanksgiving Day

Uncle Harry and his wife Dorothy made it to the reunion. I hadn't seen them since Sue and my wedding. Harry was several glasses into Oil-laced rum and Co-cola. Harry isn't a blood relative. He was once my favorite relative-by-marriage-in-law through my mother's side of the family until I realized he was an unapologetic bigot.

"Uncle Harry. Wow. How long has it been, three years?"

"Probably more than that, Jack."

"No. Three years. You were at my wedding three years ago."

"Oh yeah. You married an I-talian girl. A Yankee. I remember. Dark hair. Dark coloring. But pretty."

"Right. But it didn't work out. We got divorced."

"Sorry, Jack. I hear you're a big-time TV newsman now?"

"Small time. Newspaper. And not even that right now. I'm out of work."

"Downsized?"

"Well, sure, let's go with that, Uncle Harry."

"Oh. Hey, I hear ya. Been there, done that, about a thousand times. You're in a slump, huh? Well, you know what they say, 'when one door closes, get right back up on the horse'."

Uncle Harry is retired now but used to work at a clay pipe making factory in Akron, Ohio. He's huge. He probably weighs more than three hundred pounds. He has a big flabby belly but is actually very muscular. He tends to sit on the edge of a chair so his stomach can hang over the end. He says his big gut helped him with all the heavy lifting he had to do at the pipe factory. "I'd bend down and pick up a hundred fifty-pound pipe and raise it half way up to my Buddha belly. Let it rest there for a second and then hoist it on up onto the truck."

Just as my father was constantly being laid off at Gosling Brick Company, Harry would occasionally see months and months without work at Akron Clay Works. So he'd grab any job he could find during the layoffs, and he found some terrible ones.

He once signed on to move an old unmarked graveyard to make way for a new highway. "Man, they shot us up with every vaccine known and unknown to man and beast so we wouldn't catch something. The bodies were so decomposed there wasn't anything there but colored dirt. We'd take a shovelful as a representative sample of each corpse to bury in the new cemetery."

He said a slaughterhouse job was especially gruesome. "The hogs would be lined up one by one in a chute. Several of the hogs, behind the hog getting killed, could see what was happening. They would squeal and squeal. They say pigs are smart, y'know. Maybe they understood what was going to happen to them."

Harry's resume would show he's worked as a dishwasher, janitor, jackhammer operator, high-rise window washer and lumberjack. He worked with a traveling carnival show one summer running the Tilt-a-Whirl ride. My Unc the Carny!

One year he was a fill-in radio announcer in a small town in Florida when a longtime announcer died. The station signed on at sun up and signed off at sundown. Uncle Harry was there for both. He has a deep baritone voice that was perfect for radio and it got him the job. He'd read commercials and the news and weather and deejayed the first five hours of the broadcast day. For years afterwards, Harry would talk like an announcer by putting a smile on his face, deepening his voice, punching certain words and promoting the station. "You're listening to Don DONOVAN taking you right on into the TOP of the hour here at 77-WGTR, THE GATORRRR!"

He went by Don Donovan because the station manager decided his real name wouldn't work on the radio: Harry Crapo. "I didn't care. Crapo. What a crappy name right? It's French, y'know. Originally, Crepeaux. Damn snooty foo foo frog name. Hey, at least it's not Creepo, huh? Ha."

He said he started out making minimum wage but received a raise after working there just two weeks.

"My mick boss called me in and told me what a fine job I was doing and rewarded me with a dime an hour raise. Christ! Ten cents. You'd think he was Scottish. It was hard keeping GAS in my CADDIE," he said in his deep Don Donovan radio voice.

To Harry's mind there's only one car and it's a Cadillac.

"Only car that ought to be allowed on an American road," he said in his every day off air Harry Crapo voice.

Uncle Harry owned dozens of them over the years and traded in every two years so as to always be seen driving a new one. He may be a blue-collar worker but he and his wife, Dorothy, give the appearance of being white collar. They are always dressed nicely in Florida resort wear. He must have a dozen wide white belts.

They own a mobile home in Florida. They would usually stop by my parent's house when they used to drive from Akron to Fort Lauderdale. They'd stay at a motel since we didn't have a guest room at our house. Harry said he once drove nonstop from Akron to Fort Lauderdale in seven hours thanks to the comfort and great engine of the Cadillac. We did some road math once and determined that he'd have to average one hundred fifteen miles per hour to do that.

We always wondered how he managed to keep a new car and a house in Ohio and a trailer in Florida. Mom said it was "Dorothy money."

Aunt Dorothy was a foreigner. We could only understand about every other word she said. She sounded like Zsa Zsa Gabor.

"She's a hunky," Harry informed us one time. That's what they call Hungarians in Ohio.

"How iz (unintelligible English) Susan, Jacov?" she asked.

After I figured out her question, I answered, "Oh, jeez, Aunt Dorothy, Susan and I aren't together anymore. I know she liked you."

"I vas fahver ven (unintelligible) zabout her." Your guess is as good as mine!

They had a Pomeranian dog dressed in a skirt leashed to a table leg.

"What's her name?" I asked Dorothy even though I already knew the dog's name.

"Kitty. Iz (unintelligible) Kitty eeez nem all my dugs."

You might have translated that correctly. They had a dog named Kitty and three previous dogs were all named Kitty. Aunt Dorothy always wanted a cat but Uncle Harry wouldn't let her have one. They didn't have any kids so a Pomeranian has always been their child.

The Kitty when I was a little kid-- their second Kitty-- was a little bitch. She yapped at everything that moved and she nipped at your ankles. She wouldn't eat table leftovers like our dogs. We had a dog that was part Spitz and part Irish setter. We named him "Spitter." He liked to play with Kitty in ways that Aunt Dorothy found obscene. "Vy you no (unintelligible) ver za dug putz iz nooz?"

One of their Kittys bit me once. Drew blood. And that was one time when I swore something fierce right there in front of Mom and Dad, JJ, Bonnie, Harry, Dorothy, Spitter and Kitty. Mom told me to leave the room. Harry, dad, JJ and Bonnie laughed. Aunt Dorothy covered her mouth with her hand and said something like, "My Kitty she no nutten wrung dat Jock sez da fock verd."

Bonnie and JJ and I disliked their Kitty dogs but pretended we liked them because when Harry, Dorothy and a Kitty showed up it meant that we were going to be rich.

Uncle Harry had the practice of giving us money when he visited. It was only a quarter when we were very young but that was alot of money to us. As we got older the money got bigger: five bucks in junior high, ten in high school, fifty dollars at graduation.

He hauled out his wallet and handed me a hundred-dollar bill at the reunion.

"You don't have to give me money, Uncle Harry. I have a job. No, I don't but I did. And I'll get another one."

"Take it!"

I took it. What, you expected me to say no again? I'm out of work remember. I can always find a good place or cause for a windfall.

"I want to show you something interesting, Jack." He reached into a coat pocket and pulled out what looked like a thick six-inch long tooth. "You know what this is?"

"A whale's tooth? Driftwood?"

"Noper." I believe Uncle Harry is the only person in the world who says "noper." "This is a claw from a prehistoric giant sloth. I found this when I was digging a hole for a bush beside my house in Akron. I think there's a skeleton of a giant sloth under my house. I do."

"You should contact an archeologist or paleontologist to check it out."

"I did. I contacted a wop scientist at OSU. But I think it's mostly under my house and my house is on a concrete slab so they'd have to tear down my house to dig it up. But I'm thinking about it -- for the good of science, you know. I sure am. There might be some money in it for me. What's a prehistoric giant sloth worth to science these days? They were as big as elephants back then. I'll let the college have the house and Dorothy, Kitty and I will retire in Florida. Too damn cold in Ohio, anyhow, and too many nigerians. Too many damn kikes in Florida but, hey, whatcha gonna do about that? We'd save a fortune just on gas. The Cadillac gets terrible mileage. Don't need to give the ragheads any more money, do we?"

Absolutely in shock at hearing a negative about a Cadillac from Uncle Harry, I told him about the decent mileage I was getting on my Honda.

"Dorothy wouldn't want to be seen in no chink car, would you, dear?"

"(Unintelligible English or Hungarian) fer sure Hunda no iz Codllac."

"So, Aunt Dorothy likes Cadillacs too, huh?"

"Oh YEAH MAN," said Don Donovan. "Hunky Dorothy finds them HUNKY DORY."

Harry: Roaring laughter.

Dorothy: Deafening silence.

Me: "O--------- K. Listen, you three have fun. Nice seeing you again. Thanks for the Ben Franklin, Uncle Harry. Bye, Dorothy. Bye, Kitty. I think I'm going to the booze table and make me a vodka tonic and Oil."

Harry: "Vodka? You drink vodka?"

Me: "Yeah."

Harry: "Commie!"

Dorothy: "(Unintelligible) luv za wodka."

And then... and then... and THEN.... I distinctly heard, in the distance to my right a phrase loudly spoken in a strange English dialect I hadn't heard in three years and suddenly my headache returned with a vengeance.

MANUSCRIPT CHAPTER NINETEEN

Interviewed by a Vampire
Thanksgiving Day

"How youns doin'?"

I thought for a millisecond I might be asleep and having a nightmare in broad daylight (daymare?) when I heard that voice and that accent. *Please, if there's a God in Heaven, don't let it be...* I know, you know, who(m) I don't want it to be.

Hugging people right over there in my direct line of site was...

"Susan. How nice to see you again," I heard an apparent relative say to the person who was definitely the person I assume you assumed it was.

Well, so much for whatever religion I had left.

My mind thinking: *Now I guess I'm going to have to kill somebody for inviting Susan to the reunion. She's not even an Odum anymore! She never seemed to much like being Mrs. Odum. So, why is she all smiley and nicey... and looking very sexy as a matter of facty. She slimmed-down and attractived-up since the last time she told me she never wanted to see me again. Singlehood looks good on her. Oh brother. Here she comes.*

Hide? No.

Smile? No.

Disappear! Disappear! Disappear! . . .

"Jack. It's so nice to see you."

Well, so much for mind over matter.

"Suuuussssan!"

After a cold hug she asked, "How are you?"

"Wow. Gee. Gosh. It's you. Here. Now. Umm. I see you're here. And ah…"

"Jack. Chill. I know you're surprised to see me here. I'm surprised to see me here. I only decided to come a few days ago when Martha told me that you were definitely coming."

Let me see. How best to murder Martha? Perhaps I'll borl her in The Oral. I'll dissolve her in soap lye, I thought, but instead I said, "That was nice of Martha to invite you to the Odum Thanksgiving." My brain thought it but my mouth didn't add, *even though you're not an actual Odum anymore, Sue.*

"I'm still going by my married name, Jack. I'm still Susan Odum," she said, obviously hearing my thinker think. "But, Jack, I also rilly gotta talk to you about something that's perty imporent and I didn't wanna do it on the phone or email."

"I hope it's not something monetary because I recently had a falling out at *The Times*…"

"Fired?"

"Yeah. But I have some fires in the iron."

"You been drinking, Jack?"

At first, I wanted to say but thought instead, *No, I'm just in shock about your being here, Sue.* And then I said out loud, "No, I'm just in shock about your being here, Sue. It's a bit disconcerting. We haven't talked in, what, a year?"

"Yes, but your famly was my famly for the three years when we were together and I rilly like… some of 'em."

"What did you want to talk to me about?"

"Well, I just wanna ask you about The Oil."

"What about it?"

"How it effects ya."

"Why?"

"Because I wanna write about it."

"Who'd be interested in reading about the Odum Oil?"

"I think lotsa people might. It's an unregulated drug that a whole famly has used for generations and from what I can see it affects people in many different ways, good and bad."

"Good and Bad? Really?" I asked pronouncing "really" slowly and correctly. "How?"

"On the positive side, Jack, it made me wanna do what you do, write. I like to write. Before I met you and The Oil I had no intrest in writing. The Oil stimulated that part of my brain, I guess. 'Member hows I started writing a blog in Duck about what life is like for a northerner living in the south. Well, now I'm writing about the day-in-day-out life in western Pennsylvania. I use alot of Pennsylvania mispronunciations and my readers love it, y'know, like 'the chimley is full of soot and we hope the crick don't rise no higher', those sorts of things? On the negative side, I think The Oil affected the part of the brain that caused me to be meaner than I rilly am and maya led to our separation. I believe it also made me pee alot. So, I'm thinking maybe there might be a story to tell about the Odum Oil, Jack. Are you following me?"

"No, I'm standing right beside you."

Silence. A look of exasperation on both our faces.

"The Oil is a good thing, Susan. There's no real proof that it's harmful in any way."

"Well, I know there's no proof, Jack, but I'm gonna have it tested and write about it."

"Where are you staying in Gosling? At the Americana, I suppose?" I asked, to change the subject, which it did, temporarily.

"No, I'm staying with your Aunt Minnie. I know you two never rilly got along but she's one of my favrit Odums."

"Yeah, you two were both as mean as the other."

Nervous laughter from both of us.

"So how does The Oil affect you Jack?"

"Not very much."

"Rilly?" she asked, with a squinty-eyed-I-don't-think-so expression.

"What? Well, I suppose if I had to come up with a possible affect it would be that The Oil in my brain might help with my creative side. But it's had no negative affects on me unless saying 'no negative,' is a double negative which I do not think it is but which ain't no proper way to talk no how," I answered multi-negatively.

"C'mon Jack. Be serious," she repeated and squinted deeper.

"Okay. Let me think... *hmmm, well, ah, maybe...* maybe it's helped to make me more outgoing. I mean, look, I'm actually at a reunion for Heaven's sake."

"But not negatively, Jack. It's had no negative affects on you?"

"No, not negatively, no, none," I said quintuple negatively and shaking my head no five times.

"Jack, I would have to suggest that it has contributed to your lackadaisical attitude toward life and exacerbated your larcenous tendencies."

Phew! Now those were alot of words that hurt once I figured out what it was that she had just said. I was just openly called a thief, which I was, to a petty extent, but not anymore, thanks to modern mind altering legally prescribed drugs.

"Why would you openly say something like that to me right out in the open," I said right out loud and looking around to see if anyone heard her.

She lowered her voice a little. "C'mon, Jack, I've seen you steal things. You're in denial. You know you've taken things and I've had to take them back and apologize for your... your ... kleptomania or whatever. I think The Oil might have caused that personality flaw in you. That, or there rilly is such a thing as a thievery gene running through the Odum family. Either way, whether it's genetics or The Oil, I intend to write an article or even a whole book about the Odum Oil and its affects on your family."

"So, I've just been interviewed?"

"Ah, yeah."

"Well it's a free country with a free press and I am who I am and you are who you are and never the twain should have met. But, ah, what do you say we challenge that whole twain of thought and meet later tonight in Room #3 at The Americana? For old times' sake? You do look very nice, Susan. Sexy in fact. Maybe we should consider getting back together." She agreed and we had our own private reunion at the motel. We shared wine that I cooled in the motel's plastic ice bucket, shared laughter over some of the highlights of our married life, bumped uglies, napped a while and then shared a long warm shower before returning to JJ's Thanksgiving dinner.

Okay, ha ha, well, actually... that's not at all what happened. Ignore that last paragraph. It was just what I was thinking and should have been written in *italics*. What really happened is this:

"Well, it's a free country with a free press but I'd rather not be in your article, Sue. I should also let you know that I, too, am writing a book and I won't mention you in mine if you don't mention me in yours."

"No deal, Jack. You're the reason I know your famly and the reason I have been exposed to The Oil."

"You may not like the way I present you in my book, Sue."

"Back at ya, Jack."

"Well, I guess we're back to where we ended things three years ago."

"Yeah. I won't be here long. I've interviewed mosta your famly on the phone but there's some who never answer their phone or email. Uncle Harry for one. So, so long, Jack... again. Good luck on your book."

"Okay, bye. Um, by the way, you look very nice, Sue. I'm at the Americana Motel, Room #3. What do you say, for old times' sake, we... um ... just kidding... no I'm not... yes I am... well... maybe... ah...""?

"That hain't gonna happen, Jack. Our relationship is rilly up shit crick." She honestly said 'rilly" and "crick" and "hain't" in that quote you just read. Who'd want to read a book written by someone who talks like that, I ask you?

Is there such a thing as a thief gene? Maybe. Maybe not. If I knew the answer to that I'd write a book about it and teach at Harvard. As for The Oil, as I said way back in Chapter Three, I think it might affect some people one way and other people another way. I think more positively than negatively. Sue thinks bothly. I'm sure it's not worth an entire book. Right?

(Publisher: Right? JO)

MANUSCRIPT CHAPTER TWENTY

Hazel the Hypo
Thanksgiving Day

Right out of the blue a black cloud appeared over the reunion, not of the rainstorm variety, but my father's youngest sister, Hazel. One thing I know for sure is that everybody hoped Aunt Hazel wouldn't show. But everybody knew she would. She always shows. She doesn't seem to notice that the place comes to a screeching hush and all eyes turn her way, not out of joy about her arrival but because of dread.

Nothing is ever quite right to, or with, Hazel. She's always near death from some form of cancer and loudly explains why she's sure of it despite having never gone to a doctor in her life. "I know more than they do. All they do is put you on pills."

Yet, Aunt Hazel is a world class pill popper and daily visitor to the GNC store. She downs multiple, multiple vitamins and pills for high blood pressure and high cholesterol she's never had checked but is positive she must have. She takes a handful of herbs for loss of memory, hair, sexual desire, pain, cramps, restless leg syndrome, indigestion, skin rashes and cancer. She also self-medicates with The Oil.

Her hypochondria is-- autocorrect keeps telling me "are" instead of "is" but it's ill sounding to me-- so, okay, her hypochondria are enough to make you sick but it's her general attitude toward life that is/are especially nauseating. She attended Susan and my wedding. We didn't invite her since we knew she'd bring our big day down, but she heard about our upcoming nuptials and wrote Susan's mother a nasty note asking why her invitation had not yet arrived in the mail. Susan's mother apologized for the United States Postal Service and sent Hazel an invitation. She squeezed her in at a table with her husband's work buddies in the rear of the reception hall. Of course, Hazel was offended to be situated so near the restrooms that she left without wishing the happy couple a happy life together-- if, indeed, she knows what being happy is. We heard after our honeymoon that Hazel didn't like the food we served, the wedding cake, the music selections, the Bible verses, the minister's casual attitude and attire and the color of the bridesmaids' dresses.

At our wedding, she indicated that she was near death from spleen cancer. I about split the spleen in my gut when I heard that because Hazel also once thought she might have prostate cancer. I don't know if it's true but I heard that Hazel once noticed a lump inside her mouth and diagnosed it (diag-mouthed it?) as a mouth hemorrhoid. A neighbor, who is a dental hygienist, told her it was a natural bone growth and not to worry. Unconvinced, she rubbed Preparation H on it for a week but finally gave up convinced it was another cancer she'd have to live with until it killed her.

Apparently, her mouth, spleen and prostate cancers were in remission because there she was still alive and unwell.

Hazel sat down in the first lawn chair she saw. She's a slight woman whose clothes appear to be a size or two too large, apparently weight loss from the various phantom cancers.

Unfortunately, I fell within her line of sight, the only person to do that since everyone else somehow managed to slink away.

"Why, Jackie, look at you? Get over here and let me hug yer neck." Nobody else calls me Jackie.

"Hello, Aunt Hazel," and then without thinking I crazily asked, "How are you?"

"Oh, Jackie, you wouldn't believe what I've been through." I listened for half an hour about her recent bouts with lupus, psoriasis and shingles.

"Well, at least no cancer, Aunt Hazel," I said with a smile to counter her frown.

"I have a lump right here on my left breast that I noticed yesterday," she announced, and briskly frisked herself. I worried that she might pop one out.

"Isn't this weather just horrible?" she asked. It was 70 degrees with a slight breeze and clear blue skies.

"Yes, it's been like this for a week now, Aunt Hazel. It must be the effects of global warming."

"Oh my God, is that Jerry?" she asked, pointing to somebody who was not Jerry, who(m)ever Jerry is.

"No, that's Johnny Ames. He's the son of my mom's brother's wife's brother, I think," I think I said thoughtfully.

"Jerry looks sick, Jackie. That whole side of the family never looks well. They're not a pretty people. Our people are pretty people but they brought their homeliness into us, don't you think?"

Well, I thought, *Johnny Ames looked okay, really.* Aunt Hazel was hardly a beauty queen. At most, she might be called handsome.

"JJ isn't keeping this place up," she went on. "He used to be so particular about his yard." The yard was green for November and all the fallen leaves raked into neat piles for the kids to play in.

"How is your lovely wife, Sharon, Jackie?"

"It's Susan, Aunt Hazel, and we're divorced now. It didn't work out. We had too many differences. As a matter of fact, she was here a little while ago. You just missed…"

"I loved her very much, Jackie. I loved the unusual way she talked. She was an extraordinary young woman. She and I saw things in much the same way..."

"Aunt Hazel, can I get you some tea or lemonade?" I interrupted because I now wanted to divorce myself from Aunt Hazel, too.

"Why, yes, Jackie. Would you mind bringing me a bourbon. Straight. Make it a double. I need something to relax me some. I'm much concerned about my breast as you can imagine." I didn't want to imagine Aunt Hazel's breast but my mind went there anyway, *Jeez, Jacko. All wrinkly and low hanging.* My mind then said to me, and itself, *hurry up. Picture something else. Quick!* So, we mentally switched to Denny Roy's girlfriend's tattooed legs and apparent tattooed breasts. *Relief. Phew!*

More frisking by Aunt Hazel.

I never returned but I did get some nephew or distant cousin I didn't know to take a triple bourdon "over to that lady under the shade tree there who is, ah, adjusting her blouse."

In sneaking away from Hazel, I nearly tripped over a little girl who was sitting in the grass beside the dessert table. She had a brownie in one hand, a chocolate chip cookie in the other and a mouthful of one of them. I apologized to her and asked her who she belonged to. She was the daughter of a cousin far removed and she informed me she was three by showing me two fingers and a half-eaten brownie.

"What's your name?"

"Amy Odum."

"Is that brownie good, Amy Odum?"

A yes nod.

"Is it better than the cookie?"

A no nod.

"My name is Jack."

No nod but a cute smile.

"My name is Amy."

"I know. And that's a nice name."

"My brother's name is Josh."

"Where's Josh?"

"He's sick and daddy too."

"So, they didn't come?"

"You know what?"

"What?"

"Daddy has the foo."

"Oh, that's too bad. I had the foo once."

"You know what?"

"What?

"I'm want to be a doctor when I'm big."

"Well, Amy, that would be wonderful. I think you would be the first Odum to be a doctor. You would make us all very proud."

Nodding yes. A long pause. An expression of deep thought.

"You know what?"

"What?"

"I change my mind. When I grow up I want to be a mermaid."

"Well, Amy, you would also be the first mermaid in the family. Bye. Don't eat too many cookies or you'll get sick like Josh."

"I won't. Bye."

You know what? I badly needed that encounter with Amy the Mermaid after Hazel the Hypo.

MANUSCRIPT CHAPTER TWENTY-ONE
Holy Beer
Thanksgiving Evening

The food was running out and the alcohol was gone which meant the reunion was over and JJ was saying good-bye to us hangers on.

"Glad ya could make it, Jacko, and sorry about the surprise visit by Susan. Martha caused that. Me and her had words," JJ apologized and offered one of his normal sized melons to take home.

"I'll survive but I'll try not to kill Martha. Listen brother, it's nice, your putting this on. I had a good time."

He said, "I don't know why we don't do this every year."

I know why. Our family gatherings get too loud and liquid what with all the amplified music, rifle shooting, cannon blasting and gallons of homebrewed beer drinking. I've already documented how drinking has caused some problems for the Odum clan.

Cousin Louis has a refrigerator in his kitchen that has a beer tap on the door where the water and ice chute should be. Several Odums have mini breweries in their basements. A nephew-in-law, Larry, is the family's biggest brewer and consumer. In his house, you'll hear popping sounds every so often as beer bottles explode in his cellar. That's not all that's down there. His basement brewery shares space with his baitery: Larry Berry's Worm Farm. Larry filled a dozen children's plastic swimming pools with leaves, dirt, some of JJ's sacred chicken manure and sawdust and, of course, worms.

"Look at these beauties," he'd say as he pulled out a handful of long, slimy, squirmy, juicy red worms.

"These is gooduns. (good ones)."

Fishermen from miles around buy their bait from Larry. "Everybody hollers: 'Hey Larry! I want me some Larry Berry worms.'"

He says his homegrown basement worms are better than the run of the mill red worms (crawl of the mill?) because he hydrates them with rainwater he collects off the roof. "Even well water worms ain't as juicy as rain water worms," he claims. He also drops some Odum Oil into the worm water.

Larry said other people in Gosling have tried to wiggle their way into his bait biz. "But they ain't got the raht stuff. They don't love worms like I love 'em. I think they're loverly. Damn near as loverly as them bottles a brew over yonder."

We used to have a beer drinking game we called the Larry Berry Name Game. One person would start it off by saying something like "Larry Berry has a brother Jerry and a sister Mary" and the next person might say "his father is Barry Berry" and the next might add that he had "an uncle Perry and an Aunt Sarah-y" then "they're all Very Merry" and "they owned a Dairy in Cary" and "Mary was Hairy" and "Terry was a Fairy" and "we couldn't help but Stare at Hairy Mary" and "Harry Berry committed Hari-kari" and "Larry thought he was Jim Carrey" and "Perry had a pet Canary" and...

(Editors: I could add a hundred words to this manuscript just playing the Larry Berry Name Game if you think I need more pages. I nary wary of playing it. Let me know. JO)

Larry Berry and other family members use the home-brew beer recipe my dad's great grandfather, Orrin Owen, passed down before he passed on. Of course, The Oil is part of the recipe. Its foggy brown color makes it appear as not quite done but my relatives drink it by the case at any get together with more than four people.

Larry and a lady he planned to marry were regulars, as was I, at my Uncle Tony's monthly drink-and-singathons. Larry would usually bring a six or twelve pack of his brew. Everybody brought something, either hard or soft, to drink, something to eat and an instrument to play if they had the talent. Tony also had hundreds of bottles of his own home-brew fermenting in his cellar. His house would become what amounted to a rip-roaring beer hall.

Oddly enough, Tony was married to a hardcore teeto-taler. Aunt Laura never touched the stuff; that is, until a few weeks after the church blew-up. I'll tell you about that in a minute.

Laura, being a non-drinker, was always the odd man out (odd woman out) at these bashes. There would be twenty-five or thirty of us drinking, playing guitars and belting out country and gospel songs. Laura would be the only adult there without a drink in her hand and she was mercilessly teased about her sobriety.

"It's not tea time, Laura. It's Miller time!"

"C'mon, Lar, ain't much difference between a caffeine buzz and bein' hopped up on hops."

She would just laugh it off and had some good comebacks. "Why would I wanna drink that piss yellow evil when I can imbibe the Bible," she'd declare. "If the Good Lord wanted us to drink till we acted crazy ass silly like all y'all are doin', He woulda had His Only Son get rip roaring drunk on that wine He made from water."

Laura would drink some brand of Co-cola and join in the singing but head off to bed by 9:30 or 10.

Uncle Tony mockingly called his parties

"Laurapaboozas" in her honor.

They were alot of fun. I began Laurapaboozing, officially, when I reached my family's legal beer drinking age of fourteen.

Tony is an excellent guitarist and Laura could belt out plenty of Johnny Cash and Hank Williams songs. They should have gone on the road.

Aunt Laura stopped singing after the church blew up which I will tell you about in a minute.

My mother could sing and my dad knew some basic guitar chords. They both drank their share at Tony's but never to the point of embarrassing themselves like some of Tony's friends. And Tony. And me, sometimes. Laura would remain sober as a judge.

Tony was a detonation expert for the Logan Coal Mining Company and worked a shaft near Hindsboro. They called him TNT Tony. He learned the fine art of dynamiting as a soldier in Vietnam. The Laurapaboozas were Tony's way of letting off steam from one of the most dangerous and stressful jobs in coal mining.

There's a long line of coal mining Odums. My grandfather John, Tony's father, was injured in a mine accident and was on government disability for many years. He could easily put away a twelve pack while adding harmonica or Jews Harp to the music. Five or six beers in, he'd begin his often repeated "hard times in the mines" stories and tell everyone how easy they all have it now down there until calling it a night at about ten or eleven o'clock. My grandfather's father quit the mines because of Black Lung. I never knew him. They're both dead now. Tony's three brothers also worked for Logan Coal. They all worked side-by-side a hundred feet underground five and a half days a week. Many of them lived in identical side-by-side, weather and age-beaten row houses they bought cheap when the coal company offered them for sale.

Tony's Laurapaboozas lasted well into the wee hours of Sunday and continued for years, even after all the trouble about the church explosion, which I'll get to in a minute.

The noise level would become thunderous with drunken booming voices shouting gossip or jokes or bitching about the evils of the coal company or "the gawd damned guvmint" between the hillbilly songs. The electric guitars were amped to max. Every so often fermenting beer in the basement popped a cap adding a little offbeat percussion to the hoedown.

Uncle Tony was the life of these parties as the best guitarist and storyteller. He prided himself in telling how he supplemented his income through petty theft. He kept his truck in gas and oil by draining fuel from the mining company's equipment after dark on Sundays. One time he stole the rug from the boss' office and sold it for two hundred dollars to the manager at the A&P.

"Hope they don't never get to know each other," he'd grin.

It was during "It Wasn't God Who Made Honky Tonk Angels" late one Saturday night when the party fell to total silence. Tony and Laura were in another room arguing. He was going on about her going to church so much. She had recently started spending Saturdays and Tuesdays there, she said, "helping the preacher prepare the church for Sunday morning and Wednesday evening services."

None of us men, and only a couple of the women, ever made it to Sunday morning services at Rock Ridge Holiness Church after a Saturday night Laurapabooza. But Laura, who hated Tony's dynamite job, never missed services. "I'm blown away," she'd say, adopting Tony's favorite expression to describe the sermons of the newly hired preacher, Henry Young.

Despite her tearful denial of goings-on between her and the Rev, the very beerful Tony insisted there had to be somethings on-going.

"No damn body needs that much churchin," his voice boomed through the quiet house.

That ended the party early. Everyone was gone by midnight.

This happened in late June.

In early July, newspaper and TV reporters from as far away as Charlotte and Asheville came to write about an explosion in the small coal mining town of Hindsboro. Someone had dynamited Rock Ridge Holiness Church in the early morning hours of the Fourth of July. Cement blocks, splinters of white wood and shredded hymnals were scattered about the parking lot and adjacent cemetery. Folks heard the blast two miles away.

"FIREWORKS AND BRIMSTONE" heralded *The Salisbury Press*. "A local church gets blown to Kingdom Come," announced the anchorman at WASH-TV Action News.

Uncle Tony did it, everyone assumed and agreed. The State Police questioned him but nothing came of it. Still, everybody found it interesting that two years later, while still bragging about his petty crimes, he never claimed nor mentioned the church dynamiting. Reverend Young left town, no longer having a church in which to preach. Laura, no longer having a church in which to attend or a preacher to attend to, (ahem), gave in at last to the partying ways of Tony and the others.

I remember the night. Aunt Laura is very pretty but made the ugliest face that night when she sipped her first ever glass of Tony's homebrew. We all watched as she put the bottle to her lips. We all swallowed as she swallowed. We all laughed until we had tears in our eyes.

"To Laura's epiphany," we toasted. "No longer a beer virgin."

Aunt Laura had tears in her eyes, too, but not from laughing.

Then she drank a little more, sang a song and later drank another and laughed and sang and then left the party. I didn't see her again that night. From then on Laura would have one or two or three or four or more beers at the Laurapaboozas.

I can tell you that she sure drinks now-- religiously. At the reunion, Aunt Laura claimed a spot at the liquids table and stayed there till the end.

I said hi and goodbye to Laura although I don't think she knew who I was. And I made my rounds saying good-bye to Martha and the kids. Aaron asked me if I was going to the parade the next day. I said I hadn't planned on it but would if he'd go with me. JJ followed me to my car.

"Hey, JJ, I got something for that senior citizens' re-tirement barnyard of yours in my trunk." I had to move the copper wire to one side to get at it but you should have seen his utter (insert obvious milk cow pun here) delight at the plywood cow hiney I "found" in Turkey on the way to the reunion.

"That's beautiful. Good thing I don't have an old bull. He'd see this sexy cow's backside and perty soon I'd have me a whole herd of plywood calves runnin' 'round here. Listen, Jacko, Martha and me, we wanna thank you for helping us outta that tight spot, you hear?"

"No problem, brother. Wish I could do more. It isn't much but I put aside as much as I can. It makes me feel good to help. You know how fond I am of Aaron."

"That was plenty. It got us through. But I'll pay you back jes soon as I can."

"Don't need to pay me back. It was a gift. Just like that cow butt there. Take care, JJ. Love ya, brother."

Instead of shaking hands like we'd done forever, JJ hugged me, one of those my-right-shoulder-to-his-right-shoulder man-hugs. I'll admit right here on this page that I teared up a little as I watched JJ walking away carrying that plywood cow -- two hineys heading toward the rear of the house and into the horizon.

MANUSCRIPT CHAPTER TWENTY-TWO

Ex Rated Movie
Thanksgiving night

I went back to the Americana Motel and stopped in the office to wish Jeff Patel a happy Thanksgiving but to also complain about the TV reception. By the aroma emitting from behind a curtain behind him the Patels must have enjoyed a curry turkey.

"Happy Thanksgiving, Mr. Patel. Hope you had a pleasant day," I offered.

"Oh my, Mr. Odor. Very pleasant. Yes. Thank you. (Giggle)." Mr. Patel giggles.

He calls me Mr. Odor, I guess, because he misread my John Henry in the Registration book.

"And you, sir. A good Thanksgiving, yes?"

"Wonderful, Mr. Patel. I got to meet alot of my relatives. Many relatives. Many many Odors."

We both giggled.

"Um, Mr. Patel. The TV in my room doesn't work. I can't get any channels. Very snowy picture, y'know?"

"Oh, I am so sorry, Mr. Odor. I will have Jamal look at it tomorrow. Did you move the rabbit ears around, Mr. Odor?"

"I did. All it did was turn the snow snowier."

"Oh, I am so sorry. Did you put aluminum foil on the rabbit ears, Mr. Odor?"

"No, I didn't have any aluminum foil with me and I didn't see any foil in the room."

"Oh, I am so sorry. The people before you must have stolen the foil, Mr. Odor. It is a problem, you know. People take valuables from the rooms. It's very sad."

"Yes. I don't know why people steal things, Mr. Patel. It's sad."

He reached under the counter, found a box of Reynolds Wrap and ripped <u>off</u> a <u>foot</u> <u>of</u> <u>foil</u> <u>for</u> (offa-fo-fo-fo-fo) me. Ah, the fa-fun of reading and writing out loud. "I will give you this for a small addition to your bill. It is magical, Mr. Odor. I can't explain why."

"Okay. Well then, um, have a nice night Mr. Patel and say hi to Mrs. P."

"Oh no, sir. There is no Mrs. Patel. I have never found a Mrs. Patel but I am looking very hard, sir. I have my third eye on a future Mrs. Patel (giggle) in room 2. Praise, Krishna."

We giggled together.

Back in my room, I folded the aluminum foil around the rabbit ears and was able to watch a snowy half hour of the re-re-re-re-re-run of an old movie about a young boy in the 1940's who wanted a bb gun for Christmas but everybody kept telling him he'd shoot his eye out if he got it. He got the gun and just as the boy was about to take his first shot... there was a knock at my door. I figured it was Jamal, Jeff's brother, come to help me with the TV. It wasn't Jamal. It was the former Mrs. Odum!

"Ta da! Surprise!" she ta daed.

"I must say I am surprised, Sue. We didn't part in the best of terms today. Why are you here? What do you want?"

"I know," she said, "but your Aunt Minnie was in her pajamas by 6:30 and I'm not rilly ready to call it a day so soon. Soooo, I was wondering if you'd like to do what we used to like to do on Thanksgiving night when we were married back in Birdland-East-Duck? Go see a movie."

"Well, I was just watching a movie on my TV but the reception is so bad that the film had a scene where I think it was snowing but I couldn't tell because of all the snow. Okay. Sure. Let's catch a flick. But, you know, there's only one theater here in Birdland-West-Gosling, and it can show only one movie."

"I know. But maybe it's a new one. One we've never seen," she said.

We hopped into my Honda and it felt a little like it did in Duck when we used to get along, let the turkey or flounder dinner digest while ingesting one of Hollywood's hyped up holiday releases.

The Lyric Theater is a block off Main Street and when I saw the marquee I couldn't believe what was showing. It was that old Christmas film about the Forties kid wanting a bb gun!

I immediately thought two thoughts, but one at a time.

First thought: *Why are they showing this old film when it's on TV non-stop from Thanksgiving to Christmas?*

Second thought: *Maybe nobody gets good TV reception in Gosling since there's no cable or satellite service.*

On second thought, I see now that I had three thoughts.

Third thought: *Are there no Thanksgiving movies? Wouldn't it be a good idea for a filmmaker to make a film about Thanksgiving that everyone would want to watch around Thanksgiving?*

(Publisher: A fourth thought: Perhaps a movie about an unemployed journaller reuniting with his family after many years at a Thanksgiving reunion where he discovers how interesting/unusual they are and writes a book that becomes a bestseller and makes the journaller wealthy/famous beyond my wildest dreams. JO)

The Lyric Theater operates as if it is still 1940. Thick, dark red, dusty, moth eaten curtains surround the entire room. Then, dramatically, the curtains slowly open to reveal another curtain, a see-through, that covers the Lyric's ancient and stained screen. The projectionist starts running the first feature, a Tom and Jerry cartoon, while the see-through curtain opens ever so slowly. Next comes a Co-cola commercial for Pepsi Cola, then a request to turn off cell phones, then a request to help keep our theater clean and please refrain from throwing stuff on the floor, then seven previews, then an old black and white Fifties animated advertisement to buy expensive candy and popcorn in the lobby, then a second request to turn off cell phones and not throw stuff on the floor, then finally, "And Now Our Featured Presentation."

The film was old but the audience was young. Susan and I were the oldest people in the theater. We were surrounded by teenagers. There were so many cell phones flicking on and off in the darkened room it looked as if it was being invaded by a swarm of huge lightning bugs. The teens never stopped talking or texting. There was constant movement in the aisles and kids jumping over rows of seats and throwing popcorn at each other. Girls who looked like they were, maybe, eleven or twelve were sitting on guys' laps and making out with them. *God, I wish I was young again*, I thought, but didn't say to Susan, who was also amazed more by the audience than the movie. "Wow. Things are different, huh?"

We moved out of the way to chairs at the far right backend of the theater. The floor was a sticky mess of popcorn, candy bar wrappers and drink cups.

Surprisingly, the kids were actually paying attention to the movie called "A Christmas Story."

(Publisher: When my Thanksgiving story book becomes a major motion picture, it and "A Christmas Story" would make an excellent double feature presentation

around the holidays. Perhaps you could also run this idea past some of your many Hollywood honcho buds? JO)

The movie has been shown so often on television that the kids knew all the lines and yelled them out loud along with the film.

"YOU'LL SHOOT YOUR EYE OUT," they screamed in unison when the film's characters delivered the line-- and then back to texting or necking. They knew every character's name. When the boy named Flick in the film is 'triple dog' dared to stick his tongue on a frozen flagpole, they loudly cried in pain along with him. As did I.

This was like a Christmas movie version of "The Rocky Horror Picture Show" happenings when fans of that film repeat the lines, sing along with and dress up like the characters.

In this film, the little boy, Ralphie, says the mother-of-all-swear-words--- Cousin Louis' favorite-- but for the sake of censorship, they used the word "fudge." The teen theatergoers could barely wait for the scene. Then, all at once, and drowning out the theater speakers:

"FUUUUUDDDDDGGGGGGGGGGGGGEEEEE!"

What we thought was going to be a terrible movie experience turned out to be hilarious. The kids' response to the movie was very funny especially when they sang along when the family eats at a Chinese restaurant and the waiters attempt to sing a Christmas carol:

"FA RA RA RA RA, RA RA RA RA"

After the movie, we went out for Chinese food. Unfortunate-cookiely, there is no Chinese restaurant in Gosling and nothing was open so we went to my room and shared a slice of the pumpkin pie I brought back from the reunion and planned to have for breakfast tomorrow.

"I had a rilly good time tonight, Jack. Hey, we loved each other once remember? Let's bury the hatchet, and not into each other's skulls. Whatdaya say?"

"Sure. What the fudge. Wanta spend the night?"

"Let's not go there, Jack... yet. In fact, a little birdie told me that you managed to woo one of the many babes in Birdland-East to your little love nest in Duck."

"Ray, right?"

"Yeah, I called him the other day to see how he's doing. I hadn't talked to him in over a year. Don't give him a hard time. He told me he was jealous of you. That you were not only still, quote, on the hunt but able to find."

"Nothing came of it, Sue, just a summer romance in Birdland. And you?"

"One date one night. Disaster. My parents are after me to hurry up and meet someone and have the kids we didn't have."

"Well don't rush into it like we did and make the same mistake."

"I won't. Same with you."

"Well, then, with those wise words of advice to each other and your decision to return to Aunt Meany's house, I'll bid you goodnight and farewell. And good luck with your book, Sue."

"You too.

"Thanks."

"Um, Jack? One more thing."

"Sure. What?"

"Mind if I use your bathroom before I go. I gotta..."

"...piss like a Russian racehorse?"

MANUSCRIPT CHAPTER TWENTY-THREE

"Hello/Goodbye" to Mom, Dad, Chuckie, The Beatles and
The Beetles
Friday Morning

Out of bed at 10:30, too late to partake of the free breakfast buffet spread of hard powdered mini donuts and instant coffee at the Americana Motel. There was one bite left of the slice of pumpkin pie Sue and I nibbled on last night but it looked brown instead of orange. I flushed it out of my sight. Tired of Pearl's Diner, LOUD Aunt Ruth and Henrietta the Free Roaming Hen, I headed for "Tio's Tank & Tummy" six or seven blocks away. Tio offered breakfast all day. *Gracias Tio*, I thanked Tio in Spanish to myself.

I figured I fill up the gas tank first and then my gut. I seated myself, as the sign said, looked over the grease smeared plastic menu and when the waitress arrived I ordered a *huevos burrito*. I was *muy* hungry and, apparently, I came off somewhat grumpy to the waitress. A bonita babe in Birdland-West.

"Well, balls to you, too, señor," she said, smiling when she emphasized the word balls to me.

Oh yeah, I ohyeahed mentally in English.

I had forgotten that huevos, the word for eggs in Spanish, is also the word for balls; a running joke in the Spanglish-speaking world and especially high school *Español-Uno*, which I took but only managed a *C* (Sí?).

I laughed out loud in Spanish, "Ja Ja!"

"Sí, señor, huevos eez eggs and balls, eet eez funny, no?"

"Yes, señora, it eez," I agreed (egg-greed?)

She asked me a bunch of other questions in rapid Spanish which I didn't understand so I just kept nodding yes and sí-sí-sí-ing her.

She asked, "You like it muy caliente hot, sí?" and winked at me. I thought, *Yes. And you are muy caliente, señora, but your esposo is standing right over there and he's watching you very closely. And he doesn't look happy.*

I smiled innocently and told her "Sí, señora. Hot burrito, por favor."

She pointed at the menu's warning that all dishes with habanero required a customer signature not holding Tio responsible for burns or death. I signed.

It singed my insides! *Ah! Chihuahua, my insides screamed in Spanish.* It was a red-hot-sausage-and-balls burrito with a side of fried potatoes that were practically on fire. I think Tito took it out on me for his wife's flirting. *That's UNFAIR, Tito,* I thought, and looked around for something cold-- and something I might like as a souvenir. My mouth, tonsils and esophagus are scarred forever and I believe my voice is now gruffer.

Once recovered, I was quickly back on the road all gassed-up and gassed up, if you catch my drift, which you don't want to do, *mi amigo.*

I stopped by the cemetery to visit my parents' grave and also that of my best buddy in high school who passed away in our senior year. It was thanks to his good notes taking that I managed to graduate with a solid C+ average.

There was a crowd and television cameras in the cemetery that morning and so I moseyed on over to see what was going on. There are usually a few souls at a funeral who, despite the solemnity, gather the strength to smile. But there was outright hilarity at this funeral. Turns out it was a news event with media on the scene from Charlotte and

Asheville. A gaggle of Gosling and Jefferson County politicians had come to pay their disrespect as a local farm pest was laid to rest. It was a photo op mock funeral for the boll weevil. A paper maché modél of a huge weevil was laid out legs up in a cotton-lined coffin.

"May the Lord not allow you to rest in peace, you damned boll weevil," screamed newly appointed Jefferson County Agriculture Agent Bo Jennings who(m) I remember from junior high school as the class clown. We loved him for his humorous approach to life. He was the first person I ever saw with a Mohawk haircut and earrings when the rest of us were just trying out long hair and grow a mustache. He was always in trouble for saying or doing something hilarious or off color. Bo liked to pretend he was a car and would drive down the hallways making car sounds and pretending to be peeling out, shifting gears, taking curves too fast or braking to a screeching halt. Sometimes he'd crash into lockers and fall flat on the floor during class changes. He did it so often that students and teachers just stepped over him to prevent hallway traffic jams. He took auto shop instead of general courses and I guess we all figured he'd become a mechanic or a car salesman someday.

As the Ag agent, he told the assembled that the use of sex attractants in the cotton fields successfully brought the demise of the boll weevil in Jefferson County, among the last counties to rid itself of the bug.

"Not so long ago it seemed cotton would die out but more and more farmers are planting cotton now that we're planting the boll weevil six feet under," he eulogized. "I hope cockroaches, fleas, red ants and ticks someday join the boll weevil in purgatory."

"Vrooom... Urrrrch... Crash!" I said too loudly for a cemetery. He looked my way but I don't think he recognized me.

My parents' grave was nearby. My mother died seven years ago and my father a few months after. That my mom died first amazed everyone. She looked old and unhealthy but repeatedly claimed to be feeling "finer than a fine-tooth comb." She kept a garden, went for walks or painted a new fake something on the kitchen walls. Dad, on the other hand, was a physical wreck. He smoked unfiltered Camel cigarettes, ate everything fried, salty or sweet and drank more than his fair share of homemade beer and whiskey. Despite that, he probably never tipped the scales over one hundred seventy. He had several bathroom scales as part of his living room décor (as I described in either Chapter three or four. I haven't had time to check because I've been busy writing more chapters).

Mom managed to hide her sickness from all of us right up to the end. Her colon cancer and dad's heart disease, Alzheimer's, COPD, diabetes, prostate cancer and a couple of other diseases became outwardly serious at the same time and they ended up sharing a room at The Clearhaven Home and Rehabilitation Center for the Elderly in Gosling.

On the day they left the house for the nursing home, they gathered only their most comfortable clothes and important and prized possessions because their room had only two small closets, two dresser drawers and two nightstands.

Mom's closet was crammed tight. You couldn't have squeezed in another dress. The frilly blue dress she wanted to be buried in was on the end, wrapped in dry cleaning plastic and ready for the undertaker. Her creams, perfumes and makeup took over all the counter space. The nightstand drawer would not completely close because of the mishmash of jewelry, hair clips, pencils, puzzles, candy, magazines and paint supplies.

Dad's closet had his burial suit-- the only suit he owned-- his one tie, three shirts, a pair of jeans, a warm coat, a pair of diabetic shoes and a well-worn brown leather belt cut shorter with new holes punched in as he lost weight with age and sickness. The dresser had a week's worth of underwear and socks. He rotated a pair of pajamas and two robes. His nightstand drawer had extra razor blades, a watch that hadn't been wound in years, his expired driver's license and his Veterans Administration ID card.

There was a faded framed picture of our family of five from the 1980's above the TV. The television played all day at high volume. Loud TV's blasted from almost every room in the building. It seemed like my parents were always watching "The 700 Club" or "Cops" at a deafening volume.

There was always someone in some room moaning and groaning. One night I heard the old guy in the room across from my parents' room scream at the top of his cancerous lungs, "Bob, what the hell's the matter with you, your crazy son of a bitch? Shut up Goddamn it, Bob! Get out of here!" I asked one of my mother's female caretakers who Bob was. She said he was Bob.

Two walkers, a wheelchair, two comfortable lounge chairs and their two beds filled up the room to where visitors either had to stand, sit on their beds or in dad's wheelchair. I always chose the wheelchair and did wheelies in the hallway to the pained expressions of some residents.

It seemed like every ten minutes a caretaker came in to give my parents pills, a shot, take their blood pressure or deliver a plate of food. Both said the food was very good but neither ate hardly any of it. I sometimes ate their dinner to make them look good. "Well Ralph," the caretaker would exaggeratingly exclaim, "That's wonderful. You ate almost everything except the meat loaf. Good for you." The meat loaf was disgusting. Mostly bread. But their chocolate cake with peanut butter icing was to die for-- a phrase you probably shouldn't say out loud in a nursing home. But then, who would hear over the mass deafness and high volume TVs?

Each room was a different color. My parent's room was purple. Their undecorated wall was driving my mother up the wall. One day she painted a fake IV bottle and tubes on the wall beside her bed. It was painted-over purple again the next time we visited and her paints were gone. Humor can also die in a nursing home. Dad called the place "God's waiting room."

I'll never forget hearing the dead silence the day we watched my father being wheel chaired into the funeral home to see my mother in her casket. A caretaker helped him stand up to look into the coffin. He was pretty far gone by then. He squinted and stared at her for quite some time and finally turned to me and asked in his old weak voice, "Is that Faye?" I said, "Yeah it is, dad." He looked at her again for several more seconds without saying a word. Then, "Faye's dead, ain't she?" I nodded yes again because I had no voice. Crying and talking at the same time, my father spoke slowly and quietly to my mother, "I cain't live without you, Faye. I want to go, too. I love you. I'll be with you in Heaven. Soon. You'll see. Wait for me, Faye." Giant tears rolled down his cheeks and, with help from a caretaker and me he slowly sat back down in his wheelchair. The caretaker, also in tears, returned dad to their (his) room in Clearhaven. None of us in the viewing room could move or talk for nearly a minute. We stood in stunned silence or cried. I had never seen my father cry. I had never heard him tell my mother he loved her. I never cry. I cried.

My father built both his and my mother's coffins. Looking inside the lid of mom's casket relieved some of the stress of the funeral service. She had painted it herself. It was a replica of their bedroom ceiling, which was a scene she painted of a stormy sky of dark grey clouds with a lightning strike, some leafless tree limbs and a flock of birds escaping the coming downpour. Since they had a five-blade ceiling fan, dad installed a little battery powered fan along with a tape recording of a thunderstorm. The under-taker promised to turn them on when he finally closed the coffin's lid. She once told my father, "I can sleep real good when it's apourin'down and if I'm gonna be asleep for eternity than I want it to be rainin' raht good."

Whenever I visited my father, he would make a point of telling me he loved me. "Do you hear me, Jack? I love you. Do you hear me?"

"I hear you, dad. I love you, too." I had never told my dad that until he was at this late stage of his life. Nor had he ever said that to me until then.

When he died, the world lost another unsung hero. Ralph Odum was an Army medic in Anzio, Italy, one of the bloodiest battles of World War II. He never talked about it except to mention that he was there. He was buried with military honors complete with "Taps," gun salute, flag-draped coffin and bagpipes.

Their graves share a tombstone. Dad's side is inscribed with pictures of birds and deer because he loved to hunt, and a picture of a bathtub because of his hobby of turning bathroom fixtures into furniture. Mom's side is inscribed with a paintbrush and easel for her artistic talent. I placed a print I'd found at The Americana Motel of a vase filled with lovely orange marigolds. Orange was my mother's favorite color and I knew she'd prefer a picture of flowers instead of real ones. As a joke, I knew dad would enjoy, I planted the plunger I bought for a dollar at Miss Sarah's on his side of the tombstone. That had to set the groundskeepers to wondering.

My buddy's grave was several rows over and down from my parents. Chuckie Philip's final resting place is as unusual as was his funeral all those year ago. Chuckie's parents, aware that his favorite music was by The Beatles, played nothing but their songs at his funeral. It was disconcerting hearing "Help!" as his coffin was lowered into the ground. At the wake in their home, more Beatles tunes served up with pizza and beer. His tombstone has a button attached to it that, when pressed, plays a recording of Chuckie strumming his guitar and singing "Paper Back

Writer." Was this an omen for my attempt at novelling? If so, thank you, Chuckie.

The graveyard in Gosling should be a tourist attraction. It's a collection of buried wonders. There's one grave that contains a man's left foot, amputated in a train accident. We used to wonder if it was buried a foot deep. There's another of a British soldier standing up and saluting, his body pointed toward Great Britain. A local motorcycle enthusiast was interred with his Harley. The town's founder, Admiral Alexander Geoffrey Gosling, rests here for eternity. Another man's tombstone claims he was related to George Washington, Andrew Jackson, Blackbeard the Pirate and Admiral Alexander Georffrey Gosling. And now there is a six-foot-long paper maché bug in a cotton coffin and my parent's strange caskets. Dad's is a cast iron claw foot bathtub with a lid made of bathroom tiles. He sleeps forever on deep comfy sofa cushions and soft pillows with plumbing magazines and a monkey wrench at his side. They say you can't take it with you. Dad did. In death, he's sacked out in his living/laving room.

I want to be buried here when I die. I've prepared a will that will be read upon my death that stipulates my desire to rest eternally near mom and dad's graves if there's still room available. I wouldn't want to be buried in Duck. The cemetery there is modern with the granite tombstones flush with the ground. The landscape crews just run their mowers right over your name and dates and sometimes the wild ponies get in there and eat your grass cover and fertilize it.

My will requests that I have a small memorial service in which only the top half of my body is shown. I don't want to wear pants forevermore. Boxer shorts only. And I don't want to be shown at the viewing, or buried, wearing glasses. Why would I be wearing glasses with my eyes closed in eternal sleep when I don't wear my glasses to bed overnight while I'm alive? I want no solemn funeral music at my memorial service. Booker T and The MG's and Bob Seger would be about right. Even though I'm not Catholic, I would like to have a priest conduct the ceremony if that's permitted. Don't ask me why because I don't know. *It's just how I picture it ought to be,* in my mind, *like on TV and in the movies.* If it's okay with the Church I would like the priest to sprinkle my coffin with Holy Water. I also want a relative to sprinkle some of The Oil on me. At the wake, I would like to have my favorite foods served: southern fried chicken with garlic mashed potatoes, gravy and biscuits. Nothing green, yellow or orange. I hated vegetables when I was alive. And serve sugar bread and coffee cake for dessert. I am requesting that a copy of this book and others I'll likely write be placed in my coffin so I can share them with others in, hopefully, Heaven. But, wherever, my tombstone is to read (in large print):

> HERE LIES A TELLER OF TRUTHS
> (More or Less. Let's say 50-50)
> JACKSON PAXTON ODUM (with a "d")
> Faction Noveller and Journaller
> Born September 2, 1955
> Died

I want to write Died September 2, 2055. Alot of people are making it to a hundred now but nobody in my family that I know of.

A cemetery really gets you to thinking about your mortality, *as in you're getting up there, Jacko. You may only have ten or twenty years to go.* Don't remind me, mind! *So, change the subject.* Good idea.

There are also two unusual sites near Gosling that we locals know about but go unnoticed in tourist pamphlets-- if ever Gosling needed tourist pamphlets. Or ever saw a tourist, for that matter.

One is a small pond on private property a few miles east of Gosling. Legend has it that it was the site of a naked Civil War battle. The story we always heard was that several very tired and dirty Confederate soldiers had stripped off their greys one afternoon for a swim and a bath in the pond when Union soldiers attacked them. Most of the Rebs were able to get out of the water, grab their weapons and fight "buck nekkid" with bayonets. The Yanks won that one. Barely.

Then there is Jed's Head at a crossroads about two miles west of town. There's nothing there now except the skeletal remains of two things: an Esso gas station and Jed's head. Nobody knows who Jed was but his head was placed in the high branches of an oak tree at that intersection in the early 1900's. The skull was still there the last time I looked, the tree's large branches holding the head in place, the eye sockets staring down at the ground. I'll bet it's still a Halloween night tradition to throw candy at the skull and yell "Head's Up, Jed."

MANUSCRIPT CHAPTER TWENTY-FOUR

Whodunit Wasn't Whotheythunkit Was
Friday afternoon

On the way back to town, I re-noticed a bar I'd first noticed when I first drove into town. There were no bars in Gosling when I lived there. Jefferson County was dry. You could bring a bottle in a paper sack to a restaurant and they'd serve you some brand of Co-cola for a mixer. The county went wet just three years ago. The neon Bud sign registered with my brain and made my mouth water, which told my brain to tell me that *we sure could use a drink after a morning of mourning.*

TNT Tony's Roadhouse Tavernacle sits where the former Rock Ridge Holiness Church once stood. A sign advertised "Laurapaboozas: Last Saturday Each Month." There was nobody in the bar but the bartender, Tony's son, Joey. Joey was alot younger than me so he was a cousin I never got to know very well. Neither father nor son made it to the reunion just a half mile down the road.

I grabbed a stool at the end of the bar. And to make sure Joey was, indeed, Joey, I asked, "Joey?"

"In person."

"You probably don't remember me. I'm Jack Odum, one of your long-lost cousins. JJ's brother."

"Sure, of course, silly," he said, um, gayly. "Why, I remember you when we used to visit your parent's house and sit in Uncle Ralph's bathtub couch in the living room. Crazy fun. Ssit a sspell. Want a drink?"

"I'll have a beer. Something with a label on it. I've had enough homebrew for one day."

"I keep ssome of Larry Berry's beer in the back but how about a nice craft beer from Asheville?"

"Great," I said. *And here I thought Kraft made cheese.*

"How about ssomething to eat?"

"Yeah, something light. A sandwich. What do you recommend?"

"I'll make you my yummy specialty: Portuguese smoked bacon on foccacia bread with lettuce, tomato, aiola mayo, goat cheese, sautéed onions and dab of olive oil. How's that ssound?"

"Wonderful," I said although my stomach wanted, and my mind was thinking, *cheeseburger.*

Still, the bar smelled like a bar should: beer, sweat and grease. The place was very dark and there were booths to slink into in the far corner. Rock oldies blared from a real jukebox. Where it differed dramatically from any honky tonk I'd ever drank in was how tastefully decorated it was with plants and art and old underwear. Yes. I wrote, "old underwear." Old undies were displayed in every nook and cranny of the bar.

It had to be asked, of course. "Say, ah, Joey. What's the skinny on all the skivvies?"

Joey, the most well-groomed and impeccably dressed barkeep I've ever seen, informed me that it's his personal collection of vintage undergarments.

He said, "I'm an amateur historian. I'm trying to figure out how undies fit into American history. Women's underwear dates to Fourteenth Century Italy. Men's to Seventh Century Britain."

He said he's only been doing this a brief time and finds material on the subject quite skimpy. (My underpants puns, not his.)

"In fact," he said, "there's not much available about what the average American wore before the turn of the Twentieth Century."

"Maybe they went commando," I said.

"No, both men and women probably just wore long shirts, basically, Long Johns," he said. "The Sears and Roebuck catalogue of 1902 offered only one size: looooong. Women's underwear went all the way down to the floor. They had little pink frills along the neckline. Oh my God. Fabulouss, really!"

TMI about BVDs, Joey. I was more interested in family dynamics and why neither Joey nor his dad bothered to go to the family reunion.

Joey said that "everybody in the family assumes dad and grandpa blew up the church... ssssoooo, we don't attend family functions very often anymore."

"Did they?"

"What?"

"Dynamite the church?"

"Nope. They're innocent but nobody believes it."

"Then who...?"

"The Rev blew it up. Good ole God-fearing Pastor Henry Young bombed his Rock Ridge Holiness Church to High Heaven. Now, issn't that just a hoot and a howl? He probably figured everyone would blame my dad. The Rev was upset that nobody in the congregation was willing to handle his damn copperhead snakes. People stopped attending and switched over to the Free Methodist Church. Alsso, and don't tell dad this, but the Rev was getting tired of mom hanging all over him and not being willing to handle hissssssssnake, if you hear what I'm ssaying."

"I'm hearing ya. Ha."

If you're reading this-- and not just leafing through to see if this book might interest you-- I suppose Uncle Tony is relieved, embarrassed and laughing now.

I asked how Uncle Tony and Aunt Laura were doing. I didn't want to tell him that his mother was drunk as a skunk at the reunion. He rolled his eyes and declared them both "a mess. Especially mama. Booze. Daddy'ss on disability. But he can still pick a guitar better than most."

Joey was always bragged about as the Odum family brain. And athlete. And one of the best musicians. At least that's what we were all led to believe.

Ever since he was born, his mom, the always then-sober Laura, let the family know in her annual Christmas letter that Joey was exceptional in every way. She informed us that he was the best player on the T-Ball team and then later the baseball team and then later still the football team. She said he was a straight A student, K-12. He was in chorus and band, drama and book clubs and was taking piano and violin lessons and a member of Mensa.

My mother once wrote a Christmas letter I saved about our family that mocked Aunt Laura's holiday letter:

> *Seasons Greetings,*
> *I hope all y'all is doing good. We're not. I am suffering to no end from a bee sting on my tongue. It is as big as a basketball. Ralph said if I kept my mouth shut bees wouldn't sting my tongue. I can't hardly eat no more. I only weigh 70 pounds now. Ralph ain't good neither. By that I mean he just ain't no dang good a-tall. He ran away with a neighbor lady half his age in March and she wore him out right fast and he came home dragging his tail. I'm still mad and we ain't hardly spoken to each other since. Wolf, our hunting dog, died. Our cat killed him. A rat killed the cat. Sometimes backward things happen. Here is some good news. Bonnie is pregnant again. She is 13 and is of the marrying age now. She don't remember who the daddy is but he had a*

nice car. JJ is in a asylum. He went bat crazy in Febawary when he seen where baby cows come from. We figgerd it scared the daylights out of him seeing one cow come out the backend of another. Jacko is a heroin addict. He ran off with a city floozy. We only seen her one time. She's from Poland because Jack said she is a Pole dancer. Our house burned. Just the top two floors so we're making due in the cellar. It's cold down here because the furnace won't light. Sorry you have to pay for the 10 cent postage stamp but we're broke.

Merry Christmas and Happy New Years.
Mary, Ralph, JJ and Bonnie
PS We don't know hide nor hair where Jacko is at. Maybe Poland.

Mom never sent it. Instead of reading "A Visit from St. Nicholas" on Christmas Eve we would have her read Aunt Laura's latest bragging letter, and then her response, and have a good laugh.

"Do you still play violin, Joey?"

"Are you kidding? I'm the only member of the family that didn't get the music gene."

"I didn't either."

"Welcome to my off -key world."

"At least you got the jock gene. I didn't get that either."

"Neither did I. The only things I like about sportss are the men's fashions. I'm the gay Odum, Jack."

"No. You're. Not," I said in mock shock.

"Yesssssss," he said in a crisp lisp. "Don't tell dad."

Uncle Tony must be blind and deaf.

(Note to the Publisher: Maybe we should edit out reference to Joey's coming out. Gosling is right smack dab in the middle of the Bible Belt, y'know. Ask several of

your gay editors what they think. Also, tell them to try the sandwich Joey made for me. It was Fabulous. JO)

"The only thing even close to a sport that I'm interested in is Pigeon Rolling. Ever sseen that?" he assked.

"No, I have no idea what you're talking about."

"Well, it's a breed of pigeon that tends to fold itself up into a ball and do multiple backward ssomersaultss. They can do that in flight and they look like a ball of feathers as they fly from the sky to the ground. They're sssooo cute. I have two of them. I enter them in Rolling Pigeon Races all over the country. We roll them along the ground like bowling balls. They can roll for thirty yards before coming to a stop, and then they stand up on both feet and stretch their little wings. Ssoooo ssweet."

He said they're called Birmingham Rollers because they were first bred in Birmingham-- The British Birmingham not the Alabamaish Birmingham. Joey claims they love it and sometimes even clap their wings in satisfaction at the end of the finish line.

"C'mon over to my place tomorrow, Jack. We'll roll some pigeonss. It's a hoot. Actually, a coo. Ha-ha."

"Thanks, Joey, but I'm heading home tomorrow. I'm taking Aaron to the parade tonight so I better get going. I gotta "Get Back" to JJ's and pick up Aaron. I sing-songingly said "Get Back" because, I guess, I still had Chuckie and his Beatlemania on my mind. Joey actually knew the old Beatles song and we sang a couple verses together. And I thought *we have pretty good harmony for two guys missing the family music gene.*

MANUSCRIPT CHAPTER TWENTY-FIVE

I love a LOUD parade
Friday night

"I love a parade," I must have said a dozen times at the reunion to the question, "Do you like parades?" It was apparent that some Odums were going to be marching down uptown Gosling's main drag Friday night in the annual Thanksmas/Christgiving Parade.

I do love a parade. I do. I especially enjoy that eardrum bursting sound of a dozen marching drummers followed by the blast of brass as the horns pass. I just realized that a "blast of brass as the horns pass" has a nice Dr. Seuss AND John Phillips Sousa ring to it. It's Sousa-Seussian.

So, there I sat on a cold curb with my buddy, Aaron, waiting for what the past had shown to be a classic small town holiday parade. History also shows that Gosling cannot get a parade to start on time. 6pm is 7:15pm for Gosling's holiday parade. The annual event's longtime organizer, Mr. Thompson, the music teacher and girls' softball coach at Jefferson County High, is the annual problem. Everybody knows it but he won't step down and nobody else wants the job. The wait becomes more uncomfortable as the temperature, and the already cold concrete curb, gets colder. That can dramatically improve some people's chances of developing piles but I won't mention any names. Me. I had a blanket in the car and I wish I had brought it or a chair or a stadium pillow seat like virtually everybody else along the parade route. Several mor Odums joined us curbside. None remembered blankets.

At 7:15 or so we hear the Jefferson County Middle School Band's drummers drumming:

RATA TATA TATA TATA TATA BOOM BOOM.

I do enjoy that snare drum cadence. It makes me feel good. Young. Patriotic. Militaristic. American.

Then, to my American eardrums' dismay, the band stopped marching a block and a half away from us. I squinted my eyes to watch the trumpeters, tromboners, tubaers and fluters put their lips to the metal; and then squinted my ears to hear them blow what sounded something like "Blue Christmas." When they finished the song, the band lowered their instruments and marched past us without so much as a toot or a rata-tata-boom. All we got was marching feet sound. "C'mon," I yelled, "Play something!" but only the cymbaler looked at me in a meaningful (read: mean) way. I also received similar looks from some curb sharers.

Later on, Mr. Thompson's High School Band did exactly the same thing in the same place, and then marched by us in silence. I stayed silent this time but yelled at them through thought, *play something right here, dammit.* The high school cymbaler also looked my way. I thought at first, *she's read my mind.*

"Why is she looking at us, Aaron?" Aaron said the Middle School cymbaler probably texted the high school cymbaler and told her to throw me the evil eye. "Also, Uncle Jack, that's Julia Wright. She's my cousin. Didn't you see her at the reunion?"

"No," I said. "I didn't." But kids that age all look alike to me. *Since she's an Odum she's probably a genetically gifted musician,* I thought and was rewarded when her cymbalic excellence "crash crash crash" echoed to us from where the band had stopped to perform three blocks away.

At least the high school majorettes performed as they marched by us in their mini skirts with their legs covered in goosebumps (Goslingbumps?) from the cold. Aaron certainly liked what he saw. The lead majorette (major majorette?) tossed her baton far into the air and when it finally came down it bounced several times on the street and she had to break ranks to retrieve it. The crowd loudly applauded her botched batoning. She returned to the head of the group, regrouped, and settled on a less dramatic twirling exhibition, ignoring the snickers from some of the other obviously jealous majorettes (minorettes?) in the back row.

"Is she an Odum, Aaron?"

"No, that's Genny Neeper, the hottest girl in Gosling. She's a senior. I wish I was older."

I wish I were younger, I didn't say.

A Toyota pickup Monster truck drove by blasting bass so loud my back teeth vibrated. The truck was all engine and wheels. We had to look up to see the driver; a muscular, bald, bearded, tattooed and multi-pierced man who appeared to be paying more attention to the goose-bumped legs of the majorettes marching in front of him. Aaron advised me that it was Larry Berry's son from his first marriage driving the truck. "Don't you remember Jerry Berry, Uncle Jack?"

I did, then, remember Jerry Berry but seemed to recall a small, shy sissified little guy who didn't want to get dirty and stayed to himself. *Looks like Jerry found his inner macho.*

Cousin/Deputy Doug Humphries blew his siren and flashed his lights as he and Sheriff Reggie Moore drove by in the town's one patrol car. Doug looked at me and grinned and I thought he looked a little pie-eyed. So, did Sheriff Moore.

Aaron gave the Red Cross Blood Mobile a standing ovation.

Dance Schoolers, Brownies, Cub Scouts, War Vets, the Mayor all marched by; and then a fan favorite, the city's garbage truck and crew. They received a huge applause. The trash collectors tossed candy. Their truck was actually pretty, considering. Washed and polished, it was decorated with plastic wreaths, tinsel and garlands. Sticking out of the crusher at the back of the truck were the torso and head of The Grinch. Unfortunately, the truck's grinchy smell stole the evening's fresh air as it went by us.

The farmer whose stolen pig we enjoyed at our reunion shined up his John Deere tractor and put a red Rudolph nose and plastic antlers on it. He was pulling a wagon filled with hay and look alike teenagers who were blaring a song about Grandma getting run over by a reindeer. This had apparently become a tradition in the Gosling parade because the crowd sang along but with altered (antlered?) words: "Grandma got run over by a JOHN DEER."

Several people rode horses. A man in a clown outfit rode a donkey. A small child in a clown outfit rode a goat.

Gosling has one fire truck and it was the parade's capper with Santa atop it, his face bright red from either the cold or a bad makeup job. I looked closely and what to my wondering eyes should appear but Cousin Louis as Santa Claus.

"Ho Ho Ho," hohohoed Louis as he tossed popcorn balls to the crowd. You can be sure that, in his mind, Louis was actually saying "Ho, Ho, _____ Ho."

Being dragged behind the fire truck were the carcasses (carcassi?) of a dozen turkeys (turki?), their bony remains bouncing on the concrete to the song "Here Comes Santa Claus." It's a Gosling tradition nobody can really explain, but it is funny to watch and the crowd gobbles as they go by. This, thus, gave a symbolic (not to be confused with cymbalic) end to Thanksgiving, the start of Christmas and the end of the annual Gosling Thanksmas parade. Actually, the actual end was a city employee with a city shovel cleaning up actual droppings from the horses, the donkey and the goat. He received a huge applause. Aaron informed me that the poop scooper is an actual relative on my mother's brother's first wife's side.

Those were the highlights. The parade lasted about twenty minutes. I promised Aaron I would visit more often and told him I'd invite his dad to bring the family to Duck next summer.

That's not going to happen. Funny how those "after-party let's all get together again real soon" promises so seldom pan out when there's any distance involved.

MANUSCRIPT CHAPTER TWENTY-SIX

Bye Bye Birdyland-West
Late Saturday Morning

Check out was at 11am. I woke up at 10:15. Plenty of time to perform the four S's, pack my bags, stash Mr. Patel's two-dollar aluminum foil rabbit ears booster in my bag, pay my bill, grab three hard powdered donuts and a Styrofoam cup of Nescafé, leave before Mr. P. noticed his marigold print missing and head for home. With luck, I'd be back in Duck by nine o'cluck (another Duck cliché and rather Seussian).

The drive up and down and around the mountain roads to Brevard was uneventful and probably beautiful. The weather was dreary and it looked like it might rain or even snow. It was dark enough that I turned on my headlights. I saw that the poor white squirrel was still where I'd run over it but flat as a pancake. A possum, killed the night before, lay nearby with an ugly turkey vulture enjoying what was left of it. A gruesome scene as the bird pulled out entrails and flew away with them as my car approached. Appropriately, a road sign a few miles later told me I was leaving Transylvania County, North Carolina. You can imagine how much fun the people here have on Halloween. Some of their monster decorations were still up. In Transylvania County, this time of year you might see a Pilgrim, Santa Claus and Dracula in adjacent yards. Speaking of Dracula, US-64 takes you through the town of Bat Cave. There really is a cave full of bats there but it's protected by a nature-loving bat group, difficult to get to and next to impossible to visit. But (Bat?) why would any living person want to go there? Anyway, there are all kinds of artsy fartsy batty stuff to buy in Bat Cave but I was hell bent on getting home, so I flew through town like a bat out of there.

I decided on a quicker route home, the Interstate. I winged my way to I-40 (speed limit: seventy) where I could make good time driving the typical eighty-five miles per hour in a middle lane-- trying to ignore middle fingers but throwing a few birds myself-- while being passed on both sides by caravans of eighteen wheelers going ninety and the Damn Yankees passing them.

Flying through Winston-Salem, a long-forgotten urge came upon me from way back in my brain somewhere. It asked me, *Wouldn't a Winston or a Salem taste good right now, Jacko?* "Yes, it would, Urge. But I don't want to start that habit again. I quit smoking the same time I started the klepto cocktail and, so far, so good." *I hear you, Jacko, but "the burn." Remember the throat and chest burn? Remember that feeling?* "I do, Urge, but I am not going to give in to you this time even though that exit has a sign advertising Cheap Cigarettes (and gas, perfume and Levis)." I'm pretty much in control of my own mind and body and throat and chest now. I did not take that exit in Winston-Salem.

Then Durham came up. I instantly recalled the sweet smell of curing tobacco that would once fill your nostrils when approaching this once famous cigarette producing town. Durham bills itself today as the City of Medicine instead of Tobacco Town because Duke University and its Medical Center is so... so... omnipresent (and once again, thanks Mr. Roget whoever/whomever you are. You're always omnipresent in my presence). Only one small company still makes cancer sticks there but seeing the fading paint on the former factories advertising L&Ms and Lucky Strikes brought to mind again *"the burn."* I craved a Marlboro, my favorite brand... *Ohhhhh, Jacko, remember how nice a Marlboro went with a drink or while reading a newspaper or book or with an early morning cup of coffee or while on a long drive or long walk or after swimming or after a steak and potato dinner or after se...* exit 15, the billboard announced and featured a novelty restaurant called "Doc's Diner." Doc's sounded like just the prescription to get my mind off bellyaching for a smoke and do something about my hungry belly.

It was almost 4pm. That's too late to call it lunch, too early to call it dinner or supper (linner? dupper? sinner?) It was even too early for the Senior Citizen Blue Plate Special gang. The grey and blue hairs always show up in mass at 5pm on the dot.

The entrance door to Doc's read "In Patients." A pretty young girl dressed as a Candy Striper greeted me and asked me to please follow her. She reminded me of Peggy Lou those many years ago.

"My job is, like, triage," she explained over her shoulder as she led me through the restaurant. "I, like, prioritize and direct, like, everyone to the ER, the eating area." I followed her to my table. I would have, like, followed her anywhere if she were, like, forty years older! *God, how I wished I was young again.*

Y'know, once a regular looking guy like me reaches the age of about fifty or so he becomes invisible to women under the age of thirty. Up until then if you dress nicely, smile often, smell good and act nonchalant and noncreepy, you MIGHT get a smile returned from a younger woman. On a good night, more than that. But after fifty, no matter how hard you try, you're like that guy in the late night Rerun Channel, "The Invisible Man." That's why when I'm on the hunt for a babe in Birdland-East-Duck (Duck Hunt?), I go where alot of women my age and older spend alot of time: yoga classes. I discovered that during the meditation stage of my anti-thievery therapy, and have continued the practice. Ommmmmmmmmmm.

More often than not I am the only man in the yoga class. It's just yours truly with ten to twenty women stretching, twisting, legs up, legs out and downward facing dogging. Good karma. The women actually approach me to compliment me for being there. They say, "My husband or my ex or my late husband wouldn't try yoga. Not manly enough." I harrumph and tell them that most men don't understand how difficult the positions can be." "C'mon," I say, "how much more-manly can you get than warrior pose?" When I told my neighbor, Ray, that I practice yoga for my health but also to meet women, he said that was "just more of that damn hippy, yuppie Yankee foolishness they went and brung down here."

But I seem to have digressed again...

At my table at Doc's Diner in Durham, I immediately pocketed several packs of sugar and Equal for tsunami preparation and studied the menu, which was a nurse's chart. An obviously bored waiter dressed in scrubs asked if I would like "something to drink or an IV." I laughed. This was going to be fun. I ordered sweet tea in a glass.

When he returned with my tea he asked, "Do you feel well enough to order now, sir?" He was prepared to take my order on a prescription pad with a pen shaped as a thermometer.

In keeping with the theme, I said, "Yes, doctor." I pointed at the menu and said, "I'd like a dose of your 'Miracle Medicine,'" which was chicken soup and a salad. "And may I have a clean dressing with that please," I added cleverly, I thought.

"Hrrmmph. Never heard that sick joke before," said my bored doctor/waiter, who then fake-coughed and looked at a co-doctor/waiter beside him who rolled his eyes and also fake-coughed. I thought, *Hrmmmph. I do believe, Jacko, you are suffering from a severe case of Dukie pre-med student arrogance. Somebody needs to work on their tableside manners. You're a paying patient, Jacko, and you're not being shown proper medical procedures. That is to say, these future physicians are treating you UNFAIRLY.* I guess they didn't want we/us customers playing along.

When the soup and salad finally came, it was served on a hospital tray. The dressing was in a medicine cup.

I responded to the faux docs' sarcasm with some of my own. I asked, "Are you guys Duke students?"

"Why, yes, indeed we are," said Dukie #1. To Dukie #2 he said, "The patient is recovering nicely. He seems to be thinking logically and quite aware of the obvious. Cough." Grin. "Cough."

Interesting, I thought. *I remember Sue telling me once how I seemed unaware of the obvious. My psyche medicine really is working. But I'm annoyed at being treated as a lesser person.*

Dukie #2 said, "Our sickie must be a UNC-Chapel Hill grad."

I'm well aware of the Duke-UNC basketball rivalry but I don't follow either team and just wanted to be left alone to sip my soup. "Okay then," I said, "well, you may pretend now to remove my IV. That is, if you know how since Duke, unlike the university I attended up north, isn't IV League, isn't that right?"

I hated to play college grad, and even worse, northern, but it had to be done. *They're annoyed.*

The waiters placed my bill on the table and said I could pay at the nurse's station on the way out. No "thank you" or asking me if I might like a tea refill or dessert. I was going to order some soft ice cream or jello without fruit in it but figured they might spit in it or something. Instead I asked if I could pay with plastic and showed them my Blue Cross/Blue Shield card.

"Cough," they coughed sarcastically.

"You need to stop smoking and see a doctor about that cough dork, I mean, doc." My years of going back and forth with Susan honed my sarcasm to scalpel sharp.

My hospital food was clinically okay but I kept thinking how a Marlboro would've finished it off nicely. I fake-coughed for old times' smoking sake and left a nice tip... for the Candy Striper.

I got back on I-40 heading to Raleigh where the city's Beltline Loop system messed with my mind again. *Who came up with this Inner and Outer Loopiness? Some DOT bureaucrats who had nothing better to do than study their innie and outie navels all day?*

East of Raleigh I egressed I-40, ingressed US-64 again, ingested one of the four Peppermint Patties I swiped while paying my bill at Doc's Diner and tried to digest how best to handle long stretches of featureless flatlands that lay ahead beyond Rocky Mount and Tarboro. I resorted to using a favorite long distance driving trick of mine and came up with a great idea for this book as a result.

(Editors: I just came up with another great idea to possibly once again break literary ground by making this the world's first traffic safety public service interactive faction novel. Below is my road game trick to stay awake and stay on the road during boring stretches. JO)

I just told the editors of this book that I just came up with an idea to break literary ground by making this book the world's first traffic safety interactive faction novel.

Here's my road game trick to stay awake and, as a result, stay on the road. Many small businesses advertise their services by rolling out one of those signs-on-wheels with a lighted blinking arrow pointing to their establishment. The spelling on these signs is often atrocious (sp?):

SPAGETTY AND NEETBALWZ
CHICK N DVMPLIN$
DESERTS
All U CN EAT 4 $10.

I'll pull off the road when I see an especially good/bad one and work my brain while resting my eyes. It must be a hassle to change the message or maybe it's expensive to get new letters. For whatever reasons the signs become almost indecipherable with misspelled words and numbers used as missing letters and letters as missing numbers.

A backwards 3 makes an E and vice versa.

The number 1 is often used to make an I... and vice versa.

A U might be a V... and uice uersa.

An O might be a Q, of cqurse.

N's are almost always backwards or made with a Z placed sideways.

It's fun trying to make sense of them. Here's one I pulled off the road to study for a minute:

2 И AS   P1ZZ C $5. 9
UN GRO HO И Y WI NG
BAC   C   K

I went with: Two Nasty Pizza Crusts for 5.99? Unusually gross honey coated chicken wings? And bacon cake for dessert.

Try it. Read this sign out loud that I saw outside an auto repair shop on the way home:

BR A 3 S   3
SP I A L
$4 .   G D B   SS

A bra sale at a car shop? No, it's a brake sale special for forty some dollars. God Bless.

I'm pretty good at figuring them out now and it keeps my mind alert on long drives. It's like a whacky "Wheel of

Fortune" and much better than Pinch Buggy, especially when you're alone in the car. Pinching yourself every time you see a Volkswagen is no fun, and it hurts.

Now back to my book about the reunion and the reunioners:

All of sudden I was overcome with worry that perhaps the family and friends, I reunioned with were actually not book worthy. That's when I said out loud to myself alone in my car, "C'mon, I'm this [   ] close to having enough material for my premier book. Maybe I need more people to profile. More characters. Maybe my book is too thin to be considered a real book." Maybe it was then I thought about some other relatives and friends who didn't make it to the Thanksgiving reunion.

That's why I'm writing now about Freddy Hawks. Freddy is ugly. Gawd is he ugly. Big bug eyes and a small pug, pimply nose. He has a mouth full of small crooked teeth and his smile is all gums. He'd tell you himself he was ugly if the two of you had been at the reunion. He jokes about his looks and all things ugly. I'm a card-carrying member of Freddy's "Homely Homeboys Club of Gosling." He started the club years ago by inviting anyone he considers ugly to join and revel in their homeliness. That is, anybody he meets. No meetings, no dues. Just a card with his and your name on it:

I, _____, DO HERE-BY OWN UP TO THE UGLY FACT THAT I AM VERY UGLY AND THERE IS NOTHING I CAN DO ABOUT IT. I'M SO UGLY I CAN STOP TRAFFIC. I'M SO UG-LY MY REFLECTION BREAKS MIRRORS.

BUT NEXT TO YOU I'M DOWNRIGHT BEAUTI-FUL.

FREDDY HAWKS
UGLY PRESIDENT
HOMELY HOMEBOY'S CLUB

Lindsey Dawson, my father's sister's husband's step son wasn't there. Lindsey got the music gene. He can play a banjo upside down and backwards behind his back. I'm sure he steals the show at The Laurapaboozas at TNT Tony's now.

Maybelle Odum didn't show. I'm sure nobody really expected her to. She has a birthmark that covers half her face. Or so I'm told. I've only ever seen half her face. The birthmarkless side. She's about my age. Maybelle rarely goes outside because of the birthmark. The few times I've seen her were when she answered the door only part way, hiding the right side of her face. It's sad because the left side was pretty enough. That was many years ago. I don't think she ever married. In fact, I don't even know if she's still alive.

I just made it through a State Police radar trap set-up out in the absolute middle of nowhere. My mind reminded me that, *it's the end of the month, Jacko. Cops gotta make their quota.* But the site of the Copper got me to worrying about the copper Denny Roy put in my trunk. I suppose I felt some excitement about the loot but angry with Denny Roy and the Odum family crime gene for again leading me to no good. So, I stopped off at my sister's farm in Spivey's Corner knowing she was somewhere exotic with the highly tanned GAG the Turd. I buried my half from the copper caper exactly thirteen steps away from the door of Bonnie's corn crib and exactly thirteen steps to the right. It will remain buried there and forgotten for many years. I made a map to remember and hid it in a deep recess of my wallet where it will also remain hidden for many years to come *but then why hide it from years that have already passed*, I thought.

***

It's always nice to get back home. My ex, Susan, used to kiss the ground when we returned home despite her dislike of Duck-- the town not the bird meat. She'd say it felt good to be able to sit down and pee in her own toilet again. At least she didn't kiss the commode.

Our marriage lasted three years. The toilet and I are going on six.

***

It took several weeks but I did manage to land a new job in Duck. I took a cue from Don Donovan, my Uncle Harry. I was more or less making ends meet-- more less than more more-- working at radio station WDUK "The Mighty Duck." I worked the vampire shift from 11:30 pm to 5:30 am six days a week. My on-air name was DJ Jacko. I spun the Oldies all night long and delivered a three-minute newscast every hour.

I was very careful about my duties at the radio station. I showed up on time because the DJ on the shift before me was always so stoned and bummed out at life in general that he'd put his final song on the air and leave the station by 11:25. Okay, I was late twice and there was dead air at The Mighty Duck for twenty minutes the first time and an hour and a half the second time. Fortunate for me nobody noticed. Not even the station owner/manager who(m) I doubted ever listened to the station anyway. He was from The Big Band era and "The Mighty Duck" was Rock Oldies.

For three minutes, every hour on the hour, I was a journaller again! I would basically read the Associated Press wire copy just as the AP journallers wrote it except during the 3am newscast when I had a little fun with the news.

I livened up the copy by working music into my radio

newscasts. For instance, one morning there was a story about a shootout with police somewhere in California, I think it was. Two sheriff's deputies were injured. So, I played "I Shot the Sheriff" by Eric Clapton while I read the story. When I reported that a conflict had broken out somewhere in the world I read it to the songs "War" or "Love is in the Air" or "Don't Worry, Be Happy."

I received not a single (nor an album) complaint call. So, I kept rock'n'rollin' the 3am newscast for days and weeks.

Radio was a good gig except for the hours and pay. I made better money at the *PennySaver*. That's why I agreed to stop working at WDUK Radio after only six months when they asked me to. But I expect money will start rolling in from my book when it's published soon.

(Editors: Publication date? JO)

Since this is the last chapter, this seems a good place to pass on the knowledge I've gained in becoming an experienced writer. I would advise all wannabe authors to:

-- Write what you know but don't be afraid to wander into the unknown. Y'know?

-- Be sure your subject matter matters.

-- Know that it'll all go quickly and easily once you get past that first _____ sentence.

-- Keep yourself out of the story unless the book is about you or unless your background, life experiences, personality, loves and dislikes are needed to add drama, color and/or importance to save the story.

-- By the time the book is written and you've read what you've written a dozen times you're pretty much sick of it.

-- The rules for exactly when, why and how to use who or whom are... what, exactly?

-- Writing a book is not as daunting a task as it might seem. I knocked out this manuscript in a couple of weeks and I think it shows in the results.

MANUSCRIPT POSTFACE
MANUSCRIPT BACKWORD
MANUSCRIPT ANTILOGUE

(Editor: If a book has a Preface than it should also have a Postface. If it has a Foreword it should have a Backword. If it has a Prologue it should have an Antilogue. I'll let you all decide which word to go with.

PS: Let's breakaway from the usual and go with Post Script? JO)

PS: Okay, so here's the thing. Something inside of me says *it's time to fess up on a couple or triple of things now that I'm nearing the end of the book.*

1. First of all, I lived in Altoona, Pennsylvania for a spell when I was between jobs, that is, after the *PennySaver* job in Duck fell through and before *The Coastal Carolina Times* hired me after failing to do a proper background check.

Dad-in-law heard about a writer opening at *The Pittsburgh Press* and got me an interview. They needed an ad writer and the in-laws were sure my *PennySaver* experience would assure me the job. Unfortunately, *The Press* checks resumes. As a result, I may hold a deeply hidden slightly negative attitude toward western Pennsylvania.

So, it was back to Duck for Sue and me. And our marriage was soon in the pits (burgh?). I must add here that western Pennsylvania is actually very beautiful and it's inhabited with many interesting, literate book reading people.

I do hereby apologize to all western Pennsylvanians, here and nearby, if my comments came off harsh because I rilly want yinzes to buy my book and maybe even read it. Thank you.

Denny Roy visited us for three days during the three months we lived up north in Altoona. He and I went out howlin' one typical cold, snowy, icy, wintry night in early September, and before I knew it Denny Roy had talked me into lifting some city manhole covers to weigh down the pickup truck's back end. "I ain't got no traction, Jacko." We found eight of them and had no trouble after that maneuvering the hilly streets of Altoona. Denny Roy took them back to North Carolina. I had forgotten all about them until that Thanksgiving fishing trip and copper haul when he told me about selling them to keep him and Janice in spending money.

That Denny Roy has gotten me into more trouble. Susan never cared for him. She said she's glad Denny Roy likes to hang around bars because he's going to end up behind them someday.

2. Now, second of all, **I didn't go to JJ's reunion.** Say what, says you?

Nope, says I back. **Never went. Stayed in Duck over Thanksgiving.** Had me a Swanson's turkey dinner in my apartment and watched the Macy's Day parade on TV from Philadelphia-- which is in beautiful book buying Pennsylvania.

You see, I wasn't free to travel this year, which I'll expound upon in a minute.

So, the 100% truth is that the story I just told you in this book didn't happen in the here and now present time Thanksgiving holiday period. As I mentioned about two hundred pages ago, to quote myself, "I dislike reunions and usually diss them." So even if I had been free to go it's unlikely I would have attended.

Still, it is a somewhat true recollection (let's say 30-70) of an Odum family reunion I actually DID attended one-- EIGHT years ago. And, I'm reasonably sure the Thanksgiving gathering this year was just about as I factionally described it anyway, except that my parents were in attendance back then-- and, therefore, alive at the time. I was also unemployed eight years ago and needed a break so I went to that reunion hoping to find a job in Gosling while there. I interviewed at *The Gosling Gazette* but they must have mislocated my application, resume, phone number and email.

But I certainly thank my brother, JJ, for sending his text inviting me to Thanksgiving this year. It inspired me to get busy, *wrack my brain* and write this factional book you've just about finished reading-- unless you just skipped to the end.

JJ phoned just before Christmas to wish me a Merry One:

"We missed you, Jack. I wish you could have been here. But it's understandable. Everybody asked about you. Are you okay?"

"I'm good, under the circumstances, JJ. Lonely. But I've written that book I told you I would and expect it to hit *The New York Times* Bestsellers List someday. Hey, it might even merit a mention in *"The Coastal Carolina Crimes."*

JJ said the reunion I didn't go to was very nice with the usual crowd. He said it seems like everybody in Gosling is getting old.

Aunts Grace, Ruth, Minnie and Hazel were all there with competing picnic dishes. Hazel now has throat cancer and yakked nons-stop all day to anybody who would listen about how she probably shouldn't even be talking.

Uncle Tony was a no show, as usual. Aunt Laura was "about half there," JJ said.

Uncle Harry finally let Aunt Dorothy get a cat. They

brought both pets to the reunion. Guess what Dorothy named the cat? Surprise! Kitty! I'll bet you thought "Doggie," right? *I know I did.* Now they have a dog and a cat both named Kitty.

Of course, all of JJ's kids and their friends and their friend's friends attended, including Aaron, who is twenty now and an EMT in Asheville.

Peggy Lou told JJ to tell me not to call her anymore. Louis told him to tell me, to "_____."

Deputy Doug is running for Sheriff but will never get elected because of "several incidents."

And, now, I have a third really big confession to make.

(Editors: Let's do another interactive activity. I think the road sign game went over very well. JO)

3. I'd like to thirdly and lastly fess up with another interactive activity like we did last chapter, y'know, when we were reading those misspelled and broken road signs.

Hint: This time it's a wordplay game. *Think how the darkened words are connected.* See if you can figure out where I'm going with this and why I wasn't free to travel to the reunion-- which I wouldn't have attended anyway.

Start the game show music ♫♫:

JJ's text got me to thinking of that **TIME** with the whole **GANG** eight long **YEARS** ago. It broke my mental **BLOCK** and inspired the words and **SENTENCES** and paragraphs and pages and chapters that I expect will be my **BREAK OUT BOOK.**

The answer is on the next page:

The next page with answers:

They're **PRISON** puns. Fun with puns! More laughs than a day in solitary.

Yep, you guessed it, or maybe you didn't, **I'm in jail.** Keeping up the ole Odum family tradition.

I wrote this very book you're reading behind these very bars that you can't see since I didn't include pictures. Every last word you've read so far actually occurred eight years ago as I recall them and type them. I mentioned way back in the beginning of this book that I suddenly had alot of free time on my hands. Well, time is all I have.

I've been sent to solitary several times because the other prisoners constantly complain about my writing style of constantly saying out loud the words as I write them.

There is an angry brute in cell number three who(m) is always yelling at me to be quiet, and we've had some loud convict-style conversations:

Brute in cell number three: "SHUT THE _____ UP YOU STUPID _____ NUTCASE."

My mind: *Convicts don't swear with blanks, Jacko.*

Me: You're right, mind. "HEY, ANGRY BRUTE," I yell back. "WHO(M) ARE YOU CALLING STUPID? YOU'RE THE BRANIAC WHO ROBBED A BANK BY GIVING THE TELLER A NOTE WRITTEN ON THE BACK OF A GROCERY RECEIPT WITH YOUR DEBIT CARD NUMBER."

Angry Brute: "GUARD. WILL YOU SHUT THAT _____ UP?"

Eddie, the prison guard: "Jack. Be quiet and go back to writing. And write quiet. Do we always have to hear what you're writing? Damn. You're disturbing the fine gentleman in number three again."

Me: "Sure, Eddie, but you don't mind, do you?"

Eddie: "Actually, I do mind. Look, Jack, I jes wanna come in, sit down for eight hours, read a magazine, watch these monitors, maybe nap off a little and get on home to the missus. Okay? I don't like no trouble from y'all. And it is easier to concentrate and nap when you're in solitary and I can't hear you writing." (Eddie likes to remind us that he's sort of a prisoner, too.) "How'd y'all like to get up in the morning and hafta go to jail every damn day for goin' on eighteen years now? At least someday y'all won't have to come back to this hell hole."

Me: "I won't be back, Eddie. But the INTELLECTU-AL IN CELL THREE WILL. THAT IDIOT'S GOT A RESERVATION ON DEATH ROW." There is no death row at this county jail.

Angry brute: "SHUT THE _____ UP YOU... YOU... CRAZY ASS ...CRAZY... "

Me: "WORDSMITH OF THE CENTURY IN CELL THREE EVERYBODY..."

Eddie: "Jack! Quiet. Or it's solitary."

Me: I hope I never meet that guy in cell three in a dark alley on the outside or I'm a dead man.

Angry brute: "I SEE YOUR ASS ON THE OUT-SIDE YOUSE A DEAD MAN."

My mind: *The brainiac is a mine reader. And a north-erner!*

Me: Shush, mind.

I have trouble quieting my mind at times and more so since being assigned to this one room taxpayer funded apartment.

Actually, solitary confinement is my friend. I don't mind being sent there because I can write without anybody complaining. I take pleasure in the peace and loudness it allows me. Still, I can't help but wonder if the numbskull in cell three is right. Maybe I am going a little whacky in here. Sue used to complain that I was "scattered." She said it's no wonder I can't keep a writing job with a mind so scrambled. *That was a major put down by Sue and entirely UN-FAIR, Jacko. This book proves otherwise. We think logically. How else to have written these many pages in a row that make sense and are somewhat entertaining and somewhat true, say 20-80? Maybe 15-85.*

"That's right," I said out loud.

"What's right, Jack?"

"Oh, I was talking to myself, Eddie. Sorry."

"Well, talk to yourself to yourself, Jack. Damn. I'm trying to sleep here."

"Go to sleep, Eddie. I'll be right here. And I'll be right quiet."

I'm writing some of the following in a whisper so Eddie can guard us while catching up on his sleep. He blames "the missus."

Okay, so here's the "scoop," as journalese and we/us ex-journalese like to say, about what landed me in gated government housing.

When I lost my job at *The Crimes* newspaper and ran out of money while trying to become a successful autobiographer, I remembered that I had eight-year-old buried treasure buried in my sister's backyard in Spivey's Corner, my half of the copper from that time Denny Roy and I went on a fishing trip to Hiwassee Lake.

Recovering the copper wasn't as easy as I had expected. I knew it was exactly thirteen paces from the corn crib entrance and then thirteen steps to the right and about three feet deep. I'd kept the directions hidden in my wallet. The difficulty occurred because my sister sold her farm when she eloped and married GAG, the Turd. Bonnie and Reggie live in Cana kale. That's in-- are your ready for this? Turkey! The country Turkey. She lives in a town called Turkey and I live in a town called Duck and we're from Goosetown Gosling. Welcome to Birdland, citizens of Canakkale. Turkey. Birdland-Europe? She writes to me. Bonnie GAG says I'm to become "Uncle Jack" next March.

I approached the new owners, Bruce and Barbara Halloway, originally from Butler, (western) Pennsylvania, with the story that when I was a young'un I buried a time capsule in their backyard that I would like to unearth it to see what crazy kid stuff I put in it and how it all survived the passage of time, weather, blah, blah, blah. "Now hain't that sumpin? You buried them things when yinz lived here all them years ago? Well, go on and look. We won't be nebby."

They totally bought it and didn't neb even when I was out there digging at night. They found it "charmin'." I had to dig several nights because the Halloways tore down the corn crib to expand the barn. I had to guess and reguess where the corn crib door was and then count out thirteen paces and then thirteen to the right. It seemed like a wild goose (gosling?) chase for a while there. I dug at least twenty holes before I hit gold, er, copper. I stashed the copper in my coupe on the q-t, covered my tracks with the Halloways by showing them a stuffed unicorn I had "found" at the Gas and Grits Truck Stop and then beat-up and dirtied-up to make it look old.

"Buried in our yard!" they said. "Now hain't that just sumpin else?

I told them, "I already red-up your yard rill good. I appreciate yinz lettin' me do that." I can do a right good western Pennsylvania accent when I want to thanks to my Susan experience. Our marriage was worse than prison.

I telephoned cousin Denny Roy and told him I needed to sell my copper post haste. He said he didn't speak Greek "or whatever you're talkin'" and didn't know what that meant, and when I explained to him that it meant "raht now" he dug up his copper, too. We trucked it to an Asheville scrap yard and sold our stash for two grand. A thou each. Not bad for a one night fishing trip eight years ago. Except that the two of us, instead of fish, got reeled in this time. Asheville's Finest were watching S&J Scrappers and we just happened along at just the right wrong time. Denny Roy's doing his time in the Watauga County jail and I'm getting three free a day and a bunk in Dare County's; booked for running afoul (a-fowl?) in Birdland, North Carolina.

It's interesting as a former news reporter to find yourself in the news. Denny and I were front page material in the Asheville, Murphy, Gosling and Duck Newspapers.

The Murphy Morning Sun

DAM THIEVES COP COPPER

By Luke Wassett

(Hiwassee Lake, NC) State Police have arrested two North Carolina men in connection with an eight-year-old theft of a large amount of copper wiring and pipes from a construction site near Hiwassee Lake.

Dennis Roy Odum of Murphy and Jackson Paxton Odum of Duck, North Carolina are charged with the thefts and attempts to sell the copper at S&J Scrap Metals in Asheville. The copper was ripped out of houses scheduled for demolition to make way for expansion of the Hiwassee Dam and Lake System.

The Davis Construction Company, which owns the homes, having purchased them from former owners as part of the construction contract, estimated the copper value at approximately ten thousand dollars.

Now that was right disappointing to read. We were took.

> Police say the two men entered six houses on the Wednesday night before Thanksgiving eight years ago and tore the copper wiring and pipes from the basements. Copper prices have risen dramatically over the years and police routinely watch scrap metal dealers on the lookout for attempts to sell a large quantity of the metal.
>
> At the time of the theft there were twenty-one homes awaiting demotion in the dam site. The construction company responded by stationing security guards at the site twenty-four hours a day until the homes were removed and the area flooded over.
>
> Police at the time questioned several fishermen and campers in the area who reported seeing an older GMC model truck leaving the area very early Thanksgiving morning with a large blue tarp over the truck bed.
>
> They could not give authorities a good description of the two men in the truck except to say that they were "very loud" considering the early hour and wilderness area.
>
> Police say metal thieves usually bury the copper, hide it for several years and then sell it in small amounts to avoid suspicion. That the two suspects attempted to sell so much copper at once is what alerted authorities.

I knew better than to do that but desperate times call for desperate measures. You can "quote" me on that.

Of course, my hometown newspaper in Duck reached me at home as soon as they heard of the charges against me. The reporter had a pleasant, youthful *italics* sounding voice.

"Hello."

"Ah, hi. Is this Jack Ovum?"

"It's Jack Odum. Not Ovum, with a "d" not a "v.""

"Sorry. That's how it's written here… umm… my name is Mark Jacobs. I'm a reporter at The Carolina Times. Ernie Presenca and Sam Cooke wanted me to call you and get a reaction to the copper theft charges.

"Let me guess. Hernia and Sam think it's an awesome talker of a story?"

"Yeah. Right. That's exactly what they said. You know them well."

"I know them unwell, Mack"

"Unwell? Funny. But it's Mark. Mark Jacobs. But, ah, what do you say? How do you feel about being charged with stealing that copper?"

"How do I feel? Good Gawd, there must be a course in Journalism School called Always Ask Them How Do You Feel 101. Did you learn that in Journalism School, Marty?"

"It's Mark. I didn't go to Journalism School. This is my first job. I'm learning by doing it the old-fashioned way, I guess you might say. Go. Now. Do it. Fast."

"Right. I think I might like you, Mickey. Well. Okay. My reaction? How do I feel you might ask, which, indeed, you just did? Well. Hmmm. Look, I'll comment if you promise me one thing."

"What's that?"

"Promise me you won't misquote or exaggerate things that I tell you. I'm a bit of a stickler for exact quotes and telling the story straight and true. You can quote me on that. Mark, is it?"

"Yes, you hit it right on the mark. It's Mark. And, sure, I promise to quote you exactly."

"On the mark! I like your attitude, Markey. You remind me of me. Okay. Well, I admit my guilt. My family would disown me for saying this, if they had any money, but I think I and other family members carry a thief gene. So, well, here's my quote and you may quote my quote, Marky Mark: 'It appears that because of a genetic predisposition to steal, I performed an alcohol fueled misdeed eight years ago because of a need for money to live on. As a result, I am soon to become a prisonist.'"

"You mean prisoner."

"I mean prison-ist. Don't misquote me."

It turned out that Marco Polo was a good reporter for a news newbie.

The Coastal Carolina Times

Duck Man to Become Jail Bird

(Times Correspondent Mark Jacobs) The Duck man accused of stealing copper from abandoned houses eight years ago admitted his guilt of the crime in an exclusive interview with *The Coastal Carolina Times.* Jackson Odum told this reporter that he suffers from uncontrollable urges to occasionally steal things due to a genetic disorder. Mr. Odum claims he carries a thievery gene and that that led him to join a cousin, who may also carry the gene, to steal the copper.

The two men are charged with tearing copper wiring and pipes from several homes in the Hiwassee Lake region of Watauga County in the North Carolina mountains.

His cousin, Dennis Roy Odum,

pled guilty to that and two other copper thefts years before.

Ovum, a former employee of *The Coastal Carolina Times*, said he knows he, too, will receive jail time, and admitted that he's about to become a "prisonist." Odum purposefully mispronounced "prisoner." Changing or making up words is a hobby of his that resulted in his firing from this newspaper a year ago.

Times Executive Editor Ernie Presenca said the newspaper is also considering filing charges against Mr. Ovum for years of stealing valuable office equipment including laptop computers, recorders, staplers, paper products and many other items.

Except for a major printing error not bad journalism, Marcus.

Then, in the next day's edition:

The Coastal Carolina Times

Corrections and Omissions

In yesterday's report on theft charges against a Duck resident, *The Coastal Carolina Times* unintentionally misspelled Jackson Odum's last name as Ovum several times. We regret the errors.

"Unintentionally?" The Hernia and AweSam's revenge.

Police in Watauga County looked back over other thefts around that time and Denny Roy ended up getting blamed for some things he did and some he didn't. He got three to five. I got a year since I was just an accessory.

The Thanksgiving timing of our copper haul got the Jefferson County Sheriff's Department and the Gosling Police investigating as to whether I was up to no good in their jurisdictions back then as well. Well, the only thing they uncovered was a sarcastically written notice in the police blotter on page ten about some petty thefts that weekend.

The Gosling Gazette

The Police Blotter

(Gosling) A minor crime wave hit the Gosling area over Thanksgiving. The Gosling Police Department reports robberies at two businesses.

Tio Sanchez, owner of Tio's Tank & Tummy Drive-In on First Street told authorities that three bottles of his special habanero queso sauce were stolen Friday morning. Mr. Sanchez said the sauce sells for ten dollars a bottle.

He said a customer managed to steal the bottles by flirting and diverting the attention of his waitress at the checkout counter where the sauce is displayed. Mr. Sanchez says the waitress is his wife. Mrs. Sanchez said the customer was "muy caliente (very hot) and liked his food that way too."

That sounds like a quote I would have made up.

Meanwhile, Jagachandra "Jeff" Patel, owner of the Americana Motel on Jefferson Street also reported a holiday weekend theft. He told police that a customer removed a print from the wall of room number three valued at fifteen dollars.

The print was of a vase of marigolds. Mr. Patel said he recently purchased the picture because it reminded him of his mother in India. He said an unopened jar of Nescafe Instant Coffee and a box of fresh Hostess Donuts were also taken.

Mr. Patel added that the robber did not take seventy-five dollars in the cash register. He said he had only one guest registered last week, a Jake Odor from Slapjaw, Texas but told authorities he was a "nice funny man. This is true. Paid on time. Praise, Krishna."

In both cases, the thief left a note explaining the robbery.

The note said in part:

"Dear victim of mine,

I hope this note finds you feeling well despite having been robbed. I would like you to take note from this note that I took no money. I no longer do that thanks to modern chemistry.

The items I borrowed permanently will be put to good use or sold. Any money made from any sale will help pay high medical costs for someone I know and love and that you would like, too.

You may, or may not, be reimbursed in the future when the book I'm currently writing becomes the bestseller I expect it to be.

Wish me success.

Your Robber."

The Gosling Gazette found the old clipping comical and reprinted it under a headline "Cops in Hot Pursuit of Cold Case Thief."

I told my cousin, Deputy Sheriff Doug Humphries, that it wasn't me and he agreed that, of course, it wasn't me. Dougy is, after all, an Odum. We had a good ole laugh about it over the phone. I had sent him a bottle of the habanero queso hot sauce. And, he said Jeff Patel's marigold painting looked great at mom's grave. I think his mother wouldn't have minded. Besides, Doug said it was returned to Jeff with some fading and warping due to exposure to rain, sleet and snow.

It must have been a very slow news week because the AP included my note in an amusing article called "Not Ready for Prime-Time Crime." Newspapers across the state then carried the AP story.

A couple of old newshounds in Durham and Kinston recalled similar thefts by an apologetic, note writing thief in their towns and reprinted their eight-year-old reports:

The Durham Observer

ID Theft at Durham Restaurant

(Durham) The Durham County Sheriff's Department is looking into a report of an apologetic pickpocket stealing several hundred dollars from two waiters at Doc's Diner on Club Boulevard.

The waiters, both medical students at Duke University, said their wallets were stolen but then recovered later in the day in the restaurant's parking lot. The two wallets contained a combined amount of four hundred fifty dollars, according to the students. Also taken were the student's ID's and driver's licenses.

Waiter Trent Greenfarb of Haddenfield, New Jersey, told police that not having any identification will make things very difficult for him at Duke and around Durham.

The suspect is described as a tall, white male in his 50's, longish brown hair and dressed all in blue. The victims said that during his visit to the doctor-themed restaurant he made several "sick attempts at hospital humor." The two victims also noted that he was a terrible tipper.

The robber left a note of apology with the discarded wallets. It read:

Dear victims of mine,

You fellas are rich. Thanks. I normally don't take money thanks to modern mind calming pharmaceuticals. But as future doctors, you'll be pleased to know your cash has gone to a good cause. I donated it to the Red Cross which has helped a young person I'm very fond of who(m) has a serious blood problem.

Taking your IDs was a last-minute IDea. Get it? Idea. Ha! Unfair, perhaps, but you were unfair to me as a customer/patient in the restaurant. The temporary discomfort this causes is the only treatment I could think of to cure your cases of severe arrogance, a condition my ex-wife claimed I suffer from as well.

Oh well. Stay well,
Your friendly robber.

***

The Kinston Courier

By Ted Arnold

SIGN WITH MISSING LETTERS GOES MISSING

(Kinston) The manager at the US-64 Gas & Grits Truck Stop & Shop near Kinston reported an unusual robbery Saturday. Manager Sandy Waller told Kinston police that he discovered the store's welcome sign was stolen. He said the TRUCKERS WELCOME sign was of little value since the first two letters have been missing for years.

I'll betcha Louis proudly has that sign hanging on his front door right now. Love ya cuz.

> Mr. Waller, a former policeman, said he kept a close eye on the thief "because he looked like a thief" but that the man still managed to leave the shop with a stuffed animal. The T. Rex was priced at nineteen dollars.

I remember you saying you're into bloodthirsty dinosaurs. Love ya, Aaron.

> The stolen door sign, he said, was worthless. Mr. Waller said he can't imagine why anyone would take something so old and broken.
> "I suppose if you're going to be robbed, we were lucky to be robbed by someone who took something so minor and who even apologized for taking it," he said.
> The thief left a note for the management:
> "Dear victim of mine,
> I hope this note finds you well despite having been robbed. I know someone who'd love whatever it is I accidently took. Or I'll sell it. And please know that I don't spend the money on myself. It goes to help pay the high medical costs of someone I know and love and who(m) you would like, too.
> You may, or may not, receive another note and some cash money in the future from me because I'm authoring a novel

that should make me wealthy beyond my imagination through book sales.
Wish me luck.
Your Robber."
Meantime, The Sampson County Sheriff's Department is investigating the theft of artwork at the Wise Guys Yard Art Shop in Turkey the same day.

Unlike at the truck stop with the surveillance cameras that I forgot about, the Wise Guys apparently had no Bum-Cam at their hiney store.

Co-owner Hank Root said the missing work "is assessed at more than two hundred dollars." He described it as "a beautifully painted plywood cutout of a young woman working in her flower garden." He said the painting, titled "Maiden of Mayberry" is the work of well known Turkey artist Ed "Bubba" Goolsby.

Hold on now. I paid for that one. It was the back end of a milk cow that somehow found its way into the trunk of my car. You just can't trust some people! Enjoy the cow butt cut out, JJ. Love ya, brother.

Mr. Root said a shopper, described as a white male in his 50's, driving a grey Honda Civic, stole the painting while he and his two brothers were helping other customers.
Mr. Root said the man was "a wisecracker."
Sampson County Sheriff Buddy Gooch said he's not aware of artist Bubba

Goolsby and would "frankly be surprised if painted plywood brought such high prices" but that the investigation was ongoing.
As in the truck stop robbery, the thief said he was planning to reimburse the store owners when he becomes a successful author through the sale of his book.

Well, this jailbird is going to be out of this cage in six more months, maybe less with good behavior which probably won't happen because of my writing out loud. I'll eventually return to my apartment in Duck and await word of this book's imminent publication. Meantime-- and I can assure you that all time in prison is mean-- I've begun a second book.

Unlike in this book, where I am barely mentioned, a character resembling me will be prominently written about. My working title is "The Prisonist." I'm writing out loud the cover tease right now as you read this. It will dramatically detail the life of a journaller who accidentally broke the law through no fault of his own and served hard time at a maximum-security prison in the Deep South among rapists and murderists and druggists and worse. You'll learn how he learned to survive the daily knifings and ...

"Jack. You're being too loud!" yelled Eddie the guard, being loud himself.

"Oh, sorry, Eddie, I was on a writing hot streak there."

"Keep it down."

"Will do."

"Hey, did you like that dinner tonight, Jack?" he quietly asked.

"It was delicious, Eddie. Steak and baked potato. I wanted a cigarette afterward so badly. My compliments to the chef. When does Harvey get out?"

"He's got two years yet. Gonna hate it when they let him go. But he'll see a liquor store and be back here in no time."

"Harv may be a drunk but he's a fine cook. I've gained five pounds according to the scale in the gym."

"I'm fixin' to go on home now. You need anything tonight, Jack? A video or today's *Coastal Carolina Times*?"

"Nah, Eddie, thanks. I'm going to write some more. Quietly."

"Good. Don't wanna annoy cell number three."

"He's crazy mad. But, y'know, John in cell eight is an interesting fellow."

"Yeah. John's okay. He'll be out in four months."

"I know. We get along. Play cards. He's given me some interesting financial tips. You believe his name is actually John Doe?"

"What were his parents thinking? Listen, lights out in ten, pal. Missus says 'hey.'"

"Hey back to Denise. G'night Eddie."

A little more about John Doe: He's an accountant in here for embezzling or forgery or something. Collared for a white-collar crime. We're gonna have drinks in Duck when we're both out of here. He wants to talk about copper. I only dug up half of my copper, and from what I'm reading it's going up in value and John Doe is interested. I'll tell him where to dig and he can sell it. I'm through with it. I'm going straight… straight to the bank with the royalties from this book that you'll pay, what, $20.00 for.

$20 x 1,000,000. You do the math!

(Publisher: How much of that $20 will I get? Three-fourths? JO)

So, with the pleasant thoughts of those numbers rolling around in my brain I/we say *thank you, reader,* from the bottom of my heart and the *occipital lobe.* I do hope you enjoyed reading about my relatives, friends and acquaintances. Please tell your relatives, friends and acquaintances to buy this book in hardcover where available. Please don't just pass it around because that directly affects the revenue flow to me. Not that this is all about me.

(Editors: Music up and then fades... if we go with that book soundtrack concept. JO)

THE (MANUSCRIPT) END

(Publisher and Editors: May I suggest that we include a "Suggested Questions" page to aid teachers and book club members in their scholarly discussions of this work? JO)

SUGGESTED DISCUSSION QUESTIONS

1. What is the symbolic message suggested by the three bird-named towns of Gosling, Turkey and Duck, allegorically speaking? And do crows fly straight?

2. Should the author have included more information about himself or was keeping a low profile symbolic in some way?

3. What's up with his love of making up words? Is he symbolically criticizing accepted English word usage or he is just having a linguistically good ole time?

4. How much fun is it making fun of road signs, right?

5. Is there an overabundance of attention to bathrooms and human and animal secretions, or is it just me?

6. Does the author regret marrying Susan instead of pursuing Peggy Lou? Yes.

7. What's so bad about saying out loud what you're writing while you're writing? It's not a going-crazy-thing like moving your lips while silently reading, is it?

8. Should Ernie the Hernia spend eternity as an obituary writer for *The Hades Herald*? That would be awesomely huge.

9. What would fried pate taste like?

10. What are derivatives and who(m) should derive something from them, whatever they are?

11. Why is Jack the only Odum who(m) doesn't have a southern accent? Wasn't he born in Gosling? Yes, but I'm mid-westernizing my writing accent to make it easier for northerners to read.

12. Wolverines are very comfortable shoes.

13.   *The author's petty thievery is of little importance so there is no need of any discussion on that matter.*

Now, a preview of Noveller Jackson Odum's soon to be released: "The Prisonist: Written and to be Read Behind Locked Doors."

(Sure to become a Major Motion Picture)

Dear Readers,
Please enjoy this free sample of my upcoming master-work, "The Prisonist: Written and to be Read Behind Locked Doors."
Jack Odum

(Dear Publisher: Before I begin: May I say how much I enjoy and respect the editors and staff at White Pages Publishing Company. I'm looking forward to a long and productive relationship and further success with my follow up novel "The Prisonist: Written and to be Read Behind Locked Doors." JO)

BOOK TWO MANUSCRIPT CHAPTER ONE

Hello. My name is Jack Odum, as clearly indicated on the cover. You know me quite well if you read my first book, and not at all if you didn't. Let me begin this writing by writing about the act of writing itself.

Writing a bestseller is so easy it's a crime. Nothing to it!

Writing a novel is the simple act of creating interesting characters, placing them in interesting situations and de-scribing the circumstances in interesting words, sentences and then paragraphs to build chapters-- until there are a whole bunch of pages.

I've done it twice, as soon I finish this novel. I wrote my first book in less than a month.

Of course, it helps that I was an award-winning journalist who wrote for a living. I was employed for many years as a reporter at small newspapers in Duck, North Carolina. I resigned my position at *"The Coastal Carolina Times"* in order to write books.

Reporting local news is an excellent proving ground for writers-- especially writers of fiction. A reporter must be prepared to cover everything from so-called blood-and-guts news; that is, house fires and fatal car accidents, to minor events like a cat stuck in a tree or an obituary of an everyday citizen. He, if he's a male reporter or she if she's female, must be able to deal with humorless, no nonsense, time conscious, word conscious editors and unconscious management of all sexes on a daily basis.

Now, a word or several, about my using the word "PRISONIST" in the title: To my mind *if a lawyer is also called a jurist than why can't the prisoner, WHO MY LAWYER FAILED TO GET OFF, be called a prisonist? A juror is a member of a jury panel and is, therefore, a panelist, not a paneller.*

It just makes sense, neologistically speaking...

ACKNOWLEDGEMENTS

The author would like to thank Minnie Crane, his loving aunt and favorite elementary school teacher, for inspiring him to think for himself, do his own legwork, and never give up on his dream to become the writer he is today. Without her encouragement, and especially her research on the family background, this book would probably not have these many pages.

The author would also like to thank the staff and management at *The Coastal Carolina Times* where he was able to <u>focus</u> on <u>fiction</u> and <u>faction</u> (foc fic fac)-- say that three times fast-- writing.

Thanks, too, to White Pages Publishing Company for recognizing the potential of the author's manuscript and not punching holes in the concept and making me rewrite everything.

Thank you, brother, JJ, for Thanksgiving dinner eight years ago. It was cornucopius.

Thank you, Indians (Native Americans!), Pilgrims (Illegal Immigrants!) and President Abraham Lincoln (Damn Yankee!) for Thanksgiving.

Most of all the author wishes to thank readers like you, for without readers like you, there would be no reason for writers, like me, to exert the extraordinary amount of effort required to bring quality literature, like this, to readers, like you.

About the Author:

Jackson Odum lives in the North Carolina Outer Banks' town of Duck where he enjoys meeting tourists and leading writing seminars. His early essays brought critical acclaim and several journalism awards to Duck's local newspaper, *The Coastal Carolina Times.*

(Publisher: As per your request, I have submitted a picture (actually 25 pictures) of myself for use on the back-flap cover. I rather like the one with my arms folded and a pencil behind my left ear. I think it looks authory. JO)

White Pages Publishing
1015 Guilford Avenue
Greensboro, NC27401

Jackson Odum
2525 N. Jefferson St. Apt.2
Duck, North Carolina 27949

Dear Mr. Odum:

We have reviewed your manuscript "The Journaller: My Novel: Written and to be Read Out Loud" at least twice and have determined that it is the ideal project we have been looking for for many many years years (to borrow from your writing style.) Your manuscript works well as one of our "How To" books or, in this case, a "How NOT To" book. It presents numerous examples of how NOT to approach writing and, therefore, how NOT to get a book published. It is for those reasons we are very pleased to announce that we have decided to publish it. We see its merits as highly publishable farce.

You WERE putting us on with this manuscript, of course!? Of. Course. You. Were. Surely!

The final product, however, will be presented in a much different manner than you likely expected. We see your book, as we edit it, as a learning tool; a textbook, if you will, of a somewhat entertainingly and well-intentioned but failed attempt at novel writing. Our editors will insert comments, much as you did in your manuscript, to highlight writing approaches and errors to be avoided if one wants to get published. Our inserted text will point out to hopeful novelists (okay, novellers) such mistakes as writing without an outline, lack of plot and moral, underdeveloped characters, overwriting, confusing digressions, poor word play, lame attempts at humor and over the top pretense.

Our working title is "How to Write Wrong." We'll show, through your self-absorbed life experiences, how writing can be a very lonely, unrewarding profession leading to failed relationships, joblessness, a sarcastic outlook on life, perhaps depression and, worst case scenario, criminal activity, petty or worse.

One of the most important lessons to be taken from your work is when a writer overlooks what could have been a book's strength. For instance, you casually referred to The Oil and its role in your family's quirkiness but failed to properly research and then capitalize - CAPITAL-IZE, ha ha - on its pharmacological potential and dangers.

Incidentally, White Pages Publishing is in talks with your ex-wife, Susan, about publishing her book "The Odum Oil: A Secret Family Potion" which she coauthored with your aunt, Minnie Crane. It is a vibrant, thoroughly researched, lovely and lovingly written work we'd be proud to present to the literary world. We plan to release both Odum family books next Thanksgiving and market them as companion pieces as part of our Christmas marketing campaign.

As per your request, fifty percent of all proceeds will be paid to your brother JJ for the medical care of his son, Aaron.

Sincerely yours in neologism,

David Crapo

David Crapo
Senior Editor (no relation to your uncle)

PS: About the follow up book "The Prisonist: Written and to be Read Behind Locked Doors": We thought about it, but our collective guts, consciences, emotions and minds said "no" in **CAPS**, *italicized* with a big, **bold**, funky N.

NO!

THE END

Meet our Author
Don Ross

I am a former broadcaster taking my first steps into the print world. For thirty of my forty plus years in journalism, I wrote feature news as a reporter at WTVD-TV in Raleigh-Durham, North Carolina. I had a ninety-second time-slot each night to present amusing offbeat stories that earned me a local reputation as a humorist and led to several AP, UPI, RTNDA and regional Emmy awards and nominations. My first attempts at humor writing were at my first real TV job at WTAJ in Altoona, Pennsylvania where I always volunteered to write a "kicker" to end the newscast on a light note. The Altoona TV job was offered after I covered news for WFBG Radio in Altoona while simultaneously obtaining a degree in International Politics from Penn State. My plans to become a foreign correspondent never panned-out, but I satisfy a desire for foreign travel by going abroad at least once a year. I developed an interest in world affairs and international travel during a four-year stint in the Air Force where I was a deejay and news broadcaster with The American Forces Radio and Television Service in Pakistan and Italy. I qualified for AFRTS thanks to my experience deejaying and news reading and writing at my hometown radio station, WCPA, in Clearfield, Pennsylvania. Retired now, I live in Wrightsville Beach, North Carolina with my wife, Mary, whom I met while stationed in Italy forty years ago. I have two children who live in the Charlotte-area and they have each given us two grandchildren.